THE SUNLIGHT PILGRIMS

Also by Jenni Fagan

The Panopticon

Jenni Fagan

The Sunlight Pilgrims

WILLIAM HEINEMANN: LONDON

1 3 5 7 9 10 8 6 4 2

William Heinemann
20 Vauxhall Bridge Road
London S W 1V 2SA

William Heinemann is part of the Penguin Random House group of companies
whose addresses can be found at global.penguinrandomhouse.com.

First published by William Heinemann in 2016

www.penguin.co.uk

A CIP catalogue record for this book is available from the British Library.

ISBN 9780434023301

Typeset in 13.5/15.5 pt Perpetua
Jouve (UK), Milton Keynes
Printed and bound by Clays Ltd, St Ives plc

MIX
Paper from
responsible sources
FSC
www.fsc.org   FSC® C016897

Penguin Random House is committed to a
sustainable future for our business, our readers
and our planet. This book is made from Forest
Stewardship Council® certified paper.

For Boo,
& Christian Downes

Prologue

THERE ARE three suns in the sky and it is the last day of autumn —
perhaps for ever. Sun dogs. Phantom suns. Parhelia. They mark the
arrival of the most extreme winter for 200 years. Roads jam with
people trying to stock up on fuel, food, water. Some say it is the end
of times. Polar caps are melting. Salinity in the ocean is at an
all-time low. The North Atlantic Drift is slowing.

Government scientists say the key word is planet. They take care to
remind the media that planets, by nature, are unpredictable. What did
we expect? Icicles will grow to the size of narwhal tusks, or the long
bony finger of winter herself. There will be frost flowers. Penitentes. Blin
drift. Owerblaw. Skirlie. Eighre. Haar-frost. A four-month plummet
will conclude with temperatures as low as minus forty or even minus
fifty. Even in appropriate layers. Even then. It is inadvisable. Corpses
will be found staring into a snowy maelstrom. A van will arrive, lift
the frozen ones up, drive them to the city morgue — it takes two weeks
to defrost a fully grown man. Environmentalists gather outside embas-
sies while religious leaders claim that their particular God is about to
wreak a righteous vengeance for our sins — a prophecy foretold.

The North Atlantic Drift is cooling and Dylan MacRae has just
arrived in Clachan Fells caravan park and there are three suns in
the sky.

That's how it all begins.

On Ash Lane, along a row of silver bullet caravans, a blackbird lands on a fence post. His eyes reflect a vast mountain range. Standing at the back of no. 9 looking toward the parhelia are Constance Fairbairn, her child Stella and the Incomer. Neighbours step out onto porches and everyone is unusually quiet, nodding to each other instead of saying hello.

Stella imagines the brightest sun is for her, the second is for her mother and the last is for clarity, most recently lost. Her mother wants this back in their lives, but the child does not know why she should want it so much when clarity is no ally. It isn't any kind of a companion at all. Stella stands, arms folded, frowning – right in between her mother and the Incomer, while three suns climb higher in the sky.

Constance does not see her child in the parhelia. She sees two lost lovers and herself in the middle – reflecting light. Caleb will be in Lisbon from now on and, after this last fight, she will never speak to him again. Alistair is back with his wife. Three suns to herald the beginning of a great storm. How very fleeting – any moment of stability. Constance is weary from matters of the heart but more so from worry for her child.

Dylan MacRae shades his gaze. He wears a fisherman's jumper and a deerstalker hat, Chelsea boots, tailored trousers, he is overly tattooed, immodestly bearded – he is clearly taller than a man was ever meant to be. He rolls a cigarette and lights it. His eyes are red-rimmed in this brightness and he is dazed from seeing a woman polish the moon. In all his days. Three suns, seven mountains and so, so close to the sea.

Dylan looks up at the parhelia and he sees Constance, her child and him.

There is a curious coruscation to the Incomer's eyes. The mother stacks wood. The child has two spirits. The entire landscape repaints itself in gold – crags, gorse bushes, the burn, sheep, a glint of waterfalls, fences, stiles, whitehouses, the bothy and right up there on the seventh sister there is a stag; the train tracks curve around the lower mountains – even the scarecrows appear momentarily cast in metal.

The blackbird flies away without song.

The child gazes toward the suns.

Stella keeps her focus; this way she won't be blinded but she will not have to look away for some time. She focuses, trying to absorb the suns' energy deep into her cells so when they descend into the darkest winter for 200 years, in the quietest minutes, when the whole world experiences a total absence of light – she will glow, and glow, and glow.

Snowflakes cartwheel out of the sky – hundreds, thousands, millions – the three suns fade as caravan doors click shut, all along Ash Lane.

Part I

November 2020, −6 degrees

1

THEY ARE quite clear about it. They use short declarative statements. Capital letters. Red ink. Some points are underlined. In summation: they want everything. It is the end. Dylan uses nail scissors to trim the longest stragglers on his beard, he bends over a row of sinks in the Ladies and splashes water on his face. He has acted out many roles in front of these mirrors: Jedi, Goonie, zombie, vengeful telekinetic teen – a Soho kid growing up in an art-house cinema: he'd lie onstage in his pyjamas watching stars glide across the ceiling for hours. His grandmother used to say that they were keepers of a conclave, a place where people came to feel momentarily safe, to remember who they once were – a thing so often ignored (out there) but in here: lights, camera, action!

Dylan pulls on his jumper and heads for the empty foyer. The ticket stall is musty. A trail of empty gin glasses lead to his projection booth. He briefly recalls toasting Tom and Jerry, Man Ray, Herzog and Lynch, Besson and Bergman, the girls from the peep-show next door, Hansel, Gretel and all of their friends. He picks up the letter again. Even if she *had* told him, he couldn't have done anything. The account is empty. There is less than nothing. The deficit has so many figures he quit counting. A pile of unpaid bills are stacked neatly in Vivienne's vintage sewing box and when he got back from the crematorium he found an envelope containing the deeds for a caravan 578.3 miles away, with a pink Post-it note and her scrawl: *Bought for cash — no record in any of our accounts. Mum x.*

What kind of last words are those, exactly?

He crumples the Post-it note, drops it in the bin. It's typically Vivienne — his mother: the moirologist, every sentence delivered like a eulogy. The woman wore winkle-pickers all her days and swore the purest form of water was gin; her finger would trail along their huge medical encyclopaedia (their family bible) hoping to find a rare, incurable disease, something to penetrate her to the bone and never leave her.

There was less than six months between one passing and the next.

Gunn went first.

Then Vivienne.

Now he knows something he did not know before — there is a totality to silence.

It makes his bones ache.

His body has its habits. It is trained to listen for footsteps on the attic stairs each morning. His eyes stray toward the draining board, expecting to find mismatched mugs. The fridge probably still has sliced lemon in Tupperware boxes for a late-night session on the gin. He fills the kettle up enough for three mugs. A stack of records next to Gunn's gramophone have still not been put back in their sleeves. Their cigarette ends (or Vivienne's at least) are still in the ashtray. It's almost like he had thought if he didn't tidy the place for long enough they'd come back, out of sheer fucking irritation at him.

There is an impenetrability to absence.

He feels slighted, as if some wider trick has been played. Inconclusivity – rattles! He is a child questioning a magician's trick. Where is the rabbit? Where is her voice? Where is their laughter? How come their voices were here and now they are not? It's a basic question. Where exactly have they gone? They have made the ultimate disappearing act. Exit Stage Left – then the curtains of the magician's tent flounce shut and a *Closed* sign is placed right in front of it so the living cannot follow.

This is only grief – it will not bring them home.

He presses his fists into his eyes and swallows down hard. Repossessors will clamp metal shutters over the foyer doors in about ten hours and he will not be here to watch them. No doubt it will only be a matter of months before wealthy city types move into a well-designed property with great original features right in the middle of Soho. They're doing it to all the businesses that go bust. He picks up a glass, wanting to hurl it with enough force that it could spin all the way through to the future – while the new residents walk around wearing unsubtle signifiers of wealth, the woman (in another room) would just hear a definite clunk one day as her other half took a tumbler to the head and slid perplexed, eyes glazed, down the wall.

If he is here when the repossessors arrive with cutters.

It won't end well.

Dylan's footsteps echo in the empty building. He strides along corridors that hold memories from his childhood in each and every nook. It's all borrowed: bricks; bodies;

breathing – it's all on loan! Eighty years on the planet if you're lucky; why do they say *if you're lucky*? Eighty years and people trying to get permanent bits of stone before they go, as if permanence were a real thing. Everyone has been taken hostage. Bankers and big-business are tyrannical demigods. Where is the comeback? There is no comeback because they own the people who have the guns who are there to keep the people (bankers and big-business and governments) fucking safe and now they're saying on the news it is too little, too late. The temperature is plummeting. Four scientists murdered at the Arctic. By whom?

Vast amounts of fresh water are flooding into the ocean from melting polar caps.

Environmentalists have been campaigning outside Westminster for weeks.

Nobody wants to have sex with him (he hasn't tried, really).

He can't be bothered breathing any more.

The debt collectors have been to the door twice today. There was a minor scuffle. They said, quite seriously, they'll take the lot by force if necessary, and they seemed hopeful for that possibility; they quite fancied battering a giant bearded weirdo, just for kicks, perk of the job, a wee added bonus for them. They are gnarly, violent-looking Serbians – if he had a cat they'd likely behead the thing, spike its head on the gates of the city so it could grin at passers-by.

London is not lined with lollipops.

Businesses are closing – everywhere.

He should: TAKE THE KEYS TO THE BAILIFFS IMMEDIATELY. This is written in RED CAPITAL LETTERS. That's not going to happen. If they want his family's home then they can break in. He's not handing it to them. Banks are doing this up and down the country; any hint of weakness (which they generate by wrecking the economy) and they swoop in, put great big metal shutters right across the doors, do it up and sell it for a profit. They'll make a bomb. In all truth, he can't be in this cinema without his mother and grandmother. This was their place. Everywhere he looks another part of him hurts.

Nobody told him grief would be so physical.

Adrenaline.

Sitting down.

Each muscle aching like he has been beaten from head to toe. Grief is in his marrow. It is in his brain. It has even slowed the way he washes his hands. Dylan enters their only auditorium and presses a button on the wall. Red curtains whirr toward each other, they trail across the stage like a dancer's ballgown in an old film, and he turns on star lights so they glide across the ceiling. He will leave Cinema 1 like this. It's only right. For the first time in over sixty years there will not be a MacRae in ownership at 345a Fat Boy Lane, Soho. Babylon (the smallest art-house cinema in all of Europe) will no longer glow from the foyer chandelier as people hurry by in the rain.

Dylan pulls on socks, boots, grabs a scarf.

He packs Vivienne's old suitcase.

Art-deco ashtrays.

Clothes.

Two cinema reels.

The urns are on the popcorn stand and he tries to fit them into the suitcase but it won't close. He begins to sweat and rummages behind the counter for a plastic bag but there aren't any. He yanks open cupboards and the box-office till, he looks in the bin, wrenches open the dishwasher – there is an old ice-cream tub and a Tupperware container.

He takes them out.

Places the urns on the counter.

Gunn should go in the ice-cream tub. It's bigger. Not that she is likely to have more ashes but she would be less bothered about being in an ice-cream tub than Vivienne. Vivienne would be mighty fucking pissed off about travelling anywhere in an ice-cream tub. His grandmother wouldn't give much of a shit. Dylan wishes (not for the first time today) that he had drunk a little less last night. He picks up one urn, then puts it back down again, beginning slightly to panic. He unscrews Gunn's urn and tips the ashes into the ice-cream tub. Some fall onto the floor and he automatically rubs at them with his boot, then looks up and mouths the word *Sorry*. He lobs that empty urn into the sink and unscrews the other one. He tips Vivienne into the Tupperware container but it fills to the brim too quickly – he can't fit all of her ashes in there.

– Fuck's sake!

Dylan slams drawers and finds a spoon and carefully pats his mother's ashes down until there is a half-inch of space on top. They have to fit in. He can't take her in two different containers. It wouldn't be right and anyway there's only popcorn boxes left and they have no lids! His hands are shaky. He is too hungover for this shit. He needs sugar. Coffee. A wank. More sleep. None of these things are going to happen. He pours in the rest of his mother's ashes and pats them down, pours the last bit and smoothes them down as well; a cold slick of sweat trickles right down his back as he tries to snap on the lid. He never could get Tupperware container lids on easily. It's a skill he doesn't possess.

— What's the fucking deal with this bollocks!

The roaring and shaking his fist and stamping his feet doesn't help, so he stands on it and the Tupperware lid clicks. He gets a bit of gaffer tape and wraps it around just to make sure. He picks them up. What if he forgets which one is which? He could text himself a note: *Grandma's in the ice-cream tub, Mum's in the sandwich box.* Instead he rummages around until he finds a roll of stickers and uses a ballpoint to scrawl *Gunn* on one, then *Vivienne* with a smiley face on another. Sometimes he has no idea how he made it to thirty-eight. He is always running late, for a start, as if time is the main problem in his life. It seems pretty much all the things people are supposed to have done by his age have passed him by, while he did nothing but develop an encyclo-paedic knowledge of obscure cinema and the rudimentary skills of distilling gin.

That was fine when he was helping to keep the family business afloat.

It's unlikely to impress the job centre.

Dylan places the containers side-by-side. They fit neatly into the suitcase now — it's not the most elegant way to take his mum and grandma back to their homeland but it will do the job. He places a photograph of Gunn, Vivienne and him-self as a baby on top and clicks the suitcase shut. Dylan reassures himself that this must be the worst hangover he has ever had in his life and his brain will return to optimum (average) functioning by tomorrow, or the day after at a push. He has at least twelve hours to be vacant on the mega-bus journey. That thought is soothing. Although the megabus is no doubt a shit-fest of body odour and claustrophobia and every bit of public transport is overcrowded with people panicking, but not so many will be going north like him. There is a hard knot of muscle in his shoulder. He looks for a piece of A4 paper but there isn't any in the printer, so he grabs a flyer: *Les Français vus par (The French As Seen By), 13 minutes long, W. Herzog*. He writes carefully on the back and takes it out to place in the Upcoming Screenings sign; the bailiffs won't cover that up with metal boards:

On behalf of Gunn and Vivienne MacRae, I want to say a huge thank you to all of our faithful customers — it was my family's privilege to shine a light in the dark here for over sixty years and there is nothing we would rather have done. Running such an extraordinary cinema would not have been possible without all of you. Babylon was our family business but it was also our home. May the film reels (somewhere, for all of us) play on!

With Gratitude,
Dylan MacRae

Lights flash outside the peep-show next door. He puts his hand on the glass foyer door and steps back into the dim. Dylan has an image of his mother in his head — she is sitting in the front row wearing a miner's hat with a lamp on the front, reading in a circle of light but keeping the darkness *always* close enough to touch. They keep playing. These little film reels in his brain. He wants to go upstairs and find her jumper and put it on, so he can smell her and sit down in the front row and drink all the gin left in the cellar, but he's sure that would be a bit Bundy or some other random psychopath who had issues with their mother. He has no issues, he just misses them both more than he can take. He picks up the deeds for the caravan, the address, his bus ticket. He grabs her suitcase and pulls the old Exit door closed behind him.

It is so cold on the city streets that his skin stings and reddens; he needs to buy warmer clothes, some kind of winter boots. His throat is so tight and constricted it is hard to swallow. He checks his watch and there is still over an hour before the bus leaves, so he heads for the river – he wants to see it before he goes. Red lights flash on and off, lighting up the pavement as he walks away from Babylon. He wants to turn around, but for the very first time in his life there is absolutely nowhere to go back to. With each step forward the road behind him disappears. That's what it feels like. Just one step back and it would be an endless plummet. His shoes click on the wet pavement. His breath curls on the air. He is going to go along by the river even though it takes longer because for once in his life he has left with time to spare. Ornate lamp posts with wrought-iron fish at the bottom of them sparkle with frost. It is way too early in the year for it to be as Baltic as this, they've only just hit November. He cannot remember it ever being this bad and they are saying this is barely the beginning. He turns onto the main street, then heads along by the river toward Victoria. Bridges are lit all the way along the Thames and four naval ships sluice through black water. He runs down steps and stands at the edge of the water. He holds the key to Babylon out and drops it into the river. Somewhere nearby a busker plays the trombone and he walks quickly back into the city and he doesn't stop until he emerges up into Victoria: news-stands are covered in headlines: *Maunder Minimum / European Financial Collapse / Ice Age / Gunman at London Zoo / The Big Chill* — a group of drunk hens queue to top up their Oyster cards and they shiver, barely dressed. Dylan heads through the forecourt and out to the bus station; he boards his coach as the doors hiss closed. He sidles along the aisle, stooping as low as he can to avoid banging his head and shoulders on the bus ceiling. It is hot. Damp. Smelly. Passengers swerve out of his way. A little boy stares at him, quite clearly afraid. Dylan is grateful to spy two empty seats at the back; he takes the aisle seat so he can at least stretch his legs out. The door to the toilet cubicle behind him has a red *Engaged* sign and there is a sound of vomiting, and in between retching a man repeats the same two words.

— I die, I die, I die!

It appears to be the only words of English he knows. Dylan shrugs off his coat and puts it in the overhead storage space, glad that it is warm in here. The bus speeds up — it whirrs along, ribbons of light blur past the window: hundreds of cars, snitches-of-snatches; fat arms wearing gold bracelets; a jeep blares its horn; a woman smears on lipstick; her dog barks at the back window; four soldiers nod their heads to music. All these people on the move in a strange corporeality. A man appears in front of Dylan and he has to stand, let him into the window seat, settle himself back down. There is an unwelcome particularity to the man's odour (camphor, stale sweat, cheap deodorant) as he rummages around and finds a giant bag of Thai chilli crisps. He offers one to Dylan.

A shake of the head.

— Did you see the news today, mate? Crisp-Man asks.

— Economic collapse?

— Nah.

— Gunman at London zoo?

— Not that one.

— Sinkholes?

— Nope, though one opened up in Yarmouth yesterday.

— Did someone finally take out a contract on all the paedos in Parliament?

— No, it's an idea though, innit?

— Was it a video of a tiny baby horse? Seriously cute? I saw that one, it was amazing!

— Are you taking the piss?

Dylan grins, oddly cheery now he is on the road and going somewhere new.

— It's only a bloody Ice Age, mate, that's the front-page news today!

— Yeah, I did see that, Dylan nods.

Crisp-Man glances behind them, then leans in toward him and lowers his voice. He uses a crisp to punctuate each point and his nose has two lumps where it's been broken.

— The earth strikes back!

— The Empire Strikes Back?

— No, the fucking empire has always struck back, now it's the earth's go. It's had enough of our bullshit, we're broken. All the way down to the bone. If human bones were rock, that's what it would say right through the middle — broke-as-fuck-idiot-cunts-exterminate-exterminate. Only civilised thing we can do is nuke ourselves.

Crisp-Man takes a big mouthful of crisps and crunches on them while holding his hand out like one of those exterminators that Dylan used to watch on reruns on telly up in the attic, while it rained outside and lights from the peep-show flashed on and off.

— That's a bit excessive, mate.

— Excessive!

The guy's voice rises to a high crescendo and a boy in front of them looks back and Crisp-Man tries to smile reassuringly at the kid, which clearly freaks him out even more. Crisp-Man attempts a whisper.

— I can't take much more, mate, I tell ya. If this *is* it, if this Ice Age is because human beings are acting like a fucking cancer on this hereof beautiful planet — I, for one, think it's not before time.

— Hereof?

— Yeah, fucking hereof. Hereof from now leave the earth in peace.

He gestures at the other passengers, who all look carefully away from his rising voice. The guy reaches into his bag for a hip-flask and swigs vodka down; he pulls out max-strength painkillers, pops three, then chases those with a few Pro Plus; he offers the box to Dylan, who puts his hand up.

— No, thanks.

— We're a race of zombies fucking the earth into oblivion. Fucked-up. Beheading people like it's Bingo! Look, Mum, see me on the internet with this bloke's head in my hand and a big-fucking-knife! Say cheese! Woo hoo. It's fucking trigger-happy time mate. That shit's a medieval bloodbath. They act like they're some kind of superior breed of murderer, like they're murdering for Him upstairs so that makes them *holy* murderers. Or they're murdering for governments so they're *hero* murderers. Or for the police so they're *legal* murderers. It's all the same shit. Murder's murder. Whichever way you dress it-the-fuck-up. I'm telling you . . . Or they're murdering for governments so that's A-okay. It's all the same shit! I'm telling you, we have *had* it. You know what they're saying – it's the end of times, that's what it fucking is.

Dylan tucks his hair behind his ear and his fingers hover where his thick polo-neck is bobbled, picked at the cuffs – he is clearly just a cuff-picker sat next to a crisp-muncher in what appears to be the end of times. Along the motorway trails of yellow and orange light race each other onto a bypass where a dark shape stands on the edge of a bridge. The figure raises an arm. Dylan glances back but he cannot see the shape any more. Behind them the sound of vomiting is replaced by a steady spitting – then silence.

If someone *is* nearly dead back there.

If they are.

Dylan is tempted to stand and declare – *There's a dead man in the bog, abandon bus, abandon the fucking bus! Call an ambulance, call his family!* The passengers would turn around as one being, all hairdos and noses and fists and feet as they dealt with him. Then they'd be right back to their magazines and bags of sweets without even a rumour of emotion. The toilet cubicle is silent. Crisp-Man eyes him up. His gaze slides over Dylan's Chelsea boots, faded jeans, polo-neck, his squint-nose and the height of him. The bus engine hums loudly as countryside begins to appear – dark outlines of watermills and chimneys, and in the middle of the road they drive around a roundabout where a dining table has been set up with place mats and flowers.

– Total madness. I've seen it all now. It could be one of them programmes – they'd call it *Dinner on Location*.

It's a guffaw then – Crisp-Man – pleased with himself and more inventive than anyone might think. Looks like meat on legs but something *is* inside that rubbery dome – probably just a little drunk guy on a bicycle, cycling around, but he has a point, or two, to make. Dylan nods in some kind of a response and the guy grins widely at him.

– I'm on the oil rigs again, six weeks on this time, winter or no winter, I need the money for the missus. She goes to Brussels for lipo and that; lipo on the brain she has. New tits. New nose. She's had her sagging moaning face dragged up around her ears. I own it, though. I own that nose. I'm telling you, it's mine!

Dylan unwraps a bar of chocolate.

He's never owned someone else's nose, not someone else's sagging moaning face, certainly hasn't – not even an eye-lash. The roads are sparser and the heater filters on and on and the air is too hot. Sleep announces itself as a heaviness – a fug that he falls into – a density to it that makes it a struggle to rise back up, and the engine drones louder until noise becomes everything – night-lights shine down and distort the passengers' features while traffic signs and roadworks fly past the window.

2

EVEN IN the dark there is a clear outline of mountains. It was freezing in London but this is like the Arctic. Dylan climbs into the back of a cab with tartan seat covers and shows the driver an address and they make a U-turn. He wraps his arms around himself, already shivering as they drive out of the station past big Georgian houses, then what looks like a park and city streets, the last he imagines he will see for some time. The scenery turns into suburbia until eventually a bridge rises – defiantly lit. The driver turns the heating up but it barely warms the back of the cab. Dylan peers up at the bridge and pulls his coat tighter around himself – look at that: what a feat of engineering! The bridge is built on a solid suspension system with metal joists that criss-cross against a wide tidal estuary. As they drive onto the bridge there are flashes of criss-cross, criss-cross, criss-cross, the shadows flicker over the driver's face. The car thuds over each section and the rhythm is relaxing. Roll-thud, roll-thud, criss-cross, criss-cross. Out on the sea there is a huge cruise liner and further out what looks like oil platforms, and then a lighthouse flashes somewhere along the coast. A few seconds later another lighthouse appears to flash back a response, a little yellow light and a circle around it – right out on the water.

The cab motors up a hill. It leans into curves and dips on narrow roads so that Dylan gets butterflies. Mountains rise up on either side of them, some so big and craggy the car feels tiny on the windy roads. There are no street lights out here. The headlight beam picks out features as they turn corners; occasionally a traditional croft house or bothy is lit up, way out in the middle of a valley. What must it be like to open your front door to all that vastness each day? Dylan leans back, tired now, and after an hour or so they drive past a row of industrial estates with warehouses and Japanese car showrooms filled with four-wheel drives. The cab takes a sharp turn down a country road and through two wooden gates. Dylan takes out his wallet and removes four notes. He pays the driver and takes the receipt out of habit. She chews gum and drives away with her window down and one hand raised. A nice gesture in the dead of night.

He can make out actual planets, the skies are so clear.

This caravan park is so – quiet.

Dylan looks up at millions and millions of stars, clusters and trails, and as he turns around in a circle he finds the entire Clachan Fells region is surrounded by vast mountains. Hemmed in. When he looked online he could see Clachan Fells as a spine of land in between the sea and farmland, but he imagined it flat. He follows a route through the caravan park that seems right even though he couldn't get the address properly on his phone app.

Of all the places Vivienne could have picked.

The caravans are mostly quite big, not like the picture of the one his mother bought. An ambulance is parked outside one mobile home, an ice-cream van outside another. Some have lights flickering behind their curtains, the sounds of televisions or people talking. There is a ferry link near here that will take him up to the islands so he can scatter their ashes. That might take a week or two, then if he *can* sell the caravan maybe he could go somewhere warmer, Vietnam or Cambodia.

Dylan walks up through a car park, passes a caravan with gnomes fishing outside.

What was Vivienne doing here?

He tries to imagine his mother walking up this slope, chain-smoking, wearing a headscarf and winkle-pickers and huge sunglasses. She took three trips away last year, saying she was going to meet a film collector who had lots of rare reels, but on at least one of those trips she came here to buy a place for him. The doctor must have told her, long before she told him. She knew they were going to lose Babylon a year ago. After Gunn died, she must have been sure she wouldn't last much longer, either. All those trips she made to the hospital without telling him, it makes him angry. She never gave him the chance to look after her. She took away the last thing he could have done. She didn't want him to see her sick and deteriorating, so she'd come home in between trips to the hospital and sip gin and watch *The Wizard of Oz* in Cinema 1, wearing old paisley-pattern pyjamas. The woman was hard-as-fucking-nails. A glint materialises under a car and he crouches down to find a large frog. He scoops it up. The glassy white throat thrums and a clear membrane slides down each luminous eye. A fine black slit stares back at him, and wide pads move up and down on his palm. It pulses in his cupped hands like a heart. He places the frog carefully on the verge beneath the car and keeps walking, faster now because his ears are numb and he feels even taller next to these caravans, like he is a giant who has come here this late at night so he can peer through windows and rearrange the sleepers' dreams — blow new ones into their ears through a glass pipe.

A sign for Ash Lane is almost totally covered by briars. He pushes them back. There are five caravans on either side of a small lane. Each caravan is silver, bullet-shaped with a big bay window at the front. The first one has a sign outside that swings in the breeze: Rose Cottage. It has a crooked chimney. The air smells clean and pure with a hint of wood-smoke. His caravan is no. 7 and the gate to it is rusted shut. It is more dilapidated than the others. A BMX bike with a pirate flag flapping on the back of it leans on the neighbour's porch. A girl with black hair appears at the window and he is about to raise a hand but she is already gone. Dylan steps over the gate to no. 7. Thistles snark his coat as he makes his way along the tiny path and up a slumped set of porch steps. He lifts the mat and, in between moist soil and wriggling slaters, there is a key. He picks it up and puts it in the lock and twists. His fingers are numb; he blows on them and tries again. He can't remember what the deed said — maybe it was *Needs cosmetic attention*.

The door swings open.

He flicks the light on and steps into a hallway one footstep wide and long. Dylan pushes the door directly in front of him and it opens on a clean-looking white shower, loo, sink. He opens the bathroom cabinet. There is only paracetamol. He has a horrible feeling that his mother could be sitting in the bedroom right now, drinking gin. He did see her body but it seemed she was only sleeping, and he had so many pints before he got there that the whole thing has become hazy like a film he saw when he was tripping one time. A bad one. The kind that follows you around indefinitely.

Dylan stoops to get through the bedroom door. He can stand upright but his arm doesn't even extend halfway before he touches the ceiling. There is a double bed with brass knobs on the top and bottom headboards. Vivienne's sketchbook is on the bedside table. It used to sit next to Vivienne's bed or she'd sit sketching in it outside. Sometimes he'd wake up to find her drawing him. She must have brought it up here when she bought the place and left it for him to find. He picks it up, turns it over, slips it into a drawer. He opens the curtains and the bedroom has a view of mountains and endless skies.

He places his hand on the window.

It is only one step back through to the living room, a long thin room with an old square television with a big dial on the front. It makes a satisfying click when he switches it on. He places the suitcase down and scrolls through the fuzz on the telly until a channel mangles into life. The screen slinks away to the left, then there's a dot. Dylan sits on a blue flowery armchair and rests his hand on the arms. He switches on a Hawaiian-lady lamp, which is sitting on the wee Formica table next to him, and in the kitchenette in the corner there is a two-hob worktop Baby Belling. Fake-wood panelling adorns every available space, including the ceiling, and there is a gigantic painting of a plough horse in a gold frame on the wall. It paws the ground, come-hither long lashes frame brown eyes looking coyly at him.

How did it come to this?

A week ago he thought the family business would keep him and now he's shuffling through a sheaf of local tourist attractions: a castle, a stately home, a pottery up on Clachan Fells. Fort Harbour café does home-made banana cake and deer-burgers. He'll check that one out. A local taxidermist is giving lessons. There is an advert for stag hunting and one for hot yoga, and the timetables for a ferry that leaves from the harbour over the mountain; it will take him closer to the islands up north, where his grandmother came from. After all these years he is tracing her steps back that way. Dylan rolls a cigarette. He opens the fridge and finds four cans of cider. The thing has been switched off and it smells, but it is so cold in here they are still chilled. His mother never drank cider.

– Love is what makes it worth the utter strange!

Vivienne – the one time she took Ecstasy and got hysterical, he had to put her in a cool bath and read her nursery rhymes until she felt better. She was sixty-seven. The pills were a present from the guy she was seeing. What was she thinking? Dylan taps his fingers. He should be putting up the usual online advert, perhaps a triple-bill by Werner Herzog (*Fitzcarraldo, The Burden of Dreams* + *Bad Lieutenant: Port of Call New Orleans*) or tomorrow it could be *Nosferatu (1922)* + *evening screening: Freaks (1932)*. On Tuesday he would have gone for *The Goonies* + *Gremlins 1&2*. The television screen stops sliding to the left and the picture settles. Footage flashes. Environmental protestors outside Westminster. Rows of police officers stare through them. *Save the Planet* signs bob up and down, and one fat guy with a ginger afro and *See, We Fucking Told Youz Cunts!* scrawled across his T-shirt. Dylan rolls a cigarette.

As the camera pans along the front row, people begin to hold hands.

He takes a deep drag and exhales.

There are rows and rows of them.

Just standing by the river holding hands.

A little boy walks out to the row of police officers and places down a teddy. He holds out his hand to the policeman. The policeman is young and he looks straight ahead. The boy stands there with his hand held out. All the rows of people behind him are holding hands now and his mother puts her arms around him, leads him back. Something about it. The protestors stare back at the camera. A banner spells out *Corporatocracy is a crime*. An interactive map flashes up on the news show to pick out the potential areas that are going to be most affected by the cooling Gulf Stream. *Europe, Canada, USA, Southern America, Africa*. They all light up one-by-one. *High alert. High alert. High alert.* This message trails across the bottom of the screen in a band and he clicks it over, so the telly tries to find some more channels and Dylan closes his eyes. He falls asleep while light flickers on the walls.

It sounds like a bomber – it sputters out, then roars in again. Dylan lurches upright and grabs his phone, the LED reads 5 a.m. He stands up and pulls the net curtain back and his next-door neighbour's door is open. Trees sway wildly where a few hours ago they were still. The sound drones from somewhere further up the lane. He drags his coat on and walks out the front door. He steps easily over the rusted gate. At the end of the path a woman hoovers up the road.

Her pyjama top rides up and exposes each knot of her vertebra like a fine rope.

She is hoovering up the miles between herself and what?

Dylan looks around but nobody else is out. The sky is brighter than earlier but it is still dark – the woman aims a barefoot kick at the Hoover until it sputters out, leaving a mechanical hum on the air. She wraps the plug neatly around the handle. Her eyes have a small cat-flick or perhaps he is imagining it, her hair is neat and fine and tucked behind her ear. Her top lifts in the wind and there is a slight spit or promise of sleet.

She walks back up her pathway and puts the Hoover inside her caravan and disappears. Her door is still open. A light glares on in a caravan opposite him. There is swearing (a male voice), someone snaps open metal venetian blinds across the way, then they cling back shut and the light goes out. He's in darkness again. The wind bites at his skin, his fingers are numb. He should close the woman's door. Just go over there and push it gently shut so she doesn't freeze while sleepwalking. He is about to do exactly that when she walks back onto her porch with a rag in her hand – she reaches a pale arm up into the sky and polishes the moon.

3

STELLA SCROLLS through her phone. The LED lights up her face as she watches the YouTube video of a goth-girl in New Orleans again. Nobody could tell to look at her. She has a year-long film of her transition and at the end of it she has black lips and long hair and she is hot. Stella switches her phone off and turns over on her bunk. She has a perfect view of Clachan Fells from here. Outside haar-frost glitters across the woodshed in their back garden. Mist trails down the valleys in thin rivers of grey; it's snaking over the hills from Fort Harbour. It's 6 a.m. Frosted leaf-shapes pattern the lower corner of the bedroom window, ice-crystals trail up, with each one infinitesimally smaller until they disappear. Icicles will elongate from the bedroom windowsill soon – it happens every year, but never this early. They haven't even had Bonfire Night yet. Stella pulls her owl onesie-hood up so the beak slumps down over her forehead. If the temperature plummets quickly enough, school won't reopen. This morning is the last assembly. Stella prays snow falls so fast and heavy that school will be locked, with empty classrooms for the whole winter. She reaches up to touch the curved metal ceiling above her and it is cold but she splays her fingers out;

each nail is painted a different colour. Her mother lies on the wider platform bed below. She is still waiting for a response of some kind.

— It's not like picking a football team, Stella whispers.

— I know.

Stella walks her feet up onto the ceiling roof above her head — she grips onto her toes. A girl is a girl, is a girl, is a girl. That's all she has. Also, her obsession with Lewis is becoming creepy, she might do anything at this point — if he would kiss her again. Anything. She'd even beg. She'd take a kiss anywhere. Even on the elbow. He doesn't know what to make of her, though, does he? She could ask him out on a date. She is not afflicted with her mother's zealous self-reliance and totalitarian independence from state and fellow man — she isn't scared to say she wants something. Constance is a survivalist, she's getting more extreme each year — it's not even a joke.

— I could see Mrs Jones's brain cells grind to a halt when I explained it.

— I can't believe that woman is even allowed to be a school counsellor.

— Why?

— She's just so . . . Catholic.

— That doesn't make someone a bad person, Mum.

The light outside grows brighter. Stella passes down the muted YouTube clip to her mum on the bunk below and Constance watches it for a minute.

— Gender is closer than anyone likes to think. Men won't buy it because most of them are dickheads, she says.

— Is that the technical term, Mum?

— It is. We all share twenty-two identical chromosomes;

the twenty-third is the sex chromosome and they don't kick in for at least ten weeks. Everyone starts out female and they stay like that for months.

— What, even Dad?

— Even Jesus. Go tell that to the nuns. For some embryos the Y-chromosome creates testosterone and female organs change into male ones; about three months in, what starts out as a clitoris, in the XY gene, gets bigger until it becomes, you know, a dick.

— Mum! Can't you say penis?

— It sounds so sterile.

— Why don't they teach all of this stuff in Sex Ed?

— Gender indoctrination. It's state-imposed. The male body still holds the memory of it — the line below a scrotum is called a raphe line, and without it you'd have a vagina; every embryo has an opening at the genitals and it becomes labia and a vagina or, when male hormones kick in, the tissue fuses together and it leaves a scar, which is the raphe line.

— So, its like a vagina line?

— It's totally a vagina line.

— Fucking hell!

— Swear jar, Stella. There's plenty male-and-females in one: snails, echinoderms; a cushion sea star spends its first three years female, then three years male. There's twenty-one species of fish on the spectrum: angel fish, sea bass, snook, clown fish, wrasse — a female wrasse turns into a male if the dominant male dies. The prettiest is a butterfly, where the male side has big black wings and the female side has smaller purple wings. It's a bilateral gynandromorph, male and female in one.

— You should go back to teaching, Mum.

— Fuck that! Kids are annoying little bastards, present company excluded.

— Swear jar!

— There is a half-female, half-male cardinal bird that is pure white down one side and bright red down the other! Google it. And survival techniques — there's some great tips out there! I was chatting to a survivalist in rural Alabama, godly man but he is the-shit when it comes to foraging. I found a great website for survival skill tips — can waste hours there lately.

Stella grins.

— This sums up my entire childhood: clever shit and apocalypse-survival-skills.

— How many twelve-year-olds know how to start a fire with a battery?

— I dunno, Mum!

— You can take that in for 'special skills day' at school.

— Or I could borrow one of Alistair's corpses and show them how to dissect a body.

— That would do it.

Stella runs her hand over her stomach and vows to look in the mirror later. She would have had a vagina if it hadn't fused. She doesn't mind not having one. It's not about how they cut the meat. She should paint that on a T-shirt and wear it to church. In a minute she will get up. She will comb her hair. She will wear coconut lip gloss and drink coffee straight and black. She runs her hands over a flat, flat stomach. Stella pulls her hood up. She steps down from her bunk, imprinting her mother's mattress for a fraction of a second before thudding to the floor.

The yellow beak sits above her forehead like a cap.

Her mother looks like winter.

Constance Fairbairn is possibly the most self-reliant person on the planet. The woman clearly doesn't understand that she has to be at least half-human. Neither does her now ex-boyfriend, and soon he will be dead.

— Do you want coffee, Mum?

— Yes, please.

Constance is dozing already, drifting away with thoughts of dual-bodied butterflies and morphing fish. Her mother has fine, white hair, eyebrows so light they are barely there; her eyes are grey as late-winter skies, she looks nothing like Stella and it isn't that her own body tells a story she didn't choose. It isn't that. Stella tucks her bobbed hair under her bird hood. It is silky and straight and just as black as her irises.

Stella flicks the temperature gauge on the wall.

— Mum, it's minus six. How cold is it going to get this winter, exactly?

— Nobody knows. They say there might be icebergs.

— That's not reassuring.

— Don't worry, you can always show the other kids how to start a fire with a battery.

— I am trying to fit in, Mum!

— Sounds tedious.

Outside there is a blue, blue sky and frost has dusted the Clachan Fells mountains silver. Stella Fairbairn feels like she is going to cry, and nobody is even up yet. She is a swan wrapped in cellophane and everyone can see through her skin. Lewis will never kiss her again. She might as well forget it. She isn't pretty, and she's angular, and she has a penis.

As tick boxes go for the most popular boy in school, those attributes are probably not high on his list. He did kiss her, though, and the only two people that know about it are her and him. He won't kiss her again in case any of his friends find out and think he's weird – that is why he won't do it again. Or because he already knows he'd like it. He wants to, though. He wants to even more than she does. That feeling. A light flutter in her chest. It squeezes in. Her ribs are embracing each other. The light outside is so bright now it almost feels sinister. Clenching her teeth. Hoping someone will want her one day. If Lewis tries to kiss her again she'll shoot him down, because he's too ashamed to do it in public. Lately, fear is following her. It is two tiny pit-a-pat feet always skittering behind her. When she turns there is nothing there, just the faintest imprint of footprints in the snow.

4

DYLAN STEPS outside. His boots crunch on the light frost that is dusting everything. He needs to trample down these thistles first, so he can go in and clear all the shit he doesn't need out of the caravan. He might not go right away, he might stay for the winter and it's nothing to do with a moon-polisher. Not in the slightest. He cranes his neck to see if she is in her caravan but there's no movement next door. He begins to trample down shoulder-high thistles. First he has to aim a kick to get them flatter – then trample. It's an ungainly but efficient system. If he can clear the garden and throw out the stuff he doesn't want, he can take it over to the big bonfire stack in the park on the other side of the lane. It says it is a park, but there are no swings or flowers in it. Just a big pile of stuff for burning. If he can do that this morning then he can sort the caravan out a bit, make it more liveable, create some space for his projector and gin-still when they arrive. It's freezing but he had no idea that Clachan Fells would be as utterly beautiful as this – an arc of mountains surrounds the whole area.

— How tall are you?

The girl from the caravan next door is standing on her

BMX bike at the end of the path; she balances on it, then sits down and rests one foot on his gate. She has a gobstopper held aloft in one hand like a poison apple and she is pretty with almost-black eyes.

— Taller than most.

— That's not very exact.

— I'm six feet seven inches — how tall are you?

— I'm five feet four inches, which is tall for a girl, and I'm only twelve. I'll be thirteen soon.

— You might end up taller than me!

— I fucking hope not.

— Does your mum know you swear?

— Aye.

The girl has different-coloured nails and she rolls the front wheel of her bike back and forward. She watches him as he walks down the path with fake-wood cladding he pulled off the lounge walls earlier; he broke it apart so he could get it out the caravan and, whenever he picks up a panel, the nails get caught on his jumper.

— You're not making a very good job of that, she says.

— I know!

— I live next door, my name's Stella.

— Dylan.

He sticks out his hand and she shakes it solemnly, then glances at his arms where his sleeves are pushed up.

— Do you have tattoos everywhere?

— Not on my toes, he says.

— I want a tattoo when I'm bigger, but my mum would hate it — she hates tattoos, Stella says.

His heart sinks a little. The moon-polisher is her mother and she doesn't like tattoos. That's not great but it is winter.

He can wear a lot of jumpers. By the time she is bowled over with . . . what? . . . his knowledge of cinema? Yeah. He should probably go to Vietnam. Dylan looks at this kid and wonders for a second if his entire existence is utterly aimless.

— Where are you from?

— London, Soho, but my gran was from the Orkneys. They're that way!

Dylan points toward the mountains, then the sea, then the motorway; he is not sure quite which way they are at all and he feels stupid before he has even finished, because of course she has heard of them and after this it is definitely time for him to have breakfast and coffee and sit down and stare at a wall until he feels better.

— You are over two hundred miles away from the islands. I've not been to all of them because there are seventy, but I've been to most of the bigger ones and Papa Westray. I saw a pod of killer whales off the coast of Mull last year in September; minke whales too, porpoises and crabs, corncrakes and lots of seals, and on the last day we even got to see some sharks. They were great long things and we had to go out on a boat that went really, really fast, like really far out to sea to get to see them.

— That sounds like quite something, he says quietly.

— Your mum was called Vivienne, wasn't she?

Dylan stops trampling down thistles.

— How do you know?

— She asked about the caravans: how easy they were to heat, all that kind of stuff. She said her kid would probably come here at some point and that you were basically a giant.

— I was born in the wrong body, he says.

— No shit! she says.

— So you live with just your mum?

— Yup.

— Does she work around here?

— She works in our back garden mostly, and she keeps stuff down in a lock-up at the garages. She does shabby-shit — that's what we call it, cos we think it's funny, but officially it's called 'shabby chic'. We take furniture from dead people's houses or the city dump and she restores it. She knows a lot about furniture and beeswax and French polish and stuff. She sells it to people in the big houses. We don't tell them where we get it from.

He goes back into his caravan to get his lighter and she peers in the window at him.

— Nice suitcase, she says.

Dylan moves the suitcase into a cupboard and rolls another cigarette and looks at her through the window and she is not in the least bit embarrassed, nor does she appear to be going anywhere.

— You shouldn't go into a stranger's house, he says.

— I am not going into a stranger's house, and anyway it's a caravan. D.e.n.i.a.l. much?

Dylan steps back out onto the porch.

— It was Vivienne's suitcase, he says.

— Did you live in a caravan in London?

— No, I lived in a cinema.

— Nobody lives in a cinema.

— I did.

— It's where I grew up. My family had a little flat above it, it was my mum's — Vivienne, who you met — and also my gran's. It's a tiny art-house place called Babylon. So, your dad doesn't live with you?

— Nope, Alistair lives with his current wife.

— How many wives has he had?

— Three.

Stella scuffs her foot on the path.

— He's a commercial taxidermist — I don't like him. He's an arsehole!

She points at a tattoo on his forearm of an elaborate snake-headed lady.

— Who's that?

— Coatlicue, Aztec goddess of creation. See, she has skulls for a skirt, a great big ballgown made up of skulls — tiny ones on the belt, see there, and they get bigger and bigger all the way down and they mutter to each other. The skulls belong to the dead who couldn't escape the river of Lethe, so she's taking them on her travels across the universe until she finds a place to put them back in. Lethe is the river of forgetting — oh, you know that? Okay. Above their heads, see right there, that's the death-wish comets, they blaze through the stars intent on total self-annihilation. Sometimes they fall right out of the sky.

— Fucking hell, Stella says.

— Exactly.

— I wish I grew up in a cinema.

Dylan wants to say he had regulars that appreciated the age of the place and the films that they screened and the gin and wine. But instead he nods and imagines he must look like a strange old tattooed knob-end.

— I'm being schooled by robots, she says.

— Yup, he says.

— My classmates are robots as well, they get wound up

downstairs in the school basement each morning and marched up with matching shoes and, if one of them has something different at all – even a brass-coloured screw where all the others are silver – they just get put outside for the bin men or they get kicked around the gym hall until you can't recognise what they were in the first place.

— I bet they do, he says.

— I have a lot of brass-coloured screws, she says.

Dylan looks straight at Stella. Her jaw. Her shoulders. Her way of tapping the bell on her bike with the gobstopper and how she keeps looking up at him, a little nervous of herself, even teary.

— Sounds like you're the only real, sane person in there.

— Truth, she says.

— S'best to never let them know you've twigged they're robots, though – just keep smiling, he says.

— Is Vivienne still in Babylon?

— No.

He almost stops on the path and sinks to his knees, so overwhelmed by someone asking where she is that he has to pull himself together.

— Is your gran still there?

— No. They both, recently – you know.

He can't even say it.

— They're on holiday?

He just looks at her and she takes it as an affirmative.

— Who is going to put the films on today then?

— Nobody.

— You have to come to Bonfire Night. I'll introduce you to my mum.

— Okay.

A shot of adrenaline at the thought of being introduced to the moon-polisher.

— I'm going to start my own political party, Stella says.

— Impressive, what are your aims?

— I'm going to draw up a human-rights contract that says everyone on earth must agree we are here as caretakers of the planet, first and foremost.

— Unless the Ice Age gets us first.

— Which way would you rather go? The last great war or frozen like a fish finger?

— I dunno, they both sound so tempting!

Over at the park a cluster of kids run around the green, out playing before breakfast and the darkness lifts fully. Lights still glow in some of the caravan windows; people are getting up to make breakfast and start their day. He can smell wood-smoke and hear someone clattering around with pans. Stella stands astride her bike, looking across at the park for somebody.

— Do you have any cigarettes? she asks.

— Why?

— I'm trying to stunt my shoulders, so I don't end up big and boxy like a football player or something. I want smaller, girlier shoulders.

— I don't think there's a cigarette packet in the world that warns of stunted shoulders.

— I want to just try one.

— You're too young to smoke, but if you want to give me a hand taking all of this over to that bonfire pile, I can pay you in chocolate?

— Okay, but don't be tight. You can throw in enough tobacco for a roll-up too. Have you met Barnacle yet? He lives across the path, and then there's me and my mum. Ida is up there, you'll meet her. She's got two kids and a skinny husband. She's our resident porn star. She does adult babies on Thursdays. Down there are the lesbian schoolteachers at Rose Cottage, and up there a couple of Satan-worshipping stoner kids; and in that one right up the back there's a guy nobody sees much, and if you do see him he's on a bicycle. He's here for the aliens.

— Lot of aliens in Clachan Fells?

— Loads. They like the clear skies.

Dylan looks across to the caravan she is pointing at and to the stickers of aliens outside it.

— I thought that was left over from Halloween?

— Nope. The first thing he'll say when he meets you is: *The truth is out there, friend.* Then he'll try and figure out if you are one of them or one of us, then he might zap you on the lane. I shit-you-not.

— Interesting, he says.

— I've lived here my whole life.

— I lived in Babylon my whole life.

— My mother isn't normal.

— Neither was mine.

They eye each other warily.

— And your dad? she asks.

— My mum didn't catch his name, he says.

They grin at each other as the first snow of the year begins to fall.

— I'm not used to snow in November, Dylan says.

Stella tips her face up to feel the softness on her skin and holds her hand out to catch snowflakes. Dylan hauls stuff out of his caravan; he stacks it up on the flattened thistles. Stella helps him. He shifts the telly onto the armchair. Those are the only things that can stay. He takes the horse painting off the wall and it is so wide it almost stretches his full armspan. Stella is off with a pile of wood over to the bonfire stack. She is skinny but strong for a kid. He rips up the carpet and underneath there are ceramic tiles in a brown-and-cream pattern. It's a kind of abstract design. Could be worse. He rips the nets off the windows and shoves them in a box with the tasselled lampshade; he keeps the china Hawaiian-lady base and a light-bulb so he can read later. In the caravan across the path a telly blares, and an audience claps loudly for some morning chat show. Over at the park Stella drags the carpet along behind her, a fistful of wood in her other hand, and throws it onto the bonfire with ease. Dylan strides over with the last of the wood. The snow has eased off again as quickly as it started.

— I'll get it the rest of the way, she yells, running back to meet him.

— No, you just bring the other curtains. You've already done loads, he says.

They keep passing each other midfield and, by the time they are finished, Dylan's legs are achy and all that's left in the caravan is the armchair, telly, lamp, bedside cabinets, the bed, his mother's sketchbook and cardigan. Dylan goes back to the end of the path and hands Stella a couple of roll-ups and a box of matches. In the kitchen he finds the metal coffee-pot he used in the Bethnal Green flat when he left home to study. He sparks the camp-stove and sets it on to boil, and the smell of sulphur from the matches is soothing. He rinses out mugs and his fingers are red from the cold and he notices the sink is stained all different shades of grey-silver. Dylan goes back out into the garden and a wisp of smoke rises from a patch of thistles. He is careful on the wet porch steps because they're still green with old slippy moss. He'll scrape that off later. He hands Stella a mug of hot chocolate and half of a giant bar of Fruit & Nut.

— A nutritious breakfast, he says.

— You need proper boots or you'll die when winter really comes.

— I know, he says.

— Who's in that tattoo?

— That's my grandmother, Gunn. She's wearing a pinny and smoking outside the stage door. She always used to be there, watching for me coming home from school.

Stella looks at the tattoo — it looks like Gunn is staring right out at her.

— You really want to buy some steel-toe caps one size too big, so they fit your winter socks underneath. You can get them cheap at the Army & Navy store.

— Gunn wore those, Dylan says.

— Gunn was smarter than you.

— That's an understatement.

— You don't have winter socks, do you?

— No.

— Is your cinema house gone bust?

— Bust-as-fuck.

— Do you have an axe, no? Do you have a clean rainwater tank ordered? Do you know how to fiddle your meter so your electricity bill isn't so big that you have to live off noodles? A man in caravan eleven lived off noodles for three years. He died. Another neighbour, Ethel at number seven, died too.

— I live in number seven, he says.

— Yup. People die here. In winter it gets so fucking cold you could freeze to death in your bed. You are aware that you are living in what is essentially a metal tin at the bottom of seven mountains?

— Doesn't scare me.

— Tough guy, ay?

— Pretty fucking much, he says.

5

SHE ALWAYS knows hours before that she will log on and sometimes she tries to wait and then it is even better, but there is still a reluctance to go on and a wish that she could not even want to look; but mostly she just wants to see. Mostly. Her mother is asleep again and it is still early and she is quietly clicking on the laptop, that quick hum and click and the sign turning around and typing in her password and making sure to remember to clear the search history, taking off the parental lock, then going in.

There's three of them. A woman and a man. A third person. They pull up her skirt and take her knickers down and there it is, she is beautiful. The woman has a name and a website; she is from Rio, she is stunning, the curve of her back as she bends over, the breasts small and perfect, the woman taking a nipple into her mouth and the man gets behind her. She doesn't want to see that, just that there is a woman like her who was once a girl like her and she is confident and cool, and why is it this is the only place she can see a body like her own having sex? There was *Boys Don't Cry* and she has a few models to look up to now, but other than that she feels like she is forever searching to find girls like her who are still wanted and attractive and normal. Stella checks again that the living-room door is closed and it is and it is a kind of falling this, but she can't stop watching. A smell of cigarette smoke on her own breath. Dizzy still from inhaling. Lewis likes to smoke, he blew it in her face once and she thought she'd die right there on the ground in front of him. The woman laughs. There is an empty wine glass on the table beside her and she is wearing high-heels. Her legs are long and pretty and her hair. The screen is blue and it makes the living room feel seedy and strange and alien and she can't help herself. She is Little Red Riding Hood and her feet will walk her through the forest to the Big Bad Wolf and he will wear a frilly gown and, instead of letting him eat her, she will hack his head off with an axe. It's a foregone conclusion.

Stella opens the living-room door quietly and kicks the frost off her boots, only now realising she has still had them on the whole time.

— Why can I smell cigarette smoke?

She pauses in the hallway and looks toward the bedroom.

— I don't know.

— Where have you been?

— I said hello to our new neighbour, he's moved into number seven. I was helping him move some stuff over to the bonfire pile.

— Is he nice?

— He's a giant beatnik and his mother slept with an angel.

— Excellent.

Stella steps into a bathroom barely wider than a shower

cubicle. She sits on the loo. This is a new phase and they didn't write about it in the leaflets the doctor gave her. Once this winter is done and she is a year older she can maybe go to that group in the city for trans teens, but right now she is a pioneer. It's trial and error. Girls don't stand to take a piss no matter how much they might want to, so she is doing it like this. If she sits and pushes it down, it works. The toilet seat is freezing. Her bones have turned to mush and she is fading back into this cold, taking in the wooden cladding painted white on the walls, the slight damp in the corner that Constance keeps painting over. She is hungry. She listens to the tinkle and presses her feet flat against the wall – that's how small this space is, she can pee and keep her feet flat on the wall and spit in the sink all at the same time. In the girls' loos at school they pee like a tap. There's no subtlety. It's like a broken dam. On, then off. Full flood, little tinkle. Stella starts slow, then speeds up, then tapers off. What if someone hears her at the new coffee diner at the bookshop in town? What if someone notices in the new ladies' toilets with the hair-straighteners that cost a quid to use and the condoms and the toothbrushes that come in a little plastic ball that you chew on until your teeth are clean. If someone listened to her peeing! What kind of fucking freak would do that anyway? At home (like now) she always turns the tap on. If someone listened and said something, she could shout at them that they are obviously twisted sickos listening to a girl take a piss and then the bookshop staff would probably throw them out and then they might pat her on the back and ask if she was okay and then they might even give her a free muffin. She is paranoid. Nobody is so acutely aware of her body and how it sounds or works or looks, especially if they don't know. Lewis is aware. He holds his breath when she walks past him. It feels good. She walks slower, hoping one day he'll pass out entirely. She rips off one square of toilet roll. It takes thirty days to make a new habit. Rip off the square. Fold it. Drop it. Don't think about the rainforest. Somebody knocks on their front door and she flushes quickly, goes out to find a note has been slipped under the door. Stella bends to pick it up and turns it over to read it.

To My Darling Constance — I Am Sorry, forgive me x.

It is Alistair's handwriting.

Evidently not dead yet.

She thought her mother would kill him when he went back to this last wife one more time. So far, so not dead. The axe is still in the tree. Why did Alistair even want to reel her mother in? Why make her love him when he knew he'd never leave his wife? This wife hates Stella. She looks at her and sees Constance and it makes her feel ill. Constance is playing records every night and drinking wine and walking on the mountains for hours. Alistair's taxidermy apologies to Constance are all around their caravan. A goose head wearing pearls and tortoiseshell specs. A tiny mouse standing on a street corner under an umbrella. A bird asleep on a bible under a chandelier. Stella waits until the footsteps have gone all the way down Ash Lane before she clicks open their metal door. There is a big square box on the mat. A car starts down in the car park. She looks out but she can't see him.

— Who was that?

— Pizza delivery leaflet!

The box is too big for lumberjack shirts. Stella always

puts her father's useless gifts into the charity shop at Clachan Fells. Somewhere in the village there is a boy walking around dressed like her father's son. Stella steps out onto the porch to make sure he is gone. If he ever gives her boy-shirts again she will leave them on his step. Folded very, very neatly and no note.

Red berries on the holly bush sparkle with frost. She goes carefully down the steps and picks up a stick and jabs at the bird-bath, trying to free the leaves, but they are frozen solid. She blows on her fingers. Dogs bark somewhere down the hill. Alistair's whitehouse sits up on the mountain with smoke curling out of the chimney. She clenches her fist. He broke her mother's heart again. She is Little Red Riding Hood and there is an axe in their tree. Stella doesn't believe anyone would ever get to her with their shitty lines about big, round eyes or shiny, pointy teeth. He is toxic. He makes her mother ill.

A woman appears at the other side of her garden fence, she stops, lights a roll-up and takes a little silver bottle out of her pocket and has a drink. Through the hole at the bottom of her fence she can see the woman's old army boots stand on a pile of frosty leaves. Her hand is rammed in her pocket and the other has a thick suede glove on it, her hair is white and her eyes are a watery blue. Stella wonders if she is visiting someone because she has never seen her in the caravan park before.

— There isn't much light, she says.

— Those clouds will clear in a minute, Stella says.

The woman taps where an old heart beats under thin skin.

— You have two spirits, she smiles.

— No, I don't, Stella says.

The woman is wearing a thick donkey-jacket and even from here she smells like pickles. Behind her the mountains bathe in light as white cloud shifts and rays of sun spill out. The woman tips her head back and stares at the sun, so her eyes light up and her face softens its craggy lines and her white hair is haloed.

— Are you staring right at the sun? Stella asks.

— I'm staring right under it.

— You'll go blind.

— No, I won't. I was taught how to by the sunlight pilgrims, they're from the islands furthest north. You can drink light right down into your chromosomes, then in the darkest minutes of winter, when there is a total absence of it, you will glow and glow and glow. I do, she says.

— You glow?

— Like a fucking angel, she says.

Stella turns around to look behind her.

A gate clacks in the wind.

Dogs bark further down the caravan park.

The woman is gone.

Away over on the furthest hills the wind farm's nacelle rotate and the big white tripod legs supporting some of them look like they could just start marching toward the caravan park and trample all their homes. Like that time when the mine shafts were swallowing up caravans right into the ground and everyone was trying to move out. Pitbulls begin to scratch at the satanists' kitchen window. He sticks his head up between the curtains and scowls at Stella, points toward his dogs as if she is waking them up, and he is sweaty like he has been shagging his satanist girlfriend.

– Sorry!

– Do you know what fucking time it is? he muffles.

– Fucking sue me, she says.

Stella hurries back to her caravan and clicks the door shut. Leans against it. For a fraction of a heartbeat she gets the creepiest feeling that old pickly lady was Gunn. The air feels like glue. Like it is too thick. Like breathing is something she has to consciously invest her time and effort to do. By the kitchen are her mother's latest stacks of tins and rice and soy sauce for their apocalypse cupboard. There are four whole crates of wine. Stella picks up the box that Alistair left and she takes it into the living room and places it on the table and then, on an urge, she decides to hide it. She places it to the side of the sofa. It isn't quite hidden enough, so she drags it behind the sofa and chucks a woollen throw over it. She tidies her mum's records away.

– Mum, how many times have you played Neil Young this week?

– At least thirty.

– He's depressing.

– He's a genius.

– So, what's he so fucking depressed for then?

Stella's fingers are numb, it is too, too cold. It's the kind of biting nip that gets into your bones and the only way to get warm again is to lie in a hot bath, and they don't have one of those.

– Stella, who was at the door earlier?

– Nobody. I was looking to see how much stuff was over on the green for Bonfire Night.

Lies come so easily. Like her tongue is built for untruths. She would be a lethal spy. Stella snaps open the back air vent on the wood-stove, just enough so the paper and kindling will catch. The trick is to snap it shut before the backdraught and smoor make her throat raw. She peels newspaper pages off and wrings each into a long twisted snake, lines up ten twists and ties each one into a doughnut shape and throws them on the bottom of the grate, then she builds kindling around them in a teepee shape. As the match strikes there is a flare and the smell of sulphur as paper catches. She closes the grate, her fingers black with soot. The faded old bullet caravan next door sags. Behind Dylan's caravan there is the car park and garages and Blackfoot Burn with its sinking sand, then fields rise up toward forests and steely crags on the mountains. Winter stretches out ahead of them, a straight road with only ice and snow and one man walking along it and no other people, just that one person. It is something she saw in a horror film in a tent in the back of the white trash kids' caravan, where there were about eleven of them in one tiny skinny caravan. They made her smoke a cigarette when she was six. They all sat in this tent watching horror movies and she was so frightened she couldn't move. One came on where a girl slept in her bedroom and there were thousands and thousands of dolls in there and she put down her cigarette and it all went on fire and the dolls were alive, each and every one of them watching her as flames licked up around the room. Then they played a movie where a man walked along on an endless road. The trees were bare and the sky was white and birds were circling. He walked like that for about an hour. It was terrifying. Stella gets this horrible feeling when winter is coming in. Clachan Fells gets the deepest snow of anywhere in the region but it's not even that. Dark is following them. It's coming to cloak everything. Each day it will eat a little more light until they will wake up one morning to find the sun won't rise again. Stella feels like she is standing on the beginning of that long road and everybody is gone. The whole world frozen and nobody left but her and birds circling above her. What then? Stella looks up at the seven sisters. The tallest one has the best views. From up there you can see the whole world. Except of course you can't. But it feels like you could. On the mountain that everyone calls the fifth sister there is a long procession of willow trees, they look like Victorian women with wide bustles all setting off on a long journey.

— Go back to bed for a little while, Stella, we can leave in half an hour.

— I'm just sitting here.

— Doing what?

— Thinking.

Her mother doesn't say anything, the fire catches, it pops and crackles into flame.

6

THERE IS a message. It blinks in the bottom of the screen. Stella sits at the table with her fingers in a steeple. Wind whistles around and – even though the cavity under their caravan is weighted with scree and pebbles from the shore and its haunches are set in blocks of concrete – it feels like they will whirl away. Snowfall has been steady for twenty minutes. She clicks onto the message. Who would have thought he'd e-mail back. There is just a row of emojis: a smiley face, clapping hands, a heart.

It would be easier to be with a boy like him.

He understands.

On the lower part of the e-mail she had told him she'd be true to who she is, but she still won't be able to go to high school without being bullied. Stella glances over to the photograph of her mum with a little baby and even there she didn't look like a boy. Sometimes she catches Constance looking at her as if she's scanning her face for a sign of him. Cael Fairbairn has ceased to exist. Thirteen months ago the girl that wore his body got up and told everyone to quit calling her by the wrong pronoun. She ditched her old wardrobe in a wheelie bin. Her mother faltered for a day, then got on board. They changed Stella's name on everything and when she goes to high school people that didn't know her before would not be able to tell, except this is Clachan Fells where everybody knows what is going on with everyone else. Stella turns the photograph away because looking at it makes her feel uneasy. If she gets bullied at school and can't stop them, she'll drop out. She is not killing herself to sit a few exams in four years' time. Constance is cleverer than most of the teachers anyway. She could probably do her exams a year early and go straight to university and work so hard that one of those big old farmhouses up on the mountain, the old ones in ruins, one of those will be hers and she won't even tell her mum she bought it; she'll get it all done up and just give her the keys for Christmas because while everyone else in the world is odder than an odd thing, her mum is, in all truth, the coolest person she knows. Stella types back to the guy in Italy. Clicks *Send*. The temperature gauge on the wall now reads minus four. It is warmer than earlier. The man from no. 6 (who tells everyone his name is Alan when they all know it is Tim) walks past with a huge bag of salt for his path and marches up to his alien caravan. Ida told her that he is building a spaceship in the bay window, complete with controls and knobs, and he reckons he's going to fly right up there when the aliens come. It is one of those mornings when time elongates. One minute is an aeon all on its own. The fire crackles. A clock ticks. In the bathroom Constance brushes her teeth, spits, turns off the tap, she comes through and pours coffee. Her face is clean and bare. She never wanted a daughter, what she wanted was a son. Alistair told Stella that, the last time she spoke to him. Her mother drinks the coffee down straight and black. She wears thick fisherman's socks and tight jeans and a blue polo-neck with two long-sleeved thermal tops underneath. Wind keens down the chimney and the wood-burner glows. Stella pulls on two pairs of socks and laces her boots, and her mother soaks the porridge bowls and gets her coat on and they are both out the door without a word.

Their feet crunch on the gravel path.

— So the new guy in number seven is from London as well?

— Yup, exactly like Vivienne that was his mum; he used to live with her and his gran in a cinema called Babylon.

— Really? Maybe he's going to clean the caravan up a bit while he's here.

Constance glances at the trampled-down thistles at no. 7 as they walk by. At the end of the path there is a man bent over into a C-shape, as if he carries the whole world on his back, as if he is Atlas and he has been conned and doesn't know that if he just bends a knee and walks away the world will stay up all on its own.

— Good morning, Barnacle.

— Morning, Constance, this winter is going to be the death of us all! he says.

— We've got a new neighbour, Stella says.

— An Incomer?

— Yup.

— Is he staying?

— Looks like it.

As they walk past, Barnacle turns his head sideways to look up at Stella.

— Mum?

— Why are you whispering, Stella?

— I was wondering why Barnacle lost all his land — like what is he doing here?

— He spent all the money, he doesn't have anything now.

— On what?

— Prostitutes and drugs, that's what Ida told me.

Stella turns around and looks back at the man shuffling up his steps. Her mum is walking quickly as ever and she has to hurry to keep up. They walk away across to the garages and along a frozen path, over the burn and onto the farm road. Stella claps her hands together in her gloves and looks out over fields.

— Mum, have you noticed?

— What?

— Nobody's out, not even a dog walker.

The farm road is empty and the motorway hums nearby.

The whole place feels so bare and stark for a minute it gives Stella the creeps.

Clachan Fells mountains are gold but the sunlight is already fading to grey — fields are furrowed for winter with frozen ridges of soil and a ten-foot-tall scarecrow throws his stick-arms out against the vastness. He is dressed in a bubble jacket, with furry lapels and a pair of goggles. Up on the hills there are tall sticks with fluorescent-painted footballs on top, rags fluttering. Those are rows of poor scarecrow-cousins — not like this guy! Stella shivers, the cold already in her bones.

At the school gates Constance gives her the absence note. Down in the playground four mums are chatting outside the gym. One of them looks at Stella, then turns quickly away.

I have a friend in Italy. Stella says this to herself while trying not to pay attention to the flutter of fear she feels when they look at her. It is only one year since they thought she was a boy, and nobody has got used to it yet. All their robot children like their knobs and buttons shiny and silver and none of them understand what a real robot has to withstand, if they are to have so much rust but still be able to run as fast as the others on sports day or sing as loud at Christmas. The carols! 'Little Donkey', the verse about Mary carrying the heavy load, it always makes her cry.

– Do you want me to take the note in? Constance asks.

– No, Mum, it is fine.

– Okay, I'm only asking! Are any of those mums the parents of the boys who . . . you know?

– Who battered me at Ellie's Hole?

Her mum winces.

There are tears in the corner of her eyes.

Constance Fairbairn never cries and there is nothing worse than seeing tears in your mother's eyes and knowing you have caused them. She has to tell her something quickly to fix-it-right-now.

– I have a new friend anyway.

– Who?

– Just this guy from Italy, I met him on the trans-teen website, he sends me golden hand claps – and no, that isn't something rude.

Stella strides toward school with the note held lightly in her hand. She tries to walk like her mother. A tall walk. Easy. Assured. Those mothers are looking at her already and they give even worse looks to her mum, because she had two lovers for decades and everybody judged her for that and now she has a daughter when she used to have a son. Some of the villagers think being a Fairbairn is the devil's work. Stella is going to walk past them in a minute so she must keep her breathing steady. She won't tell Constance that every one of those mothers has a son who was at Ellie's Hole that day. The mothers know and she has to let it go because she is partly an angel but vengeance is not her job. That must be why she likes Dylan so much already. He's a smelly, tired, broken, tattooed angel who looks like his heart has ruptured with loss, but that smile – if she were her mother, she'd not go back to Alistair, she'd introduce herself to the Nephilim's offspring with his tired eyes, and there's no point in thinking this because Constance always sleeps with her father again. It makes her skin crawl. She remembers reading a book about a woman who had so much love to give the whole world, enough for everyone, bundles and bundles of it wrapped in brown paper with string and enough for the mean spirits and the sorrowful and cruel. All that love. All of it to give out into a world with people like those hard, horrible women with their shitty fucked-up sons! It is not love that Stella would deliver to them in brown paper parcels tied with string.

A haar-frost mist seeps along the playground.

The women walk up toward her and their feet and legs disappear into the mist, so they appear to begin at the knees. She walks past them and through an entrance with *Girls* written above it in stone. Everyone is filing into the last assembly for this year but it feels like they might never have one again, with the news and the Internet scares, and she watched an airport scene on the telly earlier where everybody was trying to get out to somewhere warmer and they all looked frantic. Stella runs along a corridor to the left (away from the teachers) to post her note into the *Absences* box. She walks back up through the mist and Constance is looking after the other mums with her head held up high. Her mother takes her scarf off and wraps it around Stella's neck and tucks it in and strokes her cheek with her thumb (only once).

– Are you sure you want to help me get furniture today, Stella?

– I don't want to sit in assembly with my class.

– Okay, just this once.

They march with their heads down toward Clachan Fells Tearoom.

– We need to find as much as we can today – it might be the last trip for a little while if this weather is going to get worse? Are you okay? Did someone say something to you?

– No, Mum, can you stop worrying?

They walk past a small greasy spoon with big red star-signs in the window listing a full breakfast with fourteen items. Three truckers turn their heads to look at Constance as she walks by. Their trucks are outside, stacked with long tree trunks. It takes Stella all her focus not to take down her jeans and wee on the glass, just to stop them looking at her mother. Constance opens the tearoom door and lets Stella walk through first. Heat makes their skin prickle and the windows steam up. It smells of tea and cake. Four old women sit in front of a wide flatscreen.

– I don't eat butter, I still like to keep my waist, the eldest says.

She pats her lumps and bumps and smiles at Stella, who is pointy-of-chin and lithe as a dancer. The oldest woman wears a cardigan and a vest top and no bra and her breasts droop down to her belly. Emblazoned on the vest top is the slogan *Beauty Is Only Skin Deep*. Stella grins at her and the old woman gives a toothy smirk back. The telly drones on and Constance goes up to the counter.

— It's snowing in Israel.

A tired woman at a table in the corner says this, shakes her head.

— What?

— Look, it's snowing in Israel.

— There's an iceberg coming from Norway. Bloody Ice Age, that's what it's going to be, another says.

They all stare at the television.

— Big bloody iceberg, bigger than the Wishbone Hotel.

— It's not an iceberg, you idiot, it's sea-ice. It's not coming from Norway either, it's coming from the Atlantic, Toothy says.

— It's a bloody iceberg.

— It's sea-ice from the ATLANTIC.

— What do you know about the Atlantic?

— I know it's not fucking Norway, Toothy responds.

— Well, what's the ocean around Norway then?

— It's the Norwegian Sea. I was a good sailor. Toothy adjusts her pink top.

— I don't think lying on your back constitutes sailing, the tired woman says.

— It's polar caps melting, it's cooling all the air over the sea. The Gulf Stream can't warm up any more, Stella says.

— Oh, it's not that nonsense, sweetheart, Toothy says.

— What is it then?

— It's old Mother Frost. She wants her wolves back.

Constance looks across at her and then back up at the telly.

— Fry me up two eggs, will you, Morag? I don't want to have to go across the road to the stinky cafe! Toothy says.

The tearoom owner sighs, cracks two eggs into an orange pan and they sizzle away. She wipes fat off her fingers onto her apron, spreads butter onto white bread and drops tea-bags into mismatched mugs.

— It's going to arrive here, this iceberg, at Clachan Fells? Constance asks.

Stella gets butterflies listening to her mother's tone and the news — like this is real, not just something else that is awful that they see on the news, or every time she turns on her laptop and it is all so ridiculous, it makes her teeth ache.

— That iceberg will arrive down the coast in a few weeks.

— What's to stop it crashing into land? That's what I want to know, the owner says as she places mugs down.

Stella picks through a bowl of wooden Christmas-tree decorations and little clay hearts. She turns them over and they have *Clachan Fells Pottery* stamped on one side. Alistair made them. He is useless. Not one thing in there that makes up a father at all. If he wants a boy so badly, he can make one. He probably doesn't even have that in him, now he's so old. All he's good for is embalming roadkill and baking clay fucking hearts. She puts the little heart back down and leans against her mother and just then Lewis walks by the window.

— Mum, can we go outside?

— Wait a minute.

— I'd write to my MSP but her office is closed, the smallest woman says.

— Can we go?

She tugs at her mother's sleeve.

— Wait a minute, Stella.

The oldest woman spreads butter on her scone and then jam and takes a large bite.

— What can I get you, love?

— Two teas, milk and one sugar.

— You're a nice girl, you'll be fine, mark my words, Toothy says.

Stella does not know what to say, so she nods and tries not to blush. She wants to walk outside and see Lewis and ask him why, when the other boys turned up to Ellie's Hole that night and left her with a scar on her head, why he stayed at home. They are his friends and once they were her friends, but it was always her and Lewis kicking about when they were kids, they were always together. Now he goes everywhere that they do. He kissed her! Now, when he sees her he tenses up and then laughs a bit louder and he always ignores her in class, even if she is paired up with him. It is highly irritating that he is possibly the most beautiful boy on earth, even with his big chin and his skinny legs. She wouldn't say that to him. She'd tell him he was the best gamer on the planet. They'd hold hands in a cinema and her heart would beat right through her chest like one of those pottery monstrosities. Two years ago they played football together and wore the same school strip and kicked about over at the dump, and now he doesn't know what to think when he looks at her. When he leant in and kissed her two months ago, he pushed his whole body against her and she could feel it through his trousers. He likes her just like this. Constance looks at the blueberry muffins and then into her purse and shakes her head and simply pays for the tea. Stella is hungry. It feels like ages until lunch. They wait for the owner to put their tea into styrofoam cups, while traffic outside the windows moves along, all smudged colours and a dull-muted hum.

7

STELLA AND Constance stand side-by-side at the entrance to the city dump. They scan the horizon. A doorway stands alone. Mattresses. Jagged piles of electrical goods, their wires spilled out like the entrails of hedgehogs at Alistair's, the one time he showed her how to embalm. There is a wall of fridges. A shop mannequin stands on one leg and holds her arm up like she is waiting to ask a question. The tip isn't any better than dead people's houses but at least their stuff is contained in rooms and spaces that make sense. The longer you stand in the tip, the stranger it gets. It's like the guts of the whole world have been thrown up. A mound of plastic in all different colours blurs in front of her eyes and she has to look away or it will give her a headache. They're not looking for any of this stuff. They need to get over to the other side where furniture gets dropped off. Diggers nudge in toward valleys at the north side of the tip. It smells like the end of the world. There are no lorries arriving to make drop-offs, so the two of them stand there motionless for a few more seconds.

Constance lifts up the wire fence and Stella slips under. They head for the far side, heads down, hoods up.

It is automatic to scrutinise the ground ceaselessly for wet concrete, or needles, or medication, or knives, or broken glass. All of people's lives are here. Their bills. Letters. Even their blood on bits of tissue or sanitary pads. The boys in the caravan park pointed that out to her one time when she still played with them. You can even find DNA in this place. That's what one of them said.

Her mother is wearing soft old jeans and faded leather gloves. They pause for a minute as the diggers change direction. It's always like this. The strangest game of musical statues in the world. Here I am – playing still behind a mound of several thousand tyres! Stella looks down at her boots. They are almost the same size as Constance's now. Their four boots are black, scuffed, standing in a row pointing straight ahead, steel-toe caps, boots from dead soldiers. They are the only kind her mother has ever bought her, apart from wellies.

– Come on, let's move, Constance says.

She trudges along behind her mother, the sky white and the land-gulls spiralling. That woman from Rio had the most beautiful shoes, so elegant and tall, and they made her legs look even slimmer and prettier. Stella will wear shoes like that. One day her mother will despair. On the other side of the dump, diggers roll forward. Orange warning lights blare on top of cabins. They turn west, forks raised, and plunge into waste. Whenever they pass a decent piece of furniture her mother inspects it quickly, then she leaves a little bright-coloured flag on the top so they can find it later.

Stella follows her mother, keeping up the pace, and she is warm by the time they get to the other side. If Lewis stayed home on the day she got beaten up at Ellie's Hole, then it was because he didn't want to hit her, and he didn't want to see his friends hit her either; and at one time she was pals with them all too and, when they got her on the ground, one was shouting that she'd always be a boy and not to look at him like that, cos he'd never hit a girl. They were so angry because they'd told her all their boy-secrets when they thought she was just like them and she'd slept over at Lewis's a million times and they'd eaten crisps and watched anime and played computer games and talked about girls. He knew. If he's honest about it. He liked her even then. If he would kiss her again, it would be enough to keep her happy for the rest of her life. Except that isn't true. Kissing must be like smoking. If you like it, you always want another.

Her mother takes off her gloves as they reach high cliffs made from mulched paper – she is tempted (as always) to jump. It's a thirty-foot drop. She would land in the vast basins of paper below. Stella has done it a hundred times and she can see herself leaping, an imprint of light against the sky – her outline like a negative. It's dangerous, but every time she survives it feels like being reborn. She hasn't done that for years now. Her mother's fine hair lifts in the breeze and her own head is itchy under her hat now and she has too much saliva in her mouth. She is desperate for a cold drink. The snow is falling again lightly but it won't last long. Stella's breath hovers on the air and she rubs her fingers together and blows on her gloves.

Underneath the dump there are long shafts for the unused coal mines and they stretch out around Clachan Fells. Vast hollow spaces and all that coal just wasted, and up here layers of debris stretch out for miles in every direction. On the other side of the dump are the farmers' fields, the caravan parks, the industrial parks where they have not been for ages. All the big stores are there, the warehouses, DIY stores, a garage and supermarket.

— Mum, can we go over to Ikea for lunch?

— No.

— Why not?

— We don't have any money this week.

— We didn't have any last week.

— We probably won't have any next week, either.

They giggle even though it is not funny.

Wind drags papers along the waste and there is a smell of glue on the air. She can imagine that man in the scary movie just standing on that endless road, looking forward and back and seeing nobody.

— If the snowfall is worse than last year, will it cover the entire caravan?

Her mother shades her eyes and scans the tip. She shrugs lightly but her face looks thinner and more worried than it did yesterday. Stella covers her nose for a minute and breathes in the smell of her woollen gloves, damp with snowfall. When they are scavenging for furniture at the dump she has trained herself not to react to olfactory distractions. They could be anything. It is better not to know. Metal pylons stand out starkly against the sky. There is something creepy about them jutting out of the rubble like that. Two hilled peaks of rubbish frame the road that the diggers trundle along. To the west there are vast piles of tyres all stacked on top of each other. It is dangerous over in that area. To the east is where the hospitals and old folks' homes tend to dump their stuff and they sometimes see some wired-looking junky wandering over there.

Land-gulls swoop over diggers, and snippets of cries are cut off by the wind. They sound like children crying. Stella picks her way across a pile of ceramic sinks toward an old children's wardrobe and wonders what the tips are like in Italy.

— Mum, this one's good — there's no handles but the varnish finish is still nice and there's detail on the edges.

— Any woodworm?

— Nope.

— Mould?

— Little bit, but it's not black. It has a wee ceramic sign that says *1922 c London Fellows*.

— Really?

Her mother picks her way over.

— Look at that, it's a mission design.

— Unidentified person by the cliff area — please leave the danger zone; we repeat, get out of the zone!

A man stands in a digger a hundred feet away from them. He holds the loudspeaker to shout at them again and he waves his arm. The digger's orange light flashes around and around. Constance raises her hand to let him know she has heard. Her mum puts a little fluorescent flag on top of the wardrobe, so it will be easier to find it later. They take the usual route towards farmland until they emerge at the west side of the dump. Wind snaps at any inch of bare skin it can find. Stella's glad of the fisherman's socks under her boots. Her mother's hair is so pale it blends into the skyline behind her and her skin too, like it's never seen sunlight. Alistair's traditional wee whitehouse is just up there and her mother glances that way. She has been with him on and off since she was nineteen years old. Stella has a horrible feeling it is only a matter of time before they start sleeping together again. Through every wife and fight and change in their lives, it always ends up that way. Stella will never speak to him as long as she lives. The man is hideous. There is nothing nice about him. She just knows that tonight she will dream about a hedgehog with HDMI cables for guts and land-gull eyes and it is going to be answering questions asked by a naked mannequin.

They cross over an iced pond.

Her mum tests the weight, one step ahead of her all the way and frowning.

Stella skids along behind her.

Over through the trees three parked tractors have icicles hanging off the big forks and the fat tyres and the cabins. The trees around them are all decorated with glacial spikes as well. They are appearing almost as she looks at them. Winter doing her decorating. Making the world as pretty as can be. Up on the nearest mountain a herd of fallow deer emerge from the forest and canter up the mountain, young bucks at the rear.

Constance and Stella cross the farm road. Spikes of hay crunch underfoot, there are large dark patches on the ground where hay-bales rest all summer. Stella used to roll the bales underfoot, gathering speed until she had to run to stay on top of one. She can still see that road in her mind from that film and she will dream about it again soon. She hates those nightmares. There is always a long icy track with endless fields on either side and the trees are black silhouettes; there is not one bit of green anywhere and just one person left in the whole world and they are walking along that road wearing a red coat. You'd be able to see them for miles and miles around.

A flock of birds fly low overhead.

Mossy greens and purples and red-golds have faded to brown.

Sleet billows off the mountain.

Treetops disappear in one blink as the white owerblaw races over the mountaintop and drifts down thicker and faster, painting everything white until within seconds the whole landscape is utterly changed.

8

MORNING COMES through the curtains to create a square
of sunlight on the floor. He slept on and off, then woke to
see mist creeping along the garden earlier on. Now there is
frost all over the ground and the mountains radiate all bright
and white in the morning sun. Breathing feels so clean here
it's almost making him dizzy. Dylan takes her book out
of the bedside cabinet. He has been avoiding it. He goes
through to the living room and opens the first page to find a
cutting from the *Soho Gazette*. The paper is thin and the ink
is faded. There is a photograph of his grandmother cutting a
ribbon and, if you really look, you can just make out a baby
strapped on under her coat. *Babylon, Art-House Cinema, 17th
March 1953.* A chic Soho audience smiles in black-and-white.
Beside the cutting there is a flat bit of ribbon with frayed
ends pinned to the page. Vivienne's book is musty and the
pages have grown crisper from the damp in the attic flat.
The neighbours were always trying to get her to fix the roof.
Fix the roof, they'd say. She'd smoke cigarettes and tap her
foot in irritation and ask them if they knew how many years
it was since she'd bought new shoes, let alone an entire fucking roof! Vivienne used to sit with this book on her lap,

sketching things. He turns the page. There is a sketch of Gunn. She is cleaning the projector. Her socks show above her boots. She is wearing a pinny. On the very first opening night Gunn was so nervous. She'd taught herself how to use all the equipment but she hadn't tried it all together yet. When the very first reel played, she looked out at the back of the audience's heads and held her breath. When she was sure the reel would work okay, and none of the customers were going to ask for their money back, when she saw they were all rapt and with halos around their heads, as she liked to say, she sat down and fed her baby in the projectionist booth, lulled her to sleep listening to 1920s gangsters holding a shootout in New York.

Tucked in between the pages is a folded letter. His mother's scrawled handwriting:

Dearest Dylan,

I suppose you might have sold the caravan and gone abroad and now some holidaymaker is reading this. If that is the case, then please just put this book in the bin. It's only drawings. I was never any good with words. If this is you, then I am sorry I never kept contact details for your father, but here is what I know: he is one inch taller than you. (Do you remember I used to tell you that you came from a race of giants and you would never believe me — well, here are some cuttings about tall skeletons found in Wisconsin, Bulgaria, Africa, New York, Greece, the Netherlands, Ireland. I know there are fake ones of these online but some of them are real. I do believe that somewhere down the line, these were your people.) Your father lived in Hebden Bridge. I don't imagine there are many tall men there. I don't have any wisdom for you, sorry, only a recipe for Scotch broth and some (at best) average drawings. I just wanted to tell you that holding your hand when you were a kid, watching The Wizard of Oz *on the big screen in our pyjamas, sitting on the back step eating our cheese sandwiches together or hanging out with Gunn, drinking gin — they were the very best minutes of my life. I could have travelled the world and nothing would have beat them. I'm sorry I didn't teach you how to let the world in (other than in film) but I never figured out how to do it myself.*

All my love,
Vivienne
(Mum)
xxx

He picks up a pen and a Post-it note. He writes: *Why are there no tall men in Hebden Bridge?* He focuses on breathing in through his nose and out through his mouth. He clicks on the three-bar heater, his fingers and nose already numb from cold. He flicks through a selection of newspaper clippings about tall skeletons found around the world. There is a skeleton with a 20-inch skull and dark eye sockets found in Peru. It is on display in a museum, its teeth still protruding. There is one in Greece at 7.6 feet, another in New Orleans at 8 feet 2 inches. There is a clipping about Robert Wadlow, all 8 feet 11.1 inches of him, the tallest person ever recorded. It makes his own 6 feet 7 inches seem pretty insignificant.

He clicks the kettle on.

Drops a teabag into a mug.

She never said anything nice like that while she was alive. Not once. She was probably pissed when she wrote the letter. Impending death makes people act nice out of desperation. He looks out the window. The sky is so blue. It's piercing. The caravan-site store he visited earlier was not so bad. It's in a cool old metal tractor storeroom and well stocked. He can go back later to get more supplies. The book lies open on the table. He can imagine Vivienne sitting here. Looking out at the mountains. Reading, reading, reading. Dylan opens the cupboard to try and find something to eat and the Tupperware box and ice-cream tub just sit there.

– Morning, he says.

He closes the cupboard door.

Gunn MacRae died on May Day; she curled up in her bed like a fragile child and Vivienne lay down with her and stroked her hair and sang her songs until she went over to the Other Side. Dylan watched them both from the door. He can see her now. Her profile like that of a Roman. Thin arms. A smile like she knew something about something but she wasn't telling anyone jack-shit. There is an ache he cannot shift and he is uncertain how something this physical has the remotest chance of going. Scoured out. That's what he is. He goes over to the window. There is still no sign of the moon-polisher. If he had a camera he would have filmed her and made it into a short. Maybe that's what he should be doing with his life now. Making films and living, instead of watching them and merely existing. It's a thought. He picks up Vivienne's book and find a P.S. on the next page –

P. S. Your grandmother told me she prised the keys to Babylon from a corpse's fist. He was a Lord of some kind, apparently they used to have orgies in there with laudanum and plum brandy, you know the sort. It came to the family in the worst of karma really, so of course we'd never get to keep the place for ever. I answered the door to Babylon one night to find the devil on our back step. He held a top hat in his hands. He was wearing a Savile Row suit with scruffy old trainers. He asked if Gran was home. I said no, but he could smell mince and hear her singing loudly upstairs. He asked what she was cooking, I said shepherd's pie and he said it was his favourite.

It was awkward.

Mum xxx

The field over at the park is frosty but that isn't enough to stop the locals, who are still building a bonfire. The air is crisp and it has that Guy Fawkes vibe that he almost forgot existed. The pile of broken furniture is stacked up and all the stuff he didn't need is going to burn and he supposes he isn't leaving. At least not for now. Right now he needs to walk. Dylan tucks the cuttings into the back of the sketchbook, then wraps it up in Vivienne's woollen cardigan and puts it under a pillow in the little bedroom. He rummages for a hat and yanks on a beanie that smells musty. He finds a pair of fingerless gloves. There is a toothbrush in a wrapper in the bedroom cupboard and a small travel-size tube of toothpaste. He brushes his teeth hard and takes a long drink of water. He bought two bars of chocolate from the shop and some oatcakes; it's a good enough breakfast, hits at least some of the main food groups. He eats the oatcakes and stares up at the entire Clachan Fells range. It isn't wise to walk a mountain in Chelsea boots.

Not wise at all.

The goats will laugh at him.

Or the sheep.

Or whatever it is that lives up there — wild pagans dancing naked around fires at night, wearing animal horns on their heads. That would be something. There don't appear to be any of those so far, but he did hear two people in the shop talking about a druid who owns a castle nearby and has a sex room in one wing. Dylan has not seen any druids — not that he'd know what one looks like. What he can see are some cows in the distance. What he should do is find an Army & Navy store and buy some wellies or a waterproof coat or something. That would take time, though. It might be okay to go just a little way up the mountain. All that space is too tempting. He can't resist it. It's like that clean feeling on Christmas mornings: waking up in the attic, going through to the kitchen where Gunn would have a real Christmas tree next to the old hearth, a sock hanging up that she knitted herself a hundred years ago.

The air inside the caravan is almost as cold as outside — it's a constant nip and he clicks off the fire, pulls on a jumper and grabs his jacket and he's out the door into the wind. He has to take a few steps back to see if the woman is at home, or Stella. What do you say to a woman who polishes the moon? *Pleased to meet you, Dylan MacRae, borderline-Nephil.* It is one of Vivienne's more endearing myth origins. A child created by a fallen angel and a mortal woman. Never just — one-night stand, didn't catch his name, sorry, son, love you anyway.

Dylan crunches along the lane. In this light the caravans appear tired. The two at the top of the lane have dirty windows and assorted debris stacked up in their gardens. Rose Cottage is at the end and it has flowers around the door and plastic pink flamingoes in the garden. No. 9 next door is the best-kept caravan. The silver sheen looks like it is treated with something. There is a neat, upright chimney poking out the top and smoke curling up. She has a wood-stack in her back garden and what looks like tarpaulin over random bits of furniture. He wants to knock on her door.

What if he did, though?

What if he knocked three times?

Never answer the door if someone knocks three times – Vivienne used to say that. She said demons always knock three times, but they can only gain access if you invite them in. So if someone knocks on your door three times and you shout *Come in* – well, then you're just asking for it and if it is a demon then you really are fucked. What you have to do is go to the door and look through the spy-hole and see what is standing on your doorstep and (of course) if it *is* a demon, then you tiptoe back down your hallway and put the lights out and hide behind the sofa and hope they go-the-fuck away.

His grandmother's journey is the filament Babylon grew upon. Gunn MacRae arrived in London as a pregnant run-away from the islands furthest north. She had five pounds in her pocket and she didn't know a soul. One night at the White Hart in Soho she joined an all-night poker session and proceeded to drink five grown men under the table. She was raised on the kind of home-brew that blinds by the bottle, so London gin never fazed her. She played the last man standing until his heart gave out. All the money on the table and the keys to Babylon just there in his fist.

Dylan's phone buzzes. He walks through to the bedroom but it isn't there, then back through the hall; he retraces his steps and opens the bathroom cabinet to find it buzzing next to his toothbrush: *Premises at 345a Fat Boy Lane are secured & cannot be re-entered. A. N. Brogue.*

Dylan puts his phone in his pocket. He wants to punch someone repeatedly in the face. He breathes out slowly, tries not to be so angry, tries really hard to be rational about it, not get upset like this, but it is all too fast. They were all sitting in the attic drinking tea, and chatting, and watching telly, just six months ago! Him, Gunn, Vivienne. He feels the faintest lurch, the world spinning on its axis and him tipping somehow with it.

9

WHEN HE slows down his face gets numb, it's disconcerting. He needs to walk faster. He is unsure if he can even feel his toes any more. Dylan turns onto the car park and crosses around the back of the garages. He'll need to insulate the caravan or, like the kid says, he'll just die in this. He'll need stuff. Thermals. A better fire. He really needs clothes. The landscape is layered in different shades of grey, touches of green, brown, white – all the way to the horizon. The mountains are bigger than anything he has seen before. Everywhere there is rock, stone, vastness. Dylan pauses to catch his breath. He is about to live in one of the coldest places on earth this winter. Of all the places he could have come to mourn! His boots crunch across frosty ground. His big hands flex in fingerless gloves and keeping his focus on the nearest mountain, that is the thing. Grief keeps drawing him back, though. Like something he catches out of the side of his eye. Walking down a hospital corridor. The nurse lays down her chart. She looks up and folds her hands quite carefully. Walking back out into the world after. People. Noise. Newspaper-sellers. Buses. Rain. Traffic. London. Sticking the key in the door at Babylon and just standing there in the doorway for how long?

He squeezes through a tiny path and as he comes out onto the farm road a twig skelps him in the face, a touch of blood, red on his finger and stark against a bleached-out sky – a harbinger of snow up there, even he can tell that. A sign on a fence says *Eighre*: and there is a picture of a little beach; the arrow points along a pathway and that walk is longer than he can go right now. The trees smell green and woody, the furrowed soil frozen but still with that deep earthy clarity, all undercut by brine from the nearby sea. Across the fields, soil in neat furrows and sparkling with frost for miles. There is an old crooked tree, wide on the base with bald limbs which have faded to look like bone.

The witches' tree.

It soothes him.

Flat mushrooms grow around the base, all soft and wide and potentially fatal. Dylan crosses a wooden stile. Along the side of the field his boots slip on frozen bits of ground and he makes his way up a rocky incline. Height up here. Light so bright he can almost feel his pupils dilate, even though these skies are muted.

He should go back.

While he is out here he seems to be coming back to himself somehow, though.

Also, he can't get pissed while climbing something this big.

That magician's trick.

The rabbit disappeared.

A boy at the front of the audience stares into the hat. Where has it gone? It is elsewhere or not at all. That's the only two options, kid. Elsewhere – not at all: what's your bet? Dylan swallows down hard. He reaches the top corner of the field and he is panting. His throat burns. Below him the farmland brightens from dark brown to orange. A tractor lumbers out of a barn. The tops of caravans in the park are visible now. In the distance there are long trails of light where the motorway must be and he climbs faster, turning regularly to see the world unfold like a map below him. A light smoke drifts further up the mountain from a wee traditional croft house and the air is so cold it stings his nostrils. The sun slips behind a cloud, but a few seconds later the sky brightens fractionally and even that one faint tweak of light repaints shadows and valleys on the mountains.

Dylan steadies himself, puts his hand out on a pine tree and the bark is rough to touch and a tiny spider runs down the trunk, red and quick – right across his fingers. He walks into the forest. Everything quietens. The wind cuts out. The motorway no longer hums in the distance. His breathing slows. Sun spirals down through treetops showing up sediments of silver and amber dust. A frozen pond. Curls of ice make a frost flower on a fallen bough. Each iced petal is perfectly curled and see-through. Winter has been hand-carving them overnight. Placing them here. Dylan takes a photograph on his phone, wishes for a better zoom. He had a look at the temperature on the old barometer before he left and it was minus eight. Up the slope, pine trees taper toward the light; it endlessly changes their shape and texture – sunlight illuminates one branch for a second, then dims a whole section of forest the next.

As the trees grow thicker the light dims. It is soothing. It reminds him of Babylon.

Setting up the projector.

A screen counting back, 10, 9, 8, 7, 6, 5, 4, 3, 2, 1 and that flicker.

Drinking tea.

It is so naturally dark in here that he could set up a projector right in this forest. In the summer he could tie up sheets in the clearing and send out invites to the locals to come and see movies here at night. If this winter ends. He could think about it. He wouldn't charge for admission, not at first. He could supply popcorn and gin, though, make enough doing that once a week to keep himself going. It's a thought. It would be great to see films out here at night, perhaps with some fires going in autumn, hot wine, roasted chestnuts, why not? There is something to love in this. Some people love people, some people love buildings, and he did – he burrowed in his projection booth – but this! Buildings and people – the relationship between them – childhood homes, holiday cottages, a shed in a garden, a derelict car. They showed a documentary last year about a woman who married a bridge.

– It's a long commute to see my new husband, she said.

She lived in Cologne and the bridge was in Prague.

– The heart wants what it wants, she said.

In the same documentary there was a man who wrote love letters to a cargo container and in the film he wept and seemed so genuinely grief-stricken that Dylan realised he had never loved anyone the way that man loved his cargo container, and he couldn't work out what was the most tragic part of that.

– I will not be happy until we are together again, the man said.

Another man exposed himself to lorries in lay-bys on the

motorway while their drivers slept. A young architect fell in love with the Taj Mahal; he said her beauty was unparalleled, every stone of her palace built from grief and devotion.

Birds fly up through the branches.

Dylan's heart races.

He is so high up now, he crosses over a burn and a trickle of water joins the rough swish of his jeans and a crunch of frosted pine needles as he walks. There is a new track at the bottom of the mountain and a post with a blue square on it and a green square to indicate the beginning of a heritage trail. He turns and looks back down the mountain and the landscape spreads out, vertiginous.

10

IT HAS been nearly two hours' walking already. From up here you can see the caravan site is made up of rows of vans in different shapes and sizes. Ash Lane is right at the back, it is almost separate from the rest of the park entirely. There are only ten caravans there and they are identical, all with a single, long, same-size garden space around them. To the entrance of the caravan park there is a road and a row of old miners' cottages. Up here on the mountain he is fairly close to the back garden of a traditional wee croft house and from here he can see a man skinning some kind of animal. The man looks up the mountain toward him and raises his hand. Dylan nods and turns to move on. Something about that guy is familiar. He climbs faster to see if he can make it a little higher before turning around; this is the most wintry weather he has ever felt in his life. He wants to put a kettle on to boil, make something hot to drink, toast and butter, soup. His stomach growls.

He walks up through a second, thinner layer of forest and there is a sign from the Forestry Commission. It describes all of the trees that are natural to this region. Pine, fir and larch. The sky whitens ominously and he can hear the sea but he can't see it. A steady whoosh – like bristles of the old sweeping brush across the cinema stage – that pauses just before another wave comes in – the call of a bird high up above – smaller voices of other birds below and a stillness to the air – like the land around him is waiting – ready – preparing – for winter to come. Pine. Wood-smoke. Clean air. Earth. His pores open to release alcohol from the day before yesterday and his heart thuds. He has to push his muscles to keep going until they burn and his throat aches and he has too much saliva in his mouth. He is not used to this.

He stops and spits.

There is a sense of disconnection, a nothingness and a hard-on. He heads up the next slope. His boots slip on wet bark and frosted stones. His toes are numb and so are his fingers. Then he is in a clearing with massive boulders and blackened earth where people have built fires. It begins to sleet, the cold sheets of icy pellets drive him down the mountain a few steps. He puts his head down and steps forward into the driving cold. Now would be the time to turn around, but he laughs and can't seem to stop, awed by the sheer lunacy of this weather as it beats him back. It gets wilder and he ducks his head to keep going and then he's on the ground – an awkward slip and a shooting pain through his elbow, the sleeve of his coat wet and muddy, his knee fucking hurts, the shock of it but he is up already. The sleet drives harder and faster – tells him to quit it – to get real – to go home with his stupid shoes, and that doesn't mean the caravan – it means – take a train – wait until they've put the city together after this winter and start applying for jobs in every cinema in London – get back in a burrow – where ineptitudes like you belong.

– Fuck you!

He shouts it into the wind and the sleet is furious now. His hands are red and wet and if winter was a mistress she'd be a cold, violent bitch. His jeans stick to his legs. Heavy. Awkward. He finds footholds in crags of rock, stretches an arm up, pulls himself over a hulk of stone to find a welcome canopy of trees. Dylan re-enters the forest and these boughs are thicker, more jagged – giant pines sway wildly, obliterating all but the most abstract shapes of sky. His breathing is ragged and each muscle aches. He stops and checks for his tobacco and he still has it. It's sealed enough to be good for a roll-up at the top. It shouldn't get dark until 3 p.m. but if it does, he can probably guide himself back by the lights of the motorway.

Just a little further.

He has been saying that for hours now. Isn't it always the way? Just a little further than before. Just a little more. Just one more drink. Just one more song. Down the slope twig-sculptures hang from branches, they bob and pirouette in the breeze. He takes another photograph. They're sinister. Who has been putting them all here? Maybe the man who was skinning an animal? Maybe the satanists? Or the druid with a sex room. He laughs to himself. And he'd thought Soho was full of its fair share of weird. He steps over a stile that is half-broken, the wood swollen by years of rain and snow; it crumbles beneath his weight and woodlice spill out onto the forest floor, all black scaly armour and hundreds of wriggling legs. Dylan walks along another path until he is going up the mountain vertically and, as he turns around, the view unfolds in every direction – look at that!

Layers of landscape settle everywhere.

The Sunlight Pilgrims

There are trails of white and red lights in the distance: cars emerging from a foggy sleet, and mountains below and jutting crags behind him, and down to the left valleys and peaks and a glimpse of blue further even than waves. A bank of white cloud is drifting up the hillside. It moves quickly. He stops still. Is it dangerous? What are you meant to do when a humongous cloud is coming toward you on a sheer mountain drop? He lifts his phone and there are no bars, he can't even google it. Two eagles spiral out of the cloud, calling out to each other, and one has something small gripped in its claws. They coast on the wind – each wingspan must be about three feet – and they appear almost still. The tips of their wings flutter as the wind carries them forward before they plummet back down through whiteness.

Cloud unfurls – it steals fields and trees and rocks.

Dylan sticks his hands in his pockets.

Fuck it!

It's a cloud.

What can it do?

He cricks his neck. Squares his shoulders. Plants his feet wide. The path below him is gone now and the treetops disappear; a few of the tallest Scots pines stick out, then they are gone. When the cloud reaches him the temperature drops even further and his breath is vapour on the air. Dylan sticks one hand into the cloud. It disappears. He sticks a foot out and it is gone too. The cloud goes through him – through his heart and his lungs, his ribcage, the pulse in his veins, his brain. He holds his arms out but he can't see them any more – he can't even see his jacket – when he looks down it is just a collar and his nose and his hair – then they gone.

This is a kind of flying.

Arms right out.

He is bodyless and travelling at great speed.

The cloud is so dense he could be upside down – falling off the earth – this is what it means to be chilled-to-the-bone. Anything could come at him through this. The first girl he ever kissed, with her brown eyes and upturned nose and stripy socks. A Yeti looking for a husband – ready to drag him home and tell him to put up her broken shelves or rear her Yeti children.

It. Isn't. Passing.

If anything the cloud's getting thicker.

Disoriented, he peers forward.

An endless white tunnel and if he steps into it, he will see what?

Vivienne and Gunn?

It makes him think of the magician's curtain between life and death; any minute now it will open onto an endless bar where rows of creatures with long, narrow teeth hand out cocktails, and when people sip from each straw they are actually siphoning off the last vestiges of their own humanity – the Other Side doing a great trade in soul-mining – and the lizardic bar-staff smile and nod as all that energy is siphoned down into the cellar. Sent out into the universe. Where some monstrous source of life feeds on it.

He can't breathe.

He cannot take a panic attack here!

What if the cloud won't lift?

It feels like something passes right behind him – it raises the hairs on his neck. He hears what could be footsteps or something falling out of a tree and he grips his phone. He can imagine the headline: *Tall man sucked into deadly cloud on mountain, starved to death, pulled out own hair.*

The cloud slows.

His heart hammers, but — a glimpse of a hand, his arm, his nose, coat buttons, then his jeans, his belt, his feet and there is still the same sound behind him, something walking on the rock. Dylan wills himself to turn round. Close enough that he could reach out and touch her — is a doe.

She is just one step away.

Her long neck is soft and brown, her eyes dark and long-lashed. She is unconcerned, grazing on a bit of grass, then turning to saunter up the slope. Her white tail flicks over a boulder and he exhales. When he looks back there are wide-open miles, miles and miles as far as the eye can see — light; movement; fields; farms; motorways; industrial sites with warehouse shops made by metal sheets; what looks like a quarry or a city dump; dots in the distance that are cows and sheep; clusters of rooftops where villages hunker down; and his caravan is a wee speck and he has this sensation of speed like he is standing at the top of the world so he can feel it rotate, in a way he would never experience below sea level.

He wants them to see this.

Vivienne.

Gunn.

It's a stupid want and, aside from that, his mind is always half-tilted toward a woman who polishes the moon. He wants to kiss her. That's a stupid thought as well but it is more real than the detritus of black matter that grief is hauling up in copper buckets. At some point there must, rightly, be a full stop. He scans the view, his heart beginning to slow down. He'll buy binoculars so he can come back and pick out every detail in the landscape. He walks carefully back down and the light drops as he follows the path, seeing his own footprints in the mud and retracing them. Then there is the farm, a spire of smoke curls out of the chimney. Birds flutter up from the woods and soar out across the fields.

11

STELLA UNCLIPS the metal door, it thuds off the doorstopper as she kicks frost off her boots. Up on the mountain white clouds glide over the peaks, so the top of the mountain is hidden. Constance drops her coat onto the armchair then stops, rotates, pulls the throw off a big box sitting just behind their sofa. She lifts the box up and places it on the table, opens the card. If Stella does not breathe until her mum speaks, then everything will be okay. Constance undoes the ribbon on the box. She takes the lid off and places it down and lifts out a perfect wolf-head still attached to its loose pelt. It is immaculate. Her mother hesitates and then slips the thing over her head. The eye sockets fit right over her own and the nose juts out. She is a white wolf. Her ears stick up. The wolf looks at herself in the mirror and there is a faint hint of a smile underneath her long nose. Stella squints at the note on the box again. *To My Darling Constance – I Am Sorry, forgive me x.*

— Where did Alistair get a wolf from?

— I'm guessing one died at the sanctuary.

— That's your Bonfire Night costume sorted then, Stella says.

The two of them stand side-by-side, looking in the mirror. Whatever anger was in her mum is already gone. It is always like that. Constance does clean fury and then it goes and she never stays mad for long, doesn't mince around the house in a toxic-mist of perpetual resentment like Lewis's mum always seemed to do. The two of them look at each other and smile.

— Mum, can I invite a friend for dinner before the bonfire?

— Which friend?

— A new one, Stella exhales.

— Informative.

— The Sisters are having a winter-prep meeting at the village hall, are we going?

— Yup, you better go and get ready, Stella, or we're going to be late!

The temperature gauge on the wall says minus nine — it is getting colder almost every hour right now, winter is going to come and they will be snowed in like Eskimos until spring.

The ambulance creaks its way down a dark road. Wind-screen wipers don't help much against a steady snowfall. They drive slowly. The world is a cleaner, colder, quieter place than it was a week ago. People walk along cobbled roads heading for the village hall. Constance turns the ambulance into the car park. Snow is piled on the verges already. Stella jumps down from the ambulance and it barely makes a sound. Her boots are quiet on the dustier snow on top. Lewis is going in ahead with his brother. The boys who were at Ellie's Hole won't be here, they'll be over at Fort

Hope town hall; the whole of the Clachan Fells region will be in damp rooms holding meetings like this one. Constance holds out her hand and they walk in together.

— There's a lot of extra nuns here? Stella whispers.

— The Sisters of Beathnoch — they are here as volunteers for the 2020 Winter Appeal, they want to help vulnerable people in remote communities, Constance says.

The local minister is up the back talking to the nuns. Stella's entire old class (eight people) are chatting together. She sits on the floor in front of her mum. Lewis is in the front row. He glances back and pretends not to see. What is it he can't see? Or what is it he can't deal with seeing? She isn't asking him even to speak to her. His mum barely even says hello to her now. Stella has her black hair in braids, it is getting longer. She reapplies some lip gloss and is glad she wore two pairs of socks. She can feel Constance sitting behind her and it makes her feel safe. Everyone settles and the chatter begins to peter out as the nuns file onto the stage with the local doctor and a few teachers; the minister steps up last. A weary man in a lumberjack shirt pulls his hat off and looks around. The minister stands up and raises his hand to get silence.

— Thank you all for coming along this evening to discuss forward planning regarding sub-zero conditions in the Clachan Fells region. As you all know, for once we are not alone in having an extreme winter, but this one is going to be more severe than most and so we're already putting plans together to ensure we can all get through it safely. Over by the Exit doors there are lists of jobs that we need volunteers for. The council will salt the roads but not all of them — we need to raise money to grit the smaller roads, where possible. We need extra volunteers to check on the elderly and infirm and we are looking for a roster of people who will go out and clear pathways and driveways for those who cannot do so for themselves. The third pad is for anybody who needs help of any kind this winter. Don't try to do this on your own, especially if you are elderly, or if you live alone or have any ailments. We aim to keep the church open all winter and this village hall is going to offer respite, and even somewhere to stay or get a hot meal or warm clothes or a bath, for anyone who needs it. If you need to see me afterwards, then please just say hello! I would like to introduce you all to the Sisters of Beathnoch, who are offering their time in regions all across the Highlands of Scotland this winter. There will also be basic medical aid on offer. As you know, there is only one wonderful doctor here in the village, so we want to make sure there's a back-up, should we need it!

The minister sits back down at the end of the row of nuns.

— We all need to focus on getting this community through the winter, the head nun says.

— If any of us make it through this winter! They're predicting ten feet of snowfall next month. They've said it will go down to minus forty or even colder; there is a bloody iceberg heading to our shores from Norway, a young dad says.

— Youz are all bloody nuts if you think we'll get through this, a mother agrees.

— Mercy, mercy.

This last note is uttered quietly by another nun. The Mother Superior stares over at her until she looks down at her shoes. A teacher stands up.

– We have all known global warming was occurring. The Arctic is our canary, if you like, it's going to show the rest of the world what will happen next.

– The canaries died first, the young mother says.

– Look, the Ward Hunt Ice Shelf for example is almost completely gone; that block of ice was there for three thousand years and it only started cracking in the year 2000, and here we are only twenty years later, the polar ice-cap has shrunk by thirty per cent and all that fresh water is flooding the oceans, reducing salinity.

– So now we all just freeze to death, aye? the dad asks.

– No, now we make our plans for how to get through it.

A young man puts his hand up and Stella cannot decide if the nuns are quite cute in their way, with their seriousness and their napkin heads, or if they are in fact completely ridiculous, and the village hall is full of parents and children and old people and teenagers and it is so stuffy and damp in here now that her skin prickles and she yawns widely. Lewis is giggling with a girl in the front row and, despite herself, Stella feels a hot spike of jealousy. They are passing a piece of paper to each other and folding it over. Drawing a person, when each one does a different section and passes it on. She can't remember the name of the game but they used to play it at school sometimes. She thinks it was an exquisite corpse. Stella scans the hall.

– We don't have answers long-term but we do have resources! We have drawn up a list of what we think each household needs to get them through winter, including extra water supplies, tinned goods, Mr McBride. We are telling everyone to stock up in advance: make sure you have what you need in food and water, stock your freezers. Make sure you have a back-up heating supply. We have ordered a generator for the community hall and anyone who cannot afford food or heating, especially the elderly and vulnerable, must come to the town hall, where we will be offering shelter, food and companionship for those who need it.

– I'd rather stay at home and die in front of the telly, a young mum mutters.

– We, the Sisters of Beathnoch, are going to do whatever we can to help people on the ground directly. Rising seas are affecting Louisiana, Texas, Florida, North Carolina, regions of Africa; across Europe this devastation is spreading in all directions. You are not the only community facing these problems, but if we pull together many of us will get through it.

That last sentence causes a temporary silence. The nuns look steadily ahead.

Big charts have been placed up around the hall to show exactly what is happening with the weather systems – there are signs for how to keep warm, how to avoid frostbite, how to cool and treat water from snow, how to dig your way out of a snowdrift. One shows a picture of a man digging a hole around the exhaust at the back of his car, so that even in a drift he can keep the engine running; the next picture shows what happens if he doesn't dig the hole for the exhaust fumes: him and his little boy asleep on the front seat being poisoned by the fumes. There are pictures of an Arctic family with their furry jackets open, staring into a camera. Stella is fascinated by the smallest child who looks just like her when she was little, except the girl has blonde hair rather than black.

Stella looks over at Lewis's dad and she hasn't seen him since he had that affair and got kicked out of their caravan again. He is wearing Doc boots and a thick parka and he looks thinner. She used to like going over there for sleepovers and sitting in his tiny bedroom playing computer games. It's not like she felt like this about Lewis when she was younger, or maybe only a little bit. Lewis is passing the folded drawing along the line and it is being handed up the rows toward her and that flutter of fear in her, and her skin growing hot already.

There is a slight quiet, parents nodding to each other.

— Is Santa okay at the North Pole? a wee girl asks.

— Santa is just fine, the Mother Superior says.

Elaine Brown walks past as if she's going to the toilet and drops a piece of paper in Stella's lap. She sits up on her knees and she almost doesn't want to open it. The kids from her class are facing the front, pretending they're listening. A minute ago they were just bored and picking on each other and pinching each other and hoping the adults would give up and let them all go. She unfolds the piece of paper. The bottom is a pair of sparkly Rocket Dog sneakers that she wore all summer. Then there are her skinny legs with stripy tights. The top bit has her hair in a long bob, flicked out, and bigger lips than she has, and her usual jumper with only a hint of a bump. And when she opens the middle section of paper she drops it to the floor.

Don't cry. It would be better to walk out now than to cry in a town hall in front of Lewis and the entire village and everyone from the crofts and farms. Stella scans along the row of nuns' black shoes and hopes that her mum is not unfolding the piece of paper right now, because she picked it up from the floor. Stella looks along a row of twenty-eight shiny black shoes; above those are black turn-ups and fitted trousers with a chain hanging from each belt, hanging off that a whistle and a torch and a multi-tool with knife, scissors, tweezers; the white hats are peaked like napkins and frame each nun across the middle of her forehead.

— Why don't you just spell it out: we could all be dead within months, if temperatures hit anything lower than the minus forties by December. We all know it drops another ten degrees here every January, and sometimes again in February.

Constance folds up the piece of paper. Stella can almost hear the folds and her mother running her finger along it, as if to seal the picture in. For an awful moment she thinks her mother is going to stand up and call them out. Lewis looks back and sees her expression and his face falls. On the fourth row she sees what looks like an old woman in a donkey-jacket, but when she turns it is someone's mum. Constance folds the piece of paper up and her mother's face is so steely that Stella begins to panic. She looks over to her old classmates and tries not to wish for the gift of telekinesis. The scene in *Carrie* where the girl sets the whole place on fire sums up exactly how she feels.

— Trains are still running, and most of the airports haven't closed. I think we should all fly somewhere warmer. Right now we're here like sitting ducks and nobody knows how bad it is going to get! a man says.

There are paperchains laced all across the ceiling in white and red and green and Stella can see the one she made, ready for the winter festival. Constance looks over at her and she can tell her mum is biting her tongue so hard she can probably taste blood.

— What about Year Six and Sevens: do they still need to do their prep exams for high school?

A young woman stands up to ask this; she is Tabitha the Fanny's mum. Tabitha lives with her now and she used to be the best girl football player in the whole year, until she broke her ankle and got into porn. Now she sells soiled panties to men in Tokyo, all the way from her council flat over the Clachan Fells bakery. Everyone says her mum already knows and that Tabitha's bringing money into the house, so she doesn't care. Tabitha the Fanny once sold it to a man who wanted her to cover herself in baked beans, and her dad found the towels and she had to say she was doing a project for science.

— That is Point Four of today's meeting, thank you.

A poster on the village-hall wall has a big advert up for performance night: *Raise Funds for Those without Homes!* Beside that a sign reads: *Jesus Is My Saviour!* The hall smells dank and earthy; everyone is looking at the Sisters now.

Stella flexes her toes in her welly boots and her feet are too warm. What he drew! She knows it was him. He is disgusting. Right then she knows he is more obsessed with her than she is with him. She will not think about Lewis. She is more embarrassed that her mum has seen the picture when she hid all the others. The stupid, stupid thing is that even though Constance is the most independent person, she is always trying to fix the world so it will be okay for Stella, and it is not okay. It really isn't. Her class don't believe she is a girl. Hardly anybody does anywhere. She has to stop thinking or she will cry. What if the Sisters try to stop Bonfire Night? That would be the last thing to go wrong. They couldn't. Nobody would let them. Is it unchristian for children to want to gravitate to fire like moths in the night? All the villagers look worried and that is the worst thing. Before it was just poverty, pestilence, terrorists, paedophiles, drugs, eating disorders, online grooming, meteors skimming a bit too close for comfort. Now every single person in this hall looks like they are terrified they're all about to become frozen corpses. For the first time since the news broke, Stella gets this stabbing feeling in her heart that must be some new kind of fear.

– Well, I'm telling ye right now, neither of ma girls will be staying here – we're going!

– Going where, Mr Cranston? Have you seen the global news?

The Mother Superior sits back.

The hall falls silent.

Mr Cranston is Donna-from-down-the-glen's dad; he sits down. Not one person says a thing. One of the crosses up on the mountain from last year is for his eldest boy, who had been out on his motorbike with his brother on the back when they took a corner too fast. Stella and her mum drove by last week and all along the verge there were soggy teddy bears, half-burnt candles and wilting flowers. Stella wants to go home suddenly. She wants to go to sleep. A mutter all around the hall; people exchange words and the Sisters wait for them to finish. Stella has been to the cross with her mum even though they didn't know the boys. Constance carved a flower out of wood and Stella painted it and they left it there. On the way home that day she sat right next to her mum in the ambulance, as close as she could get, so close that she could get that reassuring thing she gets when her mother is there – like not even a nun, not even an Ice Age, not even the whole community could stop her mother, if she was really angry.

A boy next to Stella picks his nose and wipes it on the floor.

He always does that.

He wipes it underneath the chairs in registration as well; he is a disgusting smelly bastard who turns his eyelids inside out. He'll sit like that until a teacher notices and then he flicks his eyelids back the right way round. He's not done it to any of the nuns yet. He told Stella he could pop his eye totally out of the socket too, but he can't. Lewis looks back at Stella again like he is trying to say sorry. She scans the hall. The nuns sit still on the stage like a painting, with eyes moving. The audience is more relaxed, quieter. It is a truce between people and the agents of everlasting peace. Her mother raises her hand.

– How long has Clachan Fells been without a library service? Is there even one at Fort Hope?

The Mother Superior looks out over the audience and faces are blank and a few parents shake their heads at Constance's question. The Mother Superior fixes her habit and, while all the other nuns have small crosses around their necks, she has a huge one on the end of her rosary. She looks up at them again and smiles, and Stella can tell the woman is pissed off about the people shaking their heads when someone mentions books and it makes her like her, despite the penguin outfit and the napkin hat.

– We want to work with the other Sisters who normally

teach at Clachan Fells Primary School and of course that involves keeping the children engaged in their education. Clachan Fells Primary School has had long-standing issues with the old boiler systems and there is no way we can heat the place with portable heaters, so we do think reinstating a library source is imperative to the health of the community. We would like donations of all appropriate texts – novels, poetry, cook books, self-help, anything you have to spare, please. Do come and leave them in the hall, we'll set up a table for them.

Appropriate texts.

The nuns look like a row of crows.

Ready to peck a few eyes out.

Constance stands up and Stella's heart falls. Stella looks at her like she is a stranger, like it is the first time she has ever seen her. There is melted snow on her mother's clothes and hair and in a slushy pool around her feet. She's not been eating enough, so she's bonier than usual, and her skin is pale except for her nose, which is red from the cold. Around the hall villagers give little glances at each other. They are looking at her mother. They are always judging her. She can take the looks at herself, curiously enough, but not at her mum. It's because she was with Caleb and Alistair for so long. She loved one and also the other, and they say you can't love more than one person so it must have been about sex, but it wasn't. Her mum really, really loved them and she is heartbroken and they should never look at her like this! *Leave her alone! She's not your mother! SO FUCKING WHAT if she had two lovers. So what! She HAD two – get fucking over it!*

— Mrs Fairbairn?

— My name is Constance. I would like to see texts in the library addressing issues of intolerance, hate-based crimes and ignorance of anything different.

The whole hall stops like all the air has gone. Stella can hear the blood in her veins and her heart and even her eyelashes drag as she looks up. Villagers are looking at her mother and she doesn't give even the remotest fuck, and Stella watches that, she takes it right in.

— We are sure that is an appropriate section for the library, Mrs Fairbairn. We could perhaps discuss it later on.

Constance walks to the front of the hall right past her classmates; she tears the picture into pieces and they flutter down into the bin like she is discarding a tissue. As she walks back she goes as close along the row of classmates as she can. Her boots are heavy and for a minute the only sound in the hall is her steady clunk as she walks by, and Stella can tell that every single one of the kids in her class is shitting their pants. None of the parents or nuns have a clue what is going on. Stella feels her cheeks burning, but she is also ready to rip Lewis's soul from his body should he ever, ever upset her mum like that again.

— We are going to personally deliver leaflets to everyone in the community this week. We will hold a meeting to discuss the upcoming fundraiser, and those of you in the community who are able to offer time or talent, please get in touch. We need your participation. There will be ideas on how to insulate and heat your homes. Those of you living nomadically will be particularly vulnerable.

— Where's the nomads, like?

— We mean the caravan community, of course — you all know that's what I meant.

— We urnay nomadic, pal, our caravans are static.

— That may be so, but you will be the most vulnerable. You are closest to the mountains and furthest from the emergency services.

— We are a bit sick of being differentiated from the rest of the village, you know. We live in a caravan park and most of the units are mobile homes; we pay our taxes, just like youz all do!

— I am sure nobody wants to make you feel there is any difference between how you are all viewed in Clachan Fells, but when it gets bad . . .

— What? We'll die first? Fucking bullshit, he mutters.

— Okay, can all volunteers please write your names on the pad at the door!

The Sisters dip their heads to pray and everybody folds their hands. Stella looks down at the floorboards, which are worn and have paint on them in green and yellow circles. The middle of the room has delineated areas for basketball and netball. Even just looking at them, like they have stored the echo of a basketball thwacking off wood. Kids shouting. Rubber shoes. White socks. Someone talking about someone else because they just got a bra, and her wanting a bra and not knowing if she'd ever get one, and the boys trying to swagger on their skinny legs and carol-practice in winter, and then going home for mince pies. Stella gazes around at the bended heads and Mother Superior is looking at her — all the heads remain bowed around them and a cross is nailed above the stage and there are smaller crosses above all the doors. Mother Superior has a freckled nose and she is looking at her and there is a faint distaste in her eyes, or is there? Stella is tired of guessing, so she does something she wouldn't do last week; she lets her hands rest in her lap so that she is relaxed and she quietly stares back at her, and after a while she realises they are simply looking at each other. Snow falls steadily, a shiny white glitter against the dark outside.

12

THE CHATTER is brighter and louder than before. Stella weaves through the adults. Parents linger, chatting it over, glancing back toward the nuns. Constance puts her hand out and Stella takes it, holds her mum's hand like when she was little.

— Lewis is a loathsome little bastard; he'll wake up one night to find me cutting off — his dick!

— Mum, have you been drinking?

— No. Is that the first time something like that has happened?

— Yup, Stella lies.

— That boy stayed over at ours hundreds of times — what happened to you being best friends? I'm going to speak to his mum about that drawing. I'm not having that.

— Don't, Mum, it will only make it worse.

Down the street a girl is walking home in the snow and she moves so lightly, so easily, Stella stashes it in her brain like she is stealing gestures to try out later or discard like old clothes.

— I got rid of that wardrobe today. How about I treat you to something from the chip shop to cheer us both up?

— Yes!

— If the weather gets too bad, we'll visit Aunt Agnes.

— Is she still alive?

— I hope so.

— If I had a sister I'd have stayed in touch with her.

— Agnes is pure Satan, as the nuns would conjecture — she is, though, through and through. You'll see what I mean if you meet her! However, if there isn't anywhere else to go, we could still try her.

Constance holds Stella's chin for just a second and looks down. They are almost the same height now. In a few more years Stella will be taller than her mum. They walk into the hot chip shop and Stella puts her hands up on the metal edge of the counter display so they get warm. The man slaps a piece of fish into a big bowl of batter. He glides it through the mixture once to the left and once to the right, then drops it into the fat. The fryer sizzles a sullen gold while bubbles jump all around the batter. He wipes his fingers on his apron and picks up another bit of pale fish. A young girl struggles through from the kitchen with a plastic vat of freshly cut chips. She places it down, then takes her place back at the till. She shovels hot chips onto greaseproof paper and asks the man in front if he wants salt and sauce. He nods and puts his hot chips into a bag and disappears out into the darkness.

— Yes?

— White-pudding supper, two pickles. Mum, do you want fish? A single fish, please — salt and sauce on everything.

They stand side-by-side watching the girl wrap their food. Stella holds onto the corner of her mum's coat. Constance's fish is picked out of the hot display with metal tongs and deluged with sauce and folded neatly into newspaper. Stella points at a Crunchie. The woman looks at her mother and she nods, so it is popped in the clear bag too, but Constance takes it out and puts it in her pocket so it doesn't melt. Constance counts out change and she even has to count out about eighty pence in five pences. When they step onto the street it is so cold that Stella can see her breath on the air.

As they walk back up to Ash Lane there is a shape ahead on the path. Stella runs on to see what it is. He is on his pathway. On his side. Like a dead spider. His boots have thick soles that are worn and rubbery and they squeak when he walks on plastic floors, and when she's over at the industrial estate with Mum, having tea in Ikea, she knows he has walked into the cafeteria without even having to turn around. He looks quite dead. Stella nudges his foot with her boot and then bends down to stare at his craggy face. It has good features. She never gets to see Barnacle from this straight-on angle – and it would seem rude to get a mirror and hold it under his chin when he is talking, just to get a better view of his expression. He has hair up his nose and his nostrils are wide and some of his white moustache-hair is ginger. His hair is long at the back and the sides and his beard is mostly white with grey and brown. He has rings on his fat fingers and a harmonica sticks out of his back pocket.

— Barnacle, are you dead?

— Not today, dear.

— Why are you lying on the path? It's freezing.

— I think I drank a little too much at lunch, with an old friend.

— Lunch was seven hours ago.

— A good lunch takes at least seven hours, sweetheart. Don't you look pretty tonight?

— Stella, take his other arm.

Constance and Stella lift him up, one arm under each shoulder, and he is heavy but he moves forward with them, silently, his head hanging even lower than usual and an apathy to his movements, like a poorly child. The steps up to Barnacle's caravan are buckled and her mum has to go through his pockets to find his key and open the door. He smells bad. He smells like his trousers need washing and maybe that he has done a wee on them at some point. Stella tries not to face him, and up on Ash Lane the caravans all have windows lit, with tellies on and people chatting behind the metal walls, so there is always a low murmur out here at night. The stars are bright and she can see Dylan putting a comb through his hair and she wonders if he likes her mum. Imagine that. Her mum just with one person, and a nice one that doesn't have a wife or go travelling or generally dick about in a triad of endless confusion. Except it wasn't Constance who used to seem that confused, was it? It was her, and she supposes what she wanted was a normal dad who lived with her and they did usual stuff, and when she became a girl he would have gone over to Fort Harbour and found the boys who beat her up and he'd make them pay. That's what dads are meant to do. She doesn't have that and she doesn't know how any of this works; being a girl isn't an easy thing, and neither is shoving Barnacle's bent-over frame through his door and her mum leading him into the living room and sitting him on an armchair and putting a blanket over him. And he is snoring already, and all around his caravan are heaps of magazines, clothes, newspapers, empty tins that haven't been thrown out, and dirty dishes.

— I'm coming over here tomorrow to clean this shit up, Constance whispers.

The two of them pull the door closed behind them.

13

THERE ARE two benches, one on each side of the table. Stella sits barefoot scuffing her feet on the wooden floor. Dylan smiles again, tucks his hair behind his ear. Constance studies both of them.

— This isn't aaaaawkward at all, Stella says.

The caravan is warm, the wood-stove crackling and the whole place nothing like his bare wee ice-box next door.

— We were just sharing some stuff from the chippy, Constance says.

— Honestly, I don't need to eat. I'm totally fine if there's not enough, Dylan says.

— There's enough, Stella says as she lays the table. — Dylan used to live in a cinema, Mum.

— Really?

— What's your favourite film? Stella asks him.

— It is too difficult to pin down. I love early Russian cinema, Yakov Protazanov, F. W. Murnau, a lot of obscure stuff, Harmony Korine, Wolf Rilla, Czech animator Břetislav Pojar, *The Goonies*, David Lynch, early Disney, even a lot of the early talkies – especially Laurel and Hardy. I don't talk about films much. I tend to like stuff that never gets a major release.

— Don't you like *WALL-E*? she asks.

— No.

— I loved that when I was little, Stella says.

Constance flicks the telly on. The way she moves, something liquid about her. Just acting cool, trying not to feel like a giant in a moon-polisher's caravan and the kid happy to see him, actually gleeful.

— Look at this, Constance says.

On the telly there are queues of people at an airport and people sleeping by chairs and a pregnant woman rubbing her tummy and everybody looking worried. The news report flicks over to a weather report. The man points as weather unfolds across Europe and Africa and bits of America — red alerts all the way round, and a band of news rolling across the bottom of the screen — flights are cancelled all across Europe. Temperatures are going to plummet faster than everyone thought. The South of England is already struggling. The Thames flashes up, all frozen over.

— There it is! Stella shouts.

Constance zooms the volume up.

Locals have named the iceberg Boo, because it is giving fishermen such a fright to see it travel over the North Sea and it is almost certain now to be heading toward the region of Clachan Fells.

Footage of the iceberg shows a hulk bigger than a hotel; it is bigger than the new shopping centre in the city. Stella drops to her knees in front of the telly, shocked.

— I didn't know it would be that big, Constance says.

— We have to go and see it, Mum!

— I'm in, Dylan says.

— You need to get snow-shoes for walking on the mountain soon, Dylan. We have ours in the shed.

Stella starts giggling.

– I think we're going to need more than snow-shoes, Mum!

– I know, Estelle, I'm going to try and get some skis as well – don't look at me like that! We might well need them. Anyway, Dylan, tell your mum I'm asking after her. We met Vivienne a few months ago – nice woman.

– She's not here.

– I know that. I mean when you speak to her.

Dylan considers leaving it at that. He is feeling guilty each day they sit in Tupperware and an ice-cream box, but when he asked about ferries from Fort Harbour they said sea-ice was going to halt all the usual trips to the islands. Stella is studying him now and he doesn't know why he finds it so hard to say it out loud.

– I mean, she's not here. She passed away two weeks ago.

– I'm really sorry to hear that, Constance says.

– So, what are you up to this week then, Stella? he asks brightly.

Constance walks back into the kitchen area, her feet bare. He is aware of everything about her: the cut of her jeans, the way she lifts up a plate, the way she is careful to not look back at him for too long. The brittle around the edges. She is jagged. It makes him want her more. She turns the telly down but leaves the footage on. The three of them eat quickly, not chatting much. Constance sprinkles salt on her chips even though there's already some on there. He helps her clear the plates away. Would that he would. Not to let her know that, though. Not to make her feel awkward.

– Nothing much, just decaying in utter boredom. Mum, that's the door!

– I can hear that, I'm not deaf!

– I'm sorry she's being a bit rude, Stella whispers.

– Come in!

– Hiya, Constance, Stella, hello!

– Hi, Ida! This is Dylan, who moved in next door.

Stella grins at him and he crosses his eyes at her.

– Love the head-to-toe latex, Ida.

– Thanks, Constance. One has to try for these events – you never know when a fan might require an autograph.

– Not every street has their own porn star, Stella says.

Ida shrugs modestly.

– Most of them do these days, sweetheart. When money's short, the tits come out!

She laughs and something about the woman relaxes Constance as well, and Dylan is lulled by the warmth of the fire and the fairy lights and sitting in here all cosy, while it gets darker and darker outside.

– I came in to see if you want to put in for the drinks kitty, Constance? I'm nipping over to the cash-and-carry.

– Just let me find my purse.

– Did you hear about this iceberg? Aye. Lobster Jack reckons he has seen it. Nearly all of the fishing boats are back in for winter already. Sea-ice everywhere – never seen the like!

– Can you see it from the harbour? Stella asks.

– Not yet, they reckon just another few weeks, though. So, where d'you move from? Ida asks.

– London-Soho-he-lived-in-a-cinema-it's-quite-boring, Stella says.

– Like she says, Dylan grins.

— Well, you are a breath of fresh air!

Ida gives him a long appreciative look from top to toe.

— See ye then, girls, she says.

Ida flounces out the door.

— I think I saw you heading up the mountain the other day, Dylan?

— I did, Constance. I went up there again today as well – I saw the coastline on the other side of the mountain. Looked choppy, though, and it is definitely being mapped over with ice. I've never seen anything like — any of this! I mean, I know it is a nightmare, but it's majestic as landscapes go. I found ice-flowers in the forest. From the top I could see a few islands out there and lighthouses? And a wee port.

— Aye, that is Fort Hope.

Constance takes a pre-rolled joint out of a tin and lights it up and her daughter scowls. So she opens the window a crack and blows the smoke out.

— When I was a kid we had a director in Babylon for a screening of his movie. I remember him saying one eye is always looking through the telescope and the other is looking through the microscope.

— Did you work in the cinema since you were young? Stella asks.

— I was checking the tickets when I was your age. I used to check the tickets for *Godzilla,* then I'd sit in the back row and watch the whole film again and again.

— It sounds better than trips to the city dump, Stella says.

Constance passes him the joint.

— Give us a minute, Dylan. I'm just going to get Stella's costume on, so she knows it fits for the bonfire party later!

Stella follows her mum through to their bedroom. He triple-drags and stands next to the fire. He had a wee look in their bedroom when he came in and it is nothing like his. It's clad in wood and painted white, with a matching upper and lower bed and handmade patchwork blankets. There are fairy lights strung all around the caravan. This caravan has the exact same layout as his – but she's painted everything white. There are clever nooks for everything; she's even drilled holes in a wide driftwood shelf, so all her wooden spoons and kitchen utensils are neatly slotted in there. He takes a roll off the table and tears it in two, chews briskly so they don't come back to find him eating at their table like a great big hairy-fucking-stoned Goldilocks. There are stuffed animals all over the place. On the wall an upside-down bat is sleeping behind a glass dome. Antlers hang above the kitchenette with tea towels and socks drying on them. Stella's drawings are tacked up all over the place and one says *Universe Closed, Take Rainbow*. Constance's bookshelf is full and from here he can read a few titles: gardening manuals, *History of French Furniture Restoration, Antiques for Beginners*, colour charts from Farrow & Ball, a *History of Burlesque*, nearly everything by Bukowski. There's one by Edgar Allan Poe, a few Stephen Kings, Cookie Mueller, Trocchi, Breece D'J Pancake, a biography of Mama Cass and one big old volume of Coleridge. She has a record player in the corner and a stack of vinyl on the floor. Neil Young's *Harvest Moon* lies with its sleeve lyric-side-up and a round red-wine stain on it. Half the room is carpeted in woven matting and there is a thick rag-rug on her real-wood kitchen floor.

Constance comes out of the bedroom and takes the joint off him and stands just – that close. She takes two or three drags, waves the smoke out of the window and hands it back to him. The wind howls over her roof and the caravan moves slightly. He can't work out what is worse: wanting a kiss and not getting one, or getting one and never getting another. She makes him feel like a teenager.

— Mum!

— I'm coming.

— Did you get the wardrobe out of the tip totally by yourself? Did you use a roller to get it into the ambulance?

Stella is asking her mother this and she's saying *Yes;* she's saying *Lift your feet up; no, stop wriggling, turn around, that's it — you look beautiful; okay, not beautiful, you look repugnant, yup, utterly foul!*

— Dylan?

— Yes, Stella.

— Our thermometer says it is minus ten, she calls through.

— Fresh, he says.

— Did they just mention that iceberg again on the radio?

— Yeah.

She is still bumping about next door, opening her bathroom cabinet, finishing things. Flames leap this way and that on her woodstove, and he wants to lie down with Constance and listen to her heartbeat. Not say a word to each other all night. Just sip wine and watch snow falling outside the window — hold hands in the dark.

14

CONSTANCE STANDS in the doorway watching him. He's
not sure how long she has been there and a frown flashes
across her, making her look older. They assess each other
formally – a contract – a measuring up.

– Don't Bogart that joint, she says.

– You know, Dennis Hopper wanted that on the sound-
track to *Easy Rider*.

– Riveting! she grins.

– You remind me of my gran, he says.

– That's a new one, she says.

– If you knew my gran, you'd take it as a compliment.
Anyway, you do furniture restoration?

– Oh, shabby-shit the-pipes-the-pipes-are-c-a-l-l-ing!
Stella bellows from the next room.

– Chic, shabby-*fucking*-chic!

Constance takes a bottle of beer out of the crate on her
front porch and opens it and has a long swig and then holds
one out for him. She glances at a photograph he is looking at,
of her and Stella who is about six years old, dressed in a
Spiderman outfit; and there is another one of her dressed as
a little boy, all in blue; and a handprint in a tiny frame and

the name Cael written underneath it. Constance takes a long drag and looks at him.

— Is that Stella when she was little?

She nods and neither of them say anything. They make more sense to him now. Constance's vague air of melancholy and sex — there is something of both about her; he couldn't place it before but she's in mourning too, for a little boy that used to be her baby.

— She made the transition thirteen months ago.

— Did you expect it?

— Not really.

— Has she been okay?

— No, she's not. You weren't what I expected, when Stella said she'd invited a pal over.

— What were you expecting?

— Someone shorter.

— Most people expect someone shorter, he says.

— And less hairy.

— You have something against hair?

They grin at each other, a quick flash and it's sealed then. She knows he likes her. Her eyes are grey with a rim around the iris in orange or gold.

— What's with the plastic birds outside Rose Cottage? he says.

Dylan squints out of her window, looking down the pathway at shadowy shapes.

— Pink flamingoes, Constance says.

— Have you seen the film?

— Aye, I have actually, I took an ex-boyfriend to see it for a midnight screening at the art-house cinema on a trip to Edinburgh once; we stayed in a hotel, went out for a meal – the whole thing. At the movie there was a guy in the row behind us, doing a lot of jerking around all the way through the film. I don't think he was epileptic.

– How did the date go after that?

– Didn't see him again. I chatted to Vivienne a few times – interesting woman.

– Oh yeah, what was she saying?

Constance is looking at him, head tilted.

– She didn't tell you she'd been here at all?

– No, she wanted to take my gran's ashes up to the islands and scatter them, but she never told me she'd visited Scotland. My gran was Gunn MacRae, she came from Orkney.

– Stella's dad's family are from up there.

– He might know them?

– Maybe, there's a lot of islands.

She looks down so her eyelashes create a slight shadow on her cheek in this light. She has no marks on her skin, no moles, no freckles; under her eyes there are lines where she has not slept and two furrows between pale brows where she frowns too much. She smiles and her eyes flash slightly luminous. They are too close to each other to be comfortable.

Stella walks in and stands at the door. She has eight bulging eyeballs sticking out from her costume, they are green and round, and her hair is a big backcombed halo, black as night. She wears a dash of pink lipstick and her chin is pointier than he ever noticed and she is exceptionally pleased with herself. She is probably the coolest kid he's met – not that he has met many. Dylan tries to focus on Stella. He tries not to appear like he thinks Constance Fairbairn is the most fuckable woman he has ever met in his entire life.

– Do you like the costume? Stella asks him.

— You look scarier than a scary thing!

— Truth, Stella says.

Constance grins at him. That urge in him to lie with her in the dark and hold her. To drink wine and read books and ignore each other, but her foot just by his, her legs, her mouth. There are herbs hanging from the kitchenette ceiling. The wooden shutters around each window are painted blue. On the wall above there's a picture of a purple dog. Stella's paintings are cool: long men with even longer arms and gadgets hanging off them, and dinosaur-heads and dog-tails.

— Your costume looks great, he says.

— You don't know what I am, though — do you?

— No.

He feels like he wants to look after the kid, and he knows she wants him here because when she asked him to come for dinner she said, please. *Please come for tea.*

— I like your caravan, he says.

— You'd never know that all of our furniture comes from the dump and dead people's houses, would you? My mum can make anything look expensive. It's a skill.

Constance uncorks a bottle and pours two large glasses of red wine.

— Cheers to that! she says.

— Do you know Lewis Brown? Stella asks.

— No, Dylan says.

— You will: he lives at the first caravan on Larch Lane with his sister and nan and their lodger, their mum and also his brother. Anyway, his uncle and granddad are in the jail and the women pad over to the phone box in their pyjamas with fags hanging out, to phone them, and who uses phone boxes anyway? They have mobile contracts, though, they just put their SIM card in and talk. We used to be best friends but we're not any more.

There is a tenseness around Constance's features.

– Lewis Brown has all the latest computer games delivered straight from Japan, but since the post only comes sometimes now, he's hardly had any, which is giving him withdrawals, cos he needs to be distracted from anything real. He can't take it. Especially in winter. He can't take the grey. Some people can't take the grey but I can – I'm built for it; it doesn't scare me but it gets so grey here in January and February especially, it makes your eyes grow tired and then your soul too, then your only choice is to get drunk, or die, or eat chocolate.

– Stella!

– Or stoned, or simply give up.

– I'd never give up, Dylan says.

– Me neither. Wait here, I'm going to do my nails in green as well.

Stella disappears back into the bathroom. Constance tears a bit of bread in two and they don't look at each other this time. The clock ticks and the fire cracks and purrs. Wind whistles against the caravan and he can feel the thing move slightly. Her arms are bare. Her neck is perfect and pale as a swan, but her shoulders are broad. It's like watching a silent-movie star. He takes three long drags of the joint and his spine moulds to the back of her chair. Light from the fire flickers on the walls. Along the other wall there are carved bookshelves, a birdcage filled with fairy lights and the skeleton of some bird with its wings flung right out.

– Is that a nest of tiny birds with yellow open beaks, sat in the middle of its feathered bird-gut?

— My ex is a taxidermist, she says.

— That explains it.

— He's Stella's father.

— I see.

— One of her exes; the other one went travelling, Stella says from down the hall.

Constance accepts the joint back from him and their fingers skim fractionally too close and dull-thud in his chest — like a pebble dropping down a well.

— Dylan doesn't need to know this, thank you, Stella.

— Mum had two boyfriends for nearly twenty years.

— I'm sure lots of mums have more than one boyfriend, Dylan says.

Stella appears at the door.

— At the same time?

— Stella, let's not go into this.

— Now she won't speak to either of them. She's single and sad and lonely!

— Stella! Stop it right now or you're not going anywhere.

— Sorry!

— The three of us didn't live together, ever. They didn't speak to each other at all in fact. It was just one of those things that happened. It wasn't a lifestyle choice, Constance says.

— Alistair and Caleb couldn't stand each other, Mum, could they?

— Alistair got married but then they separated; we were together on and off. Then he married someone else, then we were together and he got divorced, then he married his third wife.

— You were still together through that one, Stella says.

— Thanks for that, Estelle.

— I'm just saying.

— Stella came out of one of those times. Then we were together, then he went back to his last wife, then left her again. I was still with Caleb — it was one of those things, we were open about it.

— You know what Alistair really didn't like?

— What's that, Stella?

— That you called me Cael when I was a baby and it sounds like Caleb, a bit.

— No, I suppose he didn't.

— Alistair says when he dies he wants his bones ground down and made into a china teaset.

Constance and Dylan both just look at her.

— Yup!

He realises his mouth is really, really dry.

— So that is what I would inherit if he died, a bone china teaset.

— You'll get the cottage, Constance says.

— I won't. Christine won't let that happen. The woman hates me, I won't get a penny. Only a teaset. Made of bones. From a guy who has never even called me by my girl-name. I'll smash it, she says.

Stella leans into her mum for a quick hug.

— He thinks if I get the teaset, I'll sit with my own kids one day and pour a cup of builder's tea into Granddad? Fucking lovely, ay?

— Swear jar!

Dylan tries to be subtle about watching Constance, but it is compulsive. It's like watching a fire. She is the fire and her daughter the wind — howling along the rooftops, rattling at his windows all last night, warning him she could blow his house down and it is not a house, it is a caravan – d.e.n.i.a.l. It's not a river in Egypt, that's what the kid would say.

– Okay, I'll give you a clue. Everyone has what I am, Stella gestures to her costume.

– Eyes, he says.

– I'm green, I'm all green; all the eyes are just, you know, to give it a fucking edge!

– Estelle! SWEAR JAR.

The girl shrugs and Constance shakes her head and puts her feet up on the bench beside Dylan. Her toenails are all even. Square-shaped and, like her fingernails, they're unpainted.

– Something we all have?

– Aye.

– Are you a virus?

They both look at him.

– No, okay. Are you a fungus? A rare tree fungus, like the devil's cigar fungus in where was it – come on – where was it?

– Where was what? Constance says.

– It was a fungus, it was shaped like a star, they called it the devil's cigar cos it starts off as a capsule and then it opens, and it was in some humid tropical forest somewhere. It was an interesting fungus!

– As opposed to those less interesting fungi?

– I saw it on that documentary where the guy got wasted with tribes and they'd always have some shamanistic intervention, where the whole village would put on a performance to draw out his demons so he could be spiritually free!

– He got exorcised? Stella asks.

— Aye, actually I know a great preacher in Peckham who will drive the devil from your soul for a tenner, he says.

— I know a few people who could use that trick, Constance laughs.

— Never mind that, you've taken too long, Tit-head, look — I'm a bogey!

— Stella!

— *Tit* is not a swear word.

— Yes, it is — swear jar!

They both say the latter bit in unison. Stella is like the wind outside and Constance is the fire. The wind is gentle, blowing lightly to brighten the flames, to stop the fire going out. Stella picks up the remote control and slumps on the sofa, and her bogey costume swells out like it's got wire in it to make her a rounder, fatter, more luscious bogey, and she puts the telly onto a music station and taps her feet and chair-dances — she is a chair-dancing bogey and they say the word like it is a bow-gay — a bow-gay — if he was a gay he'd be a bow-gay, not just a guy who's had a few blow-jobs here and there over the years, slept with an old friend when they were drunk one night. He is in fact far too stoned right now to go outside and meet everyone else from this caravan park and his hands still keep twitching to clean a projector, stack reels, click on lights, take tickets, go back to his booth and switch the running time to *On!* Camera, action, sound-track, titles!

Stella studies him, her eyeballs jiggle slightly.

— You make a majestic bogey, he says.

— Truth (*she nods*) truth, truth, truth.

15

SHE COMES dressed as a wolf. Through the bonfire he gets glimpses of her as she steps over the back of somebody's fence. She has a wolf's head and tail and she moves like a wolf. Constance's eyes flash as a firework arcs up into the sky and cracks open into a waterfall of green and pink. She holds her girl's hand and they move like one person – each a part of the other. All the trees are bowing to the left and nobody else seems concerned by the force of the wind.

– My name is Barnacle, we haven't met.

– Dylan, pleased to meet you.

The man offers a soft paw. His back is curved and he is bent over so far he can only look up at Dylan with quick glances. The smell of grass and wood-smoke is strong. It is so cold it burns when he breathes. The mountains are dark and craggy and through the flames he can imagine people up there, naked fire-children, leaping around, half-human, half-stag, fornicating pagans offering up blood to their gods. He is getting lots of looks, standing here in his Chelsea boots and his deerstalker. He always was too tall to hide in a crowd.

– Are you a giant?

A kid runs by him, sniggers to his friend. Dylan resists an urge to knock the little shite's clown-hat right off.

— Little bastards, can't fucking stand them, Barnacle says, looking at the kids running off.

Dylan laughs.

— Stella's not a bad kid, she's starting a new political party, Dylan says.

— That girl is a diamond. What are her policies then?

— That every human vows to sign a contract as a temporary caretaker of the planet in their own lifetime, and the war against women ends.

— Well, that's never going to fucking happen, is it? She's as much chance of that as I do of walking upright again, Barnacle scorns.

— What would you put in place then?

— Free alcohol, he says.

— Interesting.

— Free prostitutes as well.

— I see. So, who will pay them, if they're free?

— I didn't think of that. Perhaps they could put it on our taxes; spend less on second homes for total cunts? Or maybe the women could just work for free?

— That's called slavery.

— Yes, yes, of course, quite right. Well, we could take all the idiots and put them on another planet. Best place for them. Of course you might think I am one of those idiots, and I am, but we are all raised in madness. The people in control have police and armies with guns and tanks, all of them trained to kill or to imprison, to restrain, to caution, to make sure what the ruling parties say goes. But we're free, right? Free to get shafted so far up the fucking arse we all just hobble our way to the shitting grave! That's how fucking free we are.

The flames on the bonfire leap this way and that; people's faces change in the firelight, they look happy one minute and sad the next. Kids race around the fire with sparklers.

– Have you been to the industrial park yet, Dylan?

– Not yet.

– There's an Ikea there, lots of fast-food places, DIY stores. You will find everything you could possibly never need over there. Giant fold-out swimming pools, dubiously named paint, dogs, budgies, Japanese cars.

Barnacle glances up at him and taps his long feet. His one concession to fancy dress is a plastic Alice-band with two long prongs and lights on the end that flash different colours.

– Did you know the woman who owns your caravan, Dylan?

– My mother, Vivienne.

– Really? She was a looker – striking woman. We had a few gins one night, it was home-made stuff with wild water mint, fucking marvellous stuff.

– My Grandma Gunn's home-brew.

– You should get the recipe for that, I'd buy it!

Gunn – distilling in their cellar. Bottles and a brass gin-still and selling it to the fancy hotel up the road for their cocktails. It is not a bad idea. He has been without a daily job for such a short time but it's already making him feel weird. The still will arrive any day now.

– I offered your mother a glass of water once, she said she couldn't possibly drink the stuff; when I asked her why, she said *Fish fuck in it, darling!*

They both laugh so loudly people look over – Barnacle

stooped in his C-shape and Dylan with his head and shoulders above everyone else. Barnacle aims to slap Dylan on the back, but gets his arse instead and that sets the two of them off again. Dylan smiles over at Stella, who has stopped for a minute to watch them in mock-horror from the other side of the bonfire.

— He's a good kid, Barnacle says.

— She's a good kid.

— That's what I said.

Dylan doesn't say anything for a minute.

— Constance is a looker, isn't she? She doesn't take any shit. I pity the kid that picks on Stella, they'll wake up to find their balls hanging from her Christmas tree. Your mother rented the caravan out to a woman called Ethel for a while, an ex-of-mine. She was an unusual woman, Ethel, like a rare, infertile peduncle. Quite unkissable, except in the right light. I knew her when she was younger. I had a Saab 900 and I'd drive back along the farm roads and there she'd be, and she was quite wonderful to look at then; and, well, something happened much more recently with her, not long before she left for a home actually. It quite freaked me out. She turned up at my caravan in the middle of the night — I never lock the door, you see — and I found her in the living room in her nightie with her pale, hairy legs quite on display, you know. I could see . . . all of heaven.

— Awkward!

— The bark, though. Where did it come from? Shameful. Barking at her. Bark, bark, bark. She scurried back over to her caravan and all her cats spilled out, to rub up and down her legs, and she slammed her door. I was furious with myself. I should have just lain down with her; should have held her and touched her cheek, and pushed her hair back off her face and told her she was the most beautiful woman I'd ever seen – should have tried to make her feel light and wanted and free, but I didn't. She freaked-me-the-fuck-out and I barked at her like a rabid beast.

– I'm sure she understood.

– She didn't. Not one bit.

– Do you know if the ferry at Fort Harbour goes as far as Orkney?

– You might need to take two ferries and a little plane. Not in these winds, though.

– I want to take my mother's and grandmother's ashes there.

– They are both gone? Dear boy, I am sorry. Did you know the women on the islands used to prepare the bodies of the dead? Aunts, sisters, mothers: they'd sing songs while they bathed their husbands or sons one last time – sing them right through to the Other Side. They had all kinds of great rituals. Like tipping the chairs over once the coffin was lifted, so the spirit of the dead couldn't sit down, or throwing the windows open as soon as someone died, so their soul could leave, but snapping it shut again quickly in case they tried to get back in. They don't do any of that now, as far as I know. You should take them both back up there for sure, young Dylan. What's your family name?

– MacRae.

– Time to burn the guy! Ida shouts.

The guy has been made out of a one-armed mannequin with a Girls' World head and a ginger afro; someone has made up the face with bright-blue eyeshadow and red lipstick and it is wearing a shell-suit.

— I can't even remember how many years it is since I saw someone wearing a shell-suit, Dylan nods at the guy.

Barnacle stares up at it intently as it blows up in flames.

— Highly flammable, shell-suits, he says.

— I think that is why they dressed the guy in it.

— I once met an ex-girlfriend's family who'd come up from some godforsaken shithole down south and we had to go into town and meet them. They drove up in a minibus and when I got there, they all got out, wearing matching shell-suits!

Dylan starts laughing.

— Matching?

— Identical and there was about fourteen of them — we had to take them all over the city like that. Absolutely morti-fied I was! Barnacle shakes his head.

Kids run around in the park with their faces bright in the firelight. Someone has set up a barbecue on the other side of the park and the smell of hamburgers wafts across the green and then sparklers — a burnt metal smell; it takes him back to being a kid and writing his name on a backdrop of night. The thrill of being able to make words and pictures on a black sky. She is on the other side of the fire. The light catches her eyes. Constance Fairbairn is a perfect wolf. The sky is clear. Two planets are outlined in a faint red. Barnacle turns his neck and looks up and the lights on the end of his Alice-band jiggle.

— Look, there's Orion. Little Bear and Big Bear; that is the Plough, Jupiter and her moons. Outstanding! I have a telescope but you don't need it here very often.

Barnacle points out constellations above them, without looking up. A star shoots straight across the sky. Constance circles around the other side of the fire. Her wolf-tail flicks behind her and Stella runs after a dalek and a clown. The kids are intimidating spirits – come to roar at the firelight, come to stamp their feet and gnash their teeth. More than a glint of red in each of their eyes. They race around in between dancers who are all variations of strange, and wholly unconcerned by it. A man pulls his wife in close to him, she has long red hair and he runs his hand down her side. The young satanist and his girlfriend stand at the edge of the fire; she is wearing contact lenses that make her eyes violet. He has a cat on a lead.

– Do they do this celebration every year? Dylan asks.

– Yeah, on Halloween the kids go trick-or-treating, and at Guy Fawkes they all dress up again and get to stay up as late as they want.

Dylan watches Constance. She is straight-up-and-down sinew and muscle and bone. Her eyes flash in the cutout of her wolf-mask and you can tell it has been made from a real wolf pelt and this Alistair guy has made it for her with skill and love.

– What did you come as, Dylan?

Stella is in front of him and staring at him, and her wolf-mother is watching him now and the man she is talking to looks a lot older than Constance.

– See that shimmer in the sky! A full aurora borealis is due, Barnacle says.

– You didn't come as anything, did you? Can you even speak?

– I didn't know it was fancy dress.

– Leave him alone, Stella, he's feeling a bit peaky. What are you anyway – are you a bogey?

— The guy's totally melting! Stella shouts.

Kids point and laugh. The plastic Girls' World head on the top is melting and Barnacle stares at his own shoes. Dylan imagines the guy must spend his whole life staring at those shoes, like he is an old man cursed for cutting off a hundred soldiers' feet in some past life, so now — no matter how beautiful the scene before him — he has to stare at his shoes before all things. Barnacle glances up at him, head turned to the left, a long face with flaccid chins.

— You don't want to go for that one, he says.

— What one?

Dylan shifts uneasily and wishes he'd brought more to drink and thinks it is time he quit his (every-other-day) attempt to not smoke any more, and he wonders if the site shop is still open.

— Constance. See the man she's talking to, that's Alistair. He's Stella's biological father. They never lived together but she was with him for a long time. He's back with his wife now, and then there's the younger one, Caleb. He goes abroad each year and then he comes back.

— She's not with either of them any more.

— Not this month.

— There's nothing to say she'll go back to either of them, Barnacle.

— No, but they're a love triangle that has lasted over twenty years, that's all I'm saying. Constance has taken so much shit for having two lovers over the years, never living with either of them, raising a child that way. The woman knows what she wants. Falling in love with a third won't change that.

Barnacle smiles and extends a paw and it looks exactly

like that, a soft curved paw, nail-less, like he's been de-clawed. Everything is stranger and warmer and wilder – the kids louder and their teeth shinier, and spirals of light against darkness and sparklers and fireworks whizzing up from miles away.

– Are you alright?

Constance is in front of him. She pulls off her wolf's head and her hair is stuck down and white and her skin is pale, so pale it glows, and she barely has eyebrows or eyelashes, which makes the grey of her eyes particularly clear. She glances at him and Barnacle looks awkwardly up at her and grins.

– Constance!

– Barnacle, you're not scaring the fresh blood, are you?

– He doesn't seem easily scared. I was just asking him why he moved – here!

The old man gesticulates, a conductor before an orchestra, his large hands palm up and drawing some strange pattern on the air. Constance, with the wolf-head in one hand, casually accepts a bottle of beer from a crate going by. She grabs a second, hands it to Dylan. They lock eyes. She tilts the bottle, still looking at him, and gestures to Stella by holding up her watch. Over on the other side of the bonfire an old couple are dancing, all stomachs and chins and an air of utter bliss as they hold each other and gently step forward – one-two, side-side, one-two. Barnacle shuffles back toward his caravan and jabs his finger up and mutters, and there are ribbons of light across the sky, billowing scarfs of purple with tiny inroads of green.

The bonfire is so hot, Dylan has to step back; flames lick around the horse painting from his caravan and it paws the ground before it goes up in flames, and the ground is mush under his sneakers. He looks up and she is not there and he looks around but he can only see the satanist kids walking their cat back to their caravan. A pitbull is up at their caravan window waiting for them.

— Do you want a sparkler, Dylan? Stella races around the fire.

— Thanks for asking me for dinner and not telling your mum it was a grown-up neighbour coming, not one of your school friends!

— I don't have school friends. Do you fancy my mum? Stella asks.

— No.

— Liar.

Barnacle has settled on his porch, waiting for the fireworks. Loud bangs echo across the green as a young guy lights them, one by one. The area is cordoned off but it's so close, if a rocket went backwards it could easily take out an eye or set a costume alight in the crowd. The young guy lights a Catherine wheel and it fizzes on the air, then sounds like a rope being pulled, and then the wheel is turning, shooting out tiny sparks in different colours until white electricity rockets up into the air, then a tiny dot exploding into arcs of sparkling light. Constance walks back over. The fire crackles but it is somehow distant and everything around them gets blurrier, and he is so high the ground is going up and down in gentle waves. What he needs is more beer.

— Where's your girlfriend then, Dylan?

— Why do you ask, Constance?

She grins and takes a swig of beer and looks away, at the fire, over the green, then back at him.

— Just making conversation, she says.

— No, you're not.

The sounds of fireworks whizz and the hiss of the fire and kids and clatter and she looks at him. Dylan resists pulling a strand of hair off her face. Constance flicks the ash off her cigarette and then she is walking away, raising her hand — a silhouette of wolf-ears and her tail flicking its way around the flames.

Part II

8th December 2020, −19 degrees

16

THERE ARE three suns in the sky. Constance raises the axe and there is a swoop-thud-crack as she brings it down. A log splits cleanly in two, falls onto a pile of softer shavings. She stacks the wood, straightens up, her hand on the small of her back.

Stella shades her eyes so she can see all three suns.

It's the most amazing thing she has ever seen in her life.

She frames the suns as if she's looking at them through an old film camera. The middle sun is the brightest and the two on either side are a tiny bit smaller and more hazy, but it is clearly suns in triplicate. The middle sun radiates a large white halo, which arcs out almost far enough to touch the suns on either side. Trails of light go up into the clouds. Stella tips her head back and narrows her eyes until sunlight makes the insides of her half-closed eyelids a warm blood-orange. Light soaks into her chromosomes.

– What are they called again, Mum?

– Parhelia. It's a phenomenon that looks like three suns, but the two on either side are just reflected light – it's something to do with ice-crystals.

She likes watching these suns and those wispy little clouds.

It does something relaxing to the eyes, like the seagulls dive-bombing down at Fort Harbour, dropping out of the sky, then the splash. Or when the mackerel are migrating, rippling the water as they swim along. Clean. Easy. Dylan appears behind them. He stares at the suns. Stella sees herself as the middle sun, but she reckons he is looking at the parhelia and seeing all three of them. If that was their life. That would be something. Adults are so stupid. It's clear they like each other. Her mum shades her own eyes and turns toward the three suns.

— They say three suns in the sky heralds the start of a great storm.

— Judging by the snowfall, they're right on cue, Dylan says.

Her mum brings down the axe again, cracking into a log where it juts out at an angle. There is snow everywhere. Piles and piles and piles of it. Smooth valleys up on the mountains that sparkle, totally untouched by anything. Constance unfolds a blue tarpaulin and fixes it over the stack of firewood to try and keep it dry. Dylan shields his eyes and stands on the other side of Stella, scanning the landscape. The seven sisters radiate! He looks up at the suns again.

— They call them sun dogs, he says.

— Why?

— I don't know.

— I met someone once who told me you can drink energy from the sun, store it in your cells so you grow strong. She said we should all do it. It's like a back-up store of it in our cells; she said there were sunlight pilgrims doing it all the time – it's how they get through the dark, by stashing up as much light as they can, Stella says.

Dylan turns to look at her.

— Who told you that?

— Just some woman I saw in the caravan park.

— My gran said those words, pretty much exactly like that, he says.

— Did she?

The two of them stare at each other and Stella notices for the first time that the shape of Dylan's eyes is exactly like Alistair's, and her heartbeat skips a little and picks up and she digs the toe of her boot into a pile of snow. Somewhere far away she can hear the motorway hum and she tries to imagine it is the sound of waves like the seashore at Fort Hope, and they need to go down there soon, to hear the boats click-clack at night and ask the fishermen when this iceberg is going to appear.

— Gunn told me there was an island close to Norway, but still part of the archipelago, that was home to a bunch of monks they called the sunlight pilgrims. All they had to eat was gannets and one year they all went mad, threw themselves off the cliffs, about seventy of them. Nobody knows what did it, but they were totally isolated from the mainland and they had one boat but they couldn't go for help until spring. They all died apart from one. They found him on the mountaintop naked, sitting in lotus, drinking light – orange to grey. That's how he said it. He said you just drink it. He said it keeps humans right. Guy claimed he hadn't eaten for weeks and the devil had taken his brothers, but he was okay, he said he got everything he needed from the sun. Apparently all the bones of the monks are still there on the island, Dylan says.

— I'd like to go there, Stella says.

— Which island is it? Constance asks.

— I don't know. It's not on the map, though; you can only get out there from spring to summer, because the sea is too rough the rest of the time. Fishermen say it moves too, sometimes it's there, other times it's not, that's how Gunn told it.

— They should have had a nuclear larder, Constance says.

— We have enough food in our apocalypse larder to be able to live solely off tins and rice and pasta for about what: six months, Mum?

— You won't be taking the piss when you don't have to eat gannets, Stella.

— It would be seagulls here, and deer.

Stella takes out her mobile and snaps a picture of the suns. She touches a tiny bit of soft down at the corner of her mouth. It's how a duckling's belly might feel. Smooth and silky but it won't stay like that. It wasn't there a month ago. Her voice is sending her odd notes. Her body is becoming a strange instrument. Her normal tone rises and dips and falls a little and nobody else has noticed yet, but any day now a tiny man is going to set up a loudspeaker in her throat and his voice will make declarations in a baritone and everyone will think it is her speaking, but it won't be. She will have to become a mute. She will carry pictures around of what she needs and point to things, or get a download where she can type words and a sexy girl-robot voice reads it all out for her. She can get the sexy girl-robot voice to say things like *arse* and *armpit* and she will call her robot the sunlight pilgrim too. She didn't think getting hair on her face or her voice changing would freak her out so deeply, but she feels like sprinting away from herself. She's just a girl who might grow a boy's face and voice, then every time she looks in the mirror who she is and who she sees won't even vaguely match – like if a big man took over her mum's body and started marching her around.

It's claustrophobic even thinking about it, and all around them winter is looking for victims and everyone is getting crazy. The darkness comes hunting an hour after lunchtime and by 3 p.m. they are plunged into twelve hours of night.

– Have you set up your gin-still? Constance asks.

– Doing it today, I'll bring you a bottle for Christmas.

– What are you going to call your gin?

– Dylan's Gin? he suggests.

– That's shit, she says.

– Call it Procrastinator's Idle, Stella mutters.

– What's in the new recipe? Constance asks.

– That would be telling!

The two of them are irritating the shit out of her. They're avoiding the issue. Even *she* knows it's clearly going to end with sex. Stella is not going to do that until she is at least eighteen and probably older, and she doesn't even know how it will work. She keeps trying to work it out. She's watched the porn but that's not real life and she can't get her head around anything other than kissing and holding hands, and if she thinks of anything more she begins to panic. Really, really panic so bad that her skin gets clammy; she really doesn't have the first clue what to do. She knows she only likes boys. That's all she knows. Stella isn't going to drink or smoke weed or do anything to stop her brain being as sharp and switched on as it can possibly be. She feels like there will be a day when she needs her wits even more than now.

The three suns rise higher in the sky.

Caravan doors open.

Neighbours come out onto their porches.

Birds on the mountains are calling. Hundreds of them lifting up as one. They swoop over the valley, the whites of their tummies flashing in the sun, and nobody speaks as the suns reach their highest point. The seven sisters' white snow-covered peaks turn yellow and colour fills the entire valley – it runs across forests, growing deeper in shade; it highlights a train track that curves out from the trees and the old Fort Hope Railway steam train motoring down the hill; smoke billows up, whitehouses turn yellow, dotted along the farmland, waterfalls glitter and even the scarecrows are momentarily cast in gold.

– There are no cows out, Stella says.

– They've been in the shed for weeks, Stella. They found two calfs frozen on the top field.

– To death?

– Yes! The farmer has taken four deer out of the forest like that already, too. I have no idea where the sheep are – they might have been taken over to Fort Hope to go into pens for the winter.

– It's deadly out there just now, Dylan says.

– Beautiful, though, Constance nods.

Stella has four layers on, thermal long-johns from head to toe, then leggings and a thin polo-neck, then a jumper and fleecy-lined waterproofs, then a jacket and her hat.

Everything settles.

Her heart.

Cells.

Breathing it in, feeling the sun on her face despite it being the coldest it has ever been in Clachan Fells. For the tiniest

second the parhelia send light all the way down inside her –
where even the wild things won't go.

Right down there in the darkest cells. Tiny dots of light!
Like little lanterns inside her veins.

Or glow-worms curling up to sleep. In the most secret
part of her – a place where she will go and sip tea one day –
and to get there she'll have to go through the darkest parts of
herself – between the pulsing aorta with its rivers of blood –
to her heart, where there is a tiny little door to for ever.

17

WHEN GROWN-UPS hear a little dark door creaking in their hearts they turn the telly up. They slug a glass of wine. They tell the cat it was just a door creaking. The cat knows. It jumps down from the sofa and walks out of the room. When that little dark door in a heart starts to go click-clack click-clack click-clack click-clack so loudly and violently their chest shows an actual beat – well, then they say they've got bad cholesterol and they try to quit using butter, they begin to go for walks.

When the tiny dark door in her heart creaks open, she will walk right through it.

She will lie down and sleep inside her own heart like a bird in the night.

If the door goes click-clack she'll take her shoes off and walk barefoot, ready for whatever comes, but all of that is a long way from now and her mother is standing in their garden, frowning and worrying about how many tins they have and how much wood and, if this is going to be an Ice Age, how will they earn any money when they can't even scavenge in the skip? There will be a lot of dead people, though. They both know that. Winter is working all of their hinges loose. A man lost in the countryside drove around in his car for four days in a snowstorm and he said he couldn't get a signal anywhere and everything looked the same. He died two streets away from home. An old couple lay down in each other's arms and left the windows open; they were frozen by morning. A whole bus full of men froze in the Sahara. Three kids fell through an ice-pond in Manchester. In Italy there have been electrical blackouts for weeks. It is so cold at the moment that her skin is already like a corpse's and the thought of it not wholly displeasing. It must be a goth-thing. After a year of finding her own look, Stella has become paler in her make-up, darker in her lipstick; she only wears tights if they're striped, even if they go under her long-johns and fleece trousers. She is obsessed with the idea of having jade-green hair.

Dylan is still standing quietly watching all three suns in the sky.

— We'll be okay, Dylan says.

— I miss clarity.

— What do you mean by that, Mum?

— I mean I miss things being clear. The weather, Stella! Not you. No, I miss a good long shit-summer, rainy autumn, miserable winter, debatable spring. Now we have this endless-fucking-Narnia and where is it all going to end?

Stella's feet flat on the deck and her fists a little clenched. Not hearing it the way it is said but hearing something else. A tiny creak in the door to her heart. The suns settle with two on either side, fading until the snow is just white, and there has been little snowfall since last night and the farm road will be packed solid. She has to get out of here.

— I'm going out on my bike.

— No, you're not, Stella.

— You can't make me stay in and you spent four days making my bike ready for the ice-roads, those tyres can handle it!

— She'll be fine, Dylan says.

— Okay, but stay on the farm road and first you need to have some breakfast. Dylan, do you want some?

Constance's voice has got higher at the end and she sounds vaguely hysterical. It's unlike her. Dylan shakes his head slowly.

— Got to go and get ingredients for gin, he says.

Stella sticks her tongue out at him and grins and he does the same as he walks away.

They didn't eat before the suns came. The kitchen clock reads 9 a.m. They must have been out there for an hour. Everyone simply flung on any old clothes and went outside to look. From the back window the three suns are still there, but the two smaller ones on either side are fading to long bright lines. They might still be there when she goes out if she hurries up, though.

— Stella, do you still want to go to the doctor's later?

— Why would I change my mind?

— I'm just asking!

— No, I don't want to go but I have to, so I'm going and I'll remember all the things we said and if I get stuck I will let you take over, I promise!

— Okay.

— I'm going for a shower.

Stella goes into the bathroom and unpeels her clothes quickly because it is freezing. The water is hot and the heat in the shower makes ice on the outside of their window crack. She dries herself with a blue towel and looks in the mirror. She has no breasts. That's okay. That's fine. A beard is less good. A deep voice is a terrifying thought. Sometimes, in quiet moments like this, she has to fight not to hate her body for threatening her with a baritone. She won't do that, though, she won't let herself hate it, because her body is a good one. It is strong. A girl is a girl is a girl. Stella unfolds a pair of ankle socks and dries her hair. She tucks one sock into each cup of her training bra. She dresses quickly and goes back into the living room. Her mother is pulling out her medical file from the kitchen cupboard. Outside the robin hops on top of his holly tree. He flits away toward the park. Stella sits back-to-front on her sofa at the window and eats the toast her mum made. It has marmalade on it, like Paddington's. She used to say that all the time when she was a kid and now that is how Stella thinks of toast and marmalade and it has to be brown bread, with only a touch of butter. Icicles elongate all the way from their window ledges to the ground. They are so thick she couldn't break them off without a hammer and chisel. They hang from all the caravans on Ash Lane, from everything now in fact. They're bony fingers, or long toothy spiky grins everywhere you look. Stella puts another pair of socks on just to be sure and then her waterproof trousers and then boots with metal grips on the bottom.

Outside the mountains are crisp and clear against the sky and the white peaks are bright. Stella unlatches the old metal window. The rubber rim is easy to lift up and underneath she can see black dirt. The air smells different, like each scent of the world is being preserved – even from here she can smell wood fires and the wild garlic under their snowy lawn. Winter is an alchemist who draws out (and heightens) the essence of scent: that was a line in a poem written on the Mother Superior's wall. She closes the window carefully before it siphons off their heat. Her mum has put draught excluders around the door and soon she'll cling-film the windows to double-insulate against the ice outside.

Down in the village church, bells ring loudly.

— Mum?

— Yes.

— Is alchemy against religion?

— Not if your religion is witchcraft.

— The Mother Superior has a quote on her wall about alchemy being kind of poetic and good.

— Alchemy is a science. Perhaps the Mother Superior is into science.

— What did alchemy create?

— Whisky, among other things. A group of alchemists were trying to create the most precious metal on earth in lots of different ways, like using lead as a base. One day a particular alchemist got liquid gold — the first hint of whisky — and he probably never looked back from there. He might as well have made pure gold. They were medieval chemists really, practising chemistry, and there are all the myths around it as an ancient spiritual science. I don't know much about it. Alistair knows more. He was down here last night.

— With you?

Constance looks out of the window and doesn't say anything.

– Are you seeing him again?

– He was asking for you.

– Why?

– He wanted to know if you're okay and if you want anything for Christmas.

– Yeah, I'd really love a vagina.

– You're getting more sarcastic by the day, Child.

– I don't want anything from Alistair; he can't even call me by my name and every time you get involved with him again you get thinner, and you drink more, and then you're ill.

– Not this time, Constance says.

– That's what you fucking said last time!

She waits for her mum to say *Swear jar* but she's even given up on that now. This winter is getting under her skin and she's just staring out the window at the snow, looking the tiniest bit frightened.

– He's making you something.

– Is it an apology?

– I think so.

– I tell you what, Mum: you tell him that I will take the old-fashioned kind of apology when you look someone in the face and you say *Sorry* and you mean it; and if he doesn't give me that, I swear I never want to stand in the same room as him again. Not fucking ever! He's a judgemental, self-rightous, self-satisfied, complete fucking arsehole! I have no time for people like that.

Stella pulls each of her fingers until they click out of their socket slightly; it's a comforting sensation, like sitting with her hands down her pyjamas at night watching telly in bed, or when she does a big shit and every part of her feels cleaner and lighter, or thinking that sex might be like that one day, a kind of emptying of herself, so she is free and less held down. She will go on the trans-teen website tomorrow. A boy will fall in love with her there. He'll be like the kind of person who founded Apple or something. Constance will loathe him until she sees how happy he makes Stella. Then they'll marry in the mountains, witnessed by her mum and Dylan and a couple of goats. They'll have a reception with rose-petal tea and candles under the wishing tree in the glen. Stella's breath leaves a circle of condensation on the window. She uses the cuff of her jumper to wipe it away. There will be deer up in the forest standing still as trees right now. She needs to go where they are. The icicles on the caravan opposite are long, but whorled like narwhal tusks — each points toward the earth and then tapers into snow. Hopefully the farm road will be packed solid. It should be, because the tractors are still trying to get the last of autumn's hay-bales out before they're all frozen and lost to winter as well.

Her mother's wolf-head sits on the shelf above the wood-stove.

Constance is in the bathroom.

Carefully tiptoeing over the floor, avoiding the creaky floorboard, Stella lifts the wolf-head up. It is surprisingly light and the fur is so soft. How can Alistair be so good at something like this and so utterly shit at being a decent human being? Stella slips the wolf over her head, and her nose and lips are framed below the long wolf-nose. The fur cloak hides her and makes her feel safe and warm straight away. It is strange looking at herself as a wolf in their silver sun-ray mirror on the wall. The wolf-cape looks even better on her than it did on her mother. Her black eyes peer out. Her lashes are long. Stella tugs the wolf-head until the ears sit perfectly; two long furry arms snake down on either side of her braids and the fur is white, like the wolf walked right out of the snow – like winter herself created it from particles of ice and dust and sent it out to find a mortal girl who isn't afraid of the big bad wolf, who knows how to use an axe and stir her own porridge, who knows that worth isn't something you let another person set for you, it is something you set yourself.

If the doctor asks her what she is most – she will tell him she is a wolf-child.

Her mother is winter.

Their neighbour is the child of Nephilim.

Her biological male donor is a future bone teapot.

Stella tips her head to the right and the wolf appears to be listening.

When the doctor asks her what she hears when she speaks (the strange tones her body stores right now), she will tell them she wants her voice to be clear as the single chime of a triangle on the top of a snowy mountain. She's not worried about breasts and she doesn't want rid of her penis, small as it is, not if it means getting an operation anyway. She just wants smooth skin and her girl-voice and to leave wolf-prints in the snow each morning.

The doctor will tell her that he is the one who owns the rights to her body and soul, that he will be the one to tell her what she can or cannot do with her own chromosomes. He will tell her about countless cancer patients who couldn't get treatment because of their postcode and he will expect her to feel bad about that, as if by being who she is, it takes medical care away from someone else with a real illness. But she is not ill. He will tell her to think herself lucky that this is something she *wants* – it's not like something she needs, like a heart transplant, or a new kidney. That's what he'll say. This isn't a want. Who would want this? She is a girl. In the wrong body. She didn't choose it and the idea of being forced to walk around in a man's body makes her want to peel her own skin off. She'll have to convince him she's always wanted to be just a girl. She will have to use the word *just*. It's important. They need girls to know their place, after all. She won't tell him not to be so dickish just because he gets to mainline testosterone for free, like a greedy, hairy bastard. On the table will be a file with her boy-name scored through and Estelle Fairbairn written in with a red biro. Alert – the red Stella. Alert, alert! Once he has reassured himself that she understands there is no decision about her body that she will ever make all on her own, that it will be teams of others, or singles, or surveys, or down to questions of budget or protocol, once he sees that register in her eyes he'll be satisfied. He'll sit back and watch her absorb the power he has over whether she can be a true thing or not. Outside there are three suns in the sky, and in the mirror there is a wolf-child with long black braids. Her mother steps out of the bathroom and Stella yanks it off her head!

18

THE WOLF is back on the shelf. Its nose points toward the door. Stella has smoothed down her braids and resumed her post back-to-front on the sofa, staring out of the window. Constance stands at the door; she does that thing where she flexes her toes — her bare feet are bony — and cricks her neck. She takes half a step to the kettle, then one turn to the bright-red cereal bowls that she bought in Italy years ago.

— Who is that from?

Stella nods toward a postcard tacked up onto the wooden saucepan rack.

— Caleb.

Her mother turns away and there's a tenseness to her when she says his name. From the back she doesn't look like an adult, but she doesn't really look like a teenager either, because she is too muscular, her frame lean, hair too short. Constance sits down at the kitchen table and puts the open cereal packet on the bunker.

— Would you take him back, and Alistair?

Her mother doesn't answer.

— What about Dylan?

Constance unfolds the paper and keeps frowning at it. Stella grabs her coat and she is out of the door, her eyes stinging. She crunches down the porch and away in the distance the village church bells chime. The snow and the ice and the cold are seeping into everybody. The whole world is getting meaner, if that is even possible. The church bells have been ringing like this for hours. It is something to do with the suns. The bells are always rung by the same old man, who took the job over forty years ago and came to the school last year to tell the pupils at Clachan Fells Primary School all about it. He told them that when they first moved to Clachan Fells, his mother warned him to be careful if he was going to get drunk in the village pub in winter. She said their neighbours would be able to tell how drunk he had been by the pattern of his footprints in the snow the next morning. That afternoon they made snowflakes by cutting little triangles out of paper and then they decorated the village hall for the Christmas party and a guy was brought in to DJ, with some flashing lights, and all of the songs were rave or pop and Stella prayed for Joy Division to materialise and stun them all. The song by Joy Division she would have had the DJ play would have been 'She's Lost Control'. That is what this winter feels like. Like everything that was once in order has unravelled, so fast nobody can keep up. Stella can hear the thwack of metal ringing from the bells all the way out here by the fields. Ropes run up into the belfry so that the bell chimes, it chimes, and chimes, and they are telling everyone to come to church, now the weather is getting worse by the day rather than weekly. They must all gather to pray. There are people in Clachan Fells village who believe this winter is the devil's work. He is wreaking revenge for being disbelieved all this time. The parhelia is still there but it is already fading. She checks her bike over; the big wheels are wide and can handle the snow as long as it is packed hard underneath, so she shouldn't go offroad, or not far anyway. The fields will be frozen as well – she'd probably be able to cycle on them too. The winter spokes are brilliant. Her mother always finds what they need out of sheer thin air. Luck and tenacity are her only employer. Constance steps out onto the porch to watch her checking over her bike.

– Stella?

– What?

Constance has put boots on and a polo-neck and the steam from her mug of tea is misting up her reading glasses.

– We need to go to the doctor's this afternoon at four p.m., okay? she says.

Her mother puts down her mug and carries a large bag of grit over to Barnacle's step. She tips it up and moves from left to right to distribute it evenly down his steps and all the way along the path to the car-park end and she does the same on the way back. She knocks on his door and he opens it and they nod and talk and laugh. Barnacle pats her mum on the arm and he points up at the mountain and she looks sad. Stella fixes her hat and her gloves, and checks that her phone is charged up enough – she has 60 per cent; it will do until she gets back. There is a haze in the upper part of the mountain and the trees along the bottom hills are mere out-lines of white. Stella walks down the path with her bike and there is just the crunch of her boots, cold air on her face and her nose red and her breath unfurling like a spectre.

– Morning, Barnacle.

– Morning, young Stella.

– I'm going out now, Mum.

– You need to be back for three, okay?

— It's not even ten yet.

— You won't get far in this anyway. Why don't you just walk?

— I'll come back if I get stuck.

Stella stamps on the ground and her boots make foot-prints in the solid snow.

— They say the aurora is coming, young Stella, and that great big bloody iceberg has been seen as close as Tanby Island now — it's definitely floating this way! Good morning, Dylan, Barnacle says across the path.

— Morning, Constance, Barnacle, Stella. The sun gods are hanging on a wee bit longer!

— Three suns! Barnacle whistles.

— See youz!

Stella hops on her bike and the pirate flag on the back flaps along. It's best to stick between the tyre treads in the snow, which are flatter and more densely packed. She has to go slowly so as not to skid. Her iPhone has enough charge to take pictures. She has her journal. She has a new hat that her mum knitted, which has big mohawk spikes in multi-colours on the top, and she has a hood like an Eskimo child. Her fur-lined boots are waterproof with spiked soles. She grips the handlebars so hard her knuckles hurt under her gloves and she turns up her iPhone to full volume, and the gloves are so thick she has to jab at the screen until a death-metal track comes on full blast. She picks up speed. Faster. Faster. She pedals harder. Air stings her few inches of bare skin, so it is colder than ice-floes on the North Sea — or even right at the bottom of the ocean where the skeletons hold hands or do the jitterbug or bang their fists on a whole roof of ice forming overhead.

19

STELLA PEDALS faster, down the back of garages; she steers
the bike between wide tractor treads and the back of her
legs begin to ache even though she is strong and too muscular. The girls changing in the gym watched her from the
other side of the room the first time she went in, and one of
the nuns was sitting there as well, just because Stella was
there. They took her into a meeting in school and she had to
say in advance that she wasn't a lesbian, or they wouldn't
have let her even try to use the girls' changing room. They
asked her if she was still a Christian. She explained that her
family are not religious. They asked her what she knew of
damnation. She asked them what they knew of autonomy.
They asked her how she knew that word. She asked if they
had met her mother. They said they would pray for her. She
said it was not necessary. They asked if she might feel different in a few months, or if perhaps she should simply change
for gym in the janitor's cupboard. She said she'd felt like this
her whole life and no amount of praying was going to change
it and she could use the janitor's cupboard to change, but
she was a person, not a broom. They said she needed to find
Jesus. She asked if that was like finding Wally? Only one

nun knew what she meant. That little drawing in those old comic strips her mum had, when you look for the dweeby guy in the stripy hat. It took nearly a year for the nuns to let her use the girls' changing room – so many meetings, all to put on white shorts and a white T-shirt and girls' gym shoes instead of the boys' blue ones. Eventually her mother said she was taking her out of school because the boys were all making Stella so self-conscious in their changing room when she took her shirt off and revealed her bra top. Her face burns even to think of Lewis and all the other boys mocking her – them sniggering, grabbing their crotches like rappers on bad videos, a horrible dark air that crept into her life that morning. Stella can't even explain how much she has dreaded gym class after that. It's worth going through an Ice Age just to not have to do that again. She could lie down in the snow like an angel and wait for winter to take her home.

At one of the meetings the Mother Superior asked her mother why her father wasn't there. Constance said he was with his wife, and she could bring her other boyfriend in if it helped any? Stella sat and felt like she was making an inconvenient fuss about nothing. Just like they wanted her to feel. Constance was furious with the nuns. It wasn't that Stella ever wanted to make anyone feel weird by being herself, but they did and ever since it has felt in school like every move she makes is exaggerated and observed and judged. It's like judging others is the absolute favourite occupation for some people in this life. Always to find the other person short on something. Just for kicks. Like how she is muscular from chopping wood since she was seven. She should be embarrassed but she's not. She wants to get some of the girls at school in a headlock sometimes – with their noses and their little mouths and their sports bras and all so lofty, yet not one of them can swing an axe. Stella can swing an axe on just the right side of freedom. That's the key to swinging an axe. Hold it with a lightness – then let it drop – so the axe does the work for you – *This is the best way to hold it; no, like this* – and her mother in the back garden showing her how to split logs, then split them again. Her mum could cut logs in her sleep, she *has* cut logs in her sleep. Every year at school they have an extracurricular skills day. Stella is daring herself for the next one. Simply go up to the blackboard and explain that we are all born female. That every man has a penis that started out as a vagina. Sketch it out. Hand out a spreadsheet for the non-believers. Probably she won't. Instead she could draw a diagram explaining that when logs are smaller, they don't need to be so hot to burn. Best not take an axe into school, though.

Or she should go and see Alistair and ask him for something dead to go and skin in front of everyone, to show them where a brain is and a heart is and that a body is just a body and if it is dead the soul is gone, nothing more to know about it until you're a spook – skulking around the living, hoping they will give you a smile. Touching them up in their bed at night. Hiding their keys. She could ask Alistair to take the body apart for her and ask him exactly why he has a problem with her being a female, when he clearly has devoted his adult life to having as many wives and girlfriends as he can manage? It was good to hang out with him, just once, or twice. She hates to even admit it. A few years ago Alistair showed her how to drain all the fluids out and take out the organs – *why do you take out the organs?* – and her mum pointing out odd things in jars then – eyeballs, hearts – showing her exactly how a heart works and *this is the main aorta, the heart valve, and this is where blood comes in to feed it with oxygen,* and our hearts not that different from squirrel hearts or our guts – not so different from hedgehog guts, and our brains not so different from eagles'. She found a hedgehog dead in the caravan park once – so dead and sad – its guts trailed around the caravan park for miles. Then he met his third wife. He married her in the same registry office where he wed the second one, but he didn't tell her that until later.

His whitehouse is just over there. If Stella knocked on the door it would be like she was a spook come to haunt them. That's how they like to think of her really. Dead. Devil spawn. Other. As if she never existed in the first place. Alistair's wife hates her. Stella reminds her of all the things that go bump in the night. She doesn't like the black nails or the stripy tights or the eyeliner, but what she hates most is that, to her, Stella is a girl who used to be a boy, and even more than that: she is her mother's daughter through and through, and Alistair's wife loathes Constance. Her husband still loves someone far more than her. She's never been able to take it, so she hated Stella and convinced him it was Stella that had the problem, it was her that wasn't right and she is so sure of it, so utterly righteous and vindictive in her piety. She doesn't want to think about them. She wants to think about clean things. Birds in flight. The noise of an axe – silent on the swing, then the thud, the crack, so satisfying – wood splitting. A whole two sheds full is what her mother has done now. Her mother smelling of oil and wax, her hands calloused. Showing her how to paint the furniture. Letting her paint the drawers that sit under the telly in the living room and each one painted a different colour and each glass knob a different colour, and on the bottom drawer two skull-head knobs found specially and kept for her birthday.

The farm road is empty. A dark blanket pulls itself across the mountains and the air grows dense and it doesn't seem like snow is going to fall, but it might begin to hail.

Stella's phone vibrates in her pocket.

Home.

Home.

– Mum?

– Are you turning back?

– Yup.

She clicks her phone off and she has one foot on the bike pedal and the other on the ground. She must talk later on. To. A. Doctor. She wishes it wasn't a doctor. It's not like she is ill. Hail snakes in a thick line down the mountains. Stella watches to see where the weather will go. She sits back on her bike and pedals even harder, and cycles past where she and Marie (the skank) made Richard's sister eat ten stalks of barley; she boaked up rough spiky bits for ages and then she trailed after them all the way home, repeatedly bleating *Am I in your gang yet?* Stella slammed the door in her face, then went and had her tea, and even now when she thinks about it – even in this cold – her face stings red. It's a thing that makes her cycle further than she should each time she goes out. Better to be alone. At least it is honest. She takes her metal spikes off so she can cycle easier, slings them over the handlebars. She cannot help this thing in her that makes her always wants to go further, to keep going, and as the first drops of hail begin to fall she is by the forest where trees sway – they shake, tall skinny boughs, and snow slides off them. It is too dark to go through the forest in this weather, but she can go over the stile instead, away from the mulched forest floor: that bit where you can fall through the false roof at the buried cottage and not get back out. A place to break your ankle or your leg and get trapped like an animal. In the summer there are always kids doing something down in that cottage that is sunk under the ground. Something disgusting. Or even pirates. Or even worse than pirates: paedophiles, or child murderers. It makes her sad. What's wrong with people?

She's up high now. She can see the old water pump, it's how you know where the cottage roof is on the forest floor – right there, because it is only uncovered in summer and in autumn is hidden by leaves and the mulch is dangerous and sometimes a dog or a walker falls through it. This whole area is built over old mine shafts too, massive hollow things. Leaves fall between exposed wooden beams in the cottage, come spring, and then you can look down and see the whole building has just dropped into the forest floor, under the ground like a troll lair that no self-respecting troll would be seen dead in. The place is full of pornos and the remnants of fires. Richard's sister said a man once caught her in the cottage and he made her pull her top up and then he got his dick out and made her touch it. He still lives in the village. Kids still go to his house to get drunk. All the kids know who he is and half the parents, so how come he still gets to live there? Stella cycles as close to the cottage as she dares but she can't see anything. All the walls are crumbly with a faded imprint of flowery wallpaper and swear words daubed on them. Sometimes the older kids get wasted and play music in there. This year there was a drum kit set up for months, and a boy gave her a joint last time and she held it like she was going to smoke it, and he stared at her top like he was trying to see tits through it. The smell of weed is disgusting. She pretended to smoke some, then handed it back. The farmer's old scarecrow is in that cottage and he's going to be down there all winter – laid out on a brass bed-stead over broken springs. The boys turned it into a Mrs Scarecrow and one of the older boys kept bending it over and saying he was doing it up the arse and he'd show them how to bukakke. Stella had to pretend it was funny, the same as the other girls did, but her heart was beating so fast and nobody from her class made one mention about her being anything than just a straight girl that day; they didn't want the older kids to turn on her. That was some-thing. She wanted those boys to let the scarecrow be. There's something wrong with her. She even feels empathy for stones.

A shower of hail clatters off the frozen snow on the ground and it bounces back up, gets bigger every second. The hail-stones batter off the earth – it's a comforting sound. Stella tucks her head down now and cycles fast and she should be heading for home, but she wants to see where they've kept the cows. If snow starts she'll have to get off and walk. In a field below a tractor snaps its lights onto full beam and farm buildings in the distance are flooded yellow. Stella picks up speed and she does not look back to where the fallen cottage is. She doesn't think about an outhouse, or six pairs of girl knickers stuffed down a rabbit hole. They were her first girly ones and she stole them all from Morag who lived on Oak Tree Lane. Stella's mum found out and it made her cry. She'd never seen her mother cry before. There is a clatter of hail on the ground, but it thins and the second and third sun disappear from the sky. Her boots slip on the pedals as she cycles toward the farm, tractors in the distance. The hail ceases and right through the middle of Clachan Fells silence builds until twenty deer bolt from the forest. They curve across the fields — the fawns big now, their hooves barely touch the ground. Stella races them down through the white valley.

Hooves clatter off the ground.

The deer gain speed and she is only yards from them now, her chest burns and for a fraction of a second she is flying! They arc ahead of her and she careens after the fleeing herd. The hailstorm has come back right overhead now. Round white pellets batter the ground as the deer disappear into a big empty cowshed. Her muscles burn. She skids into the big old shed behind them. It is dark enough that it takes her a few minutes until her eyes adjust and she breathes in the smell of hay and manure. As her vision adjusts to the light inside the barn, she sees the deer all clustered together at the far end of the echoey old corrugated-iron building. Hail beats on the tin roof and the deer all watch her. She stops so they know she is not anything to worry about. Water drips off her chin. She checks her phone and finds no signal. The barn doors are wide open and it is so, so cold. She will have to find her way back before dark. If the snow begins to fall and doesn't stop, then she's in trouble. Stella unzips her jacket and wrings the damp out of it. She throws it over a pen to dry.

20

CONSTANCE THUDS back out of the caravan and shuts the door behind her and leans against it. Dylan nods at the axe she left sticking out of a tree.

— You couldn't do that in London, he says.

— Stella's still not answering my texts.

— We'll find her.

— I'm going to finish painting this one really quickly and then we can go, okay?

Hail is battering off the tarpaulin in her back garden. The bones in Constance's wrist jut out and her brush swishes up and down furiously as she attacks the dresser, and the air smells of oil and wet wood and she sits back for a minute to appraise her work. He can't figure out how she doesn't know he wants to touch her. Trying not to think about it. Circles of other thoughts. Setting up the projector in his caravan to see if it is still working and finding a bit missing, and wondering if Babylon has had her guts ripped out and thinking he should set up his old media website to see if he can track down any old friends from Soho because there were a few, and how this morning he opened the kitchen cupboard and the smiley sticker on Vivienne's Tupperware urn was already looking faded. If Constance or Stella knew what he found in Vivienne's sketchbook. If they did. He will have to tell them. If he is completely, totally honest, he doesn't want to tell Constance until he knows if she will sleep with him. If they just lay down. If she was on top. Dragging him further into her. Sweat against the cold air even in their caravans. A bed as a refuge. Just to lie there. Pass ownership of your body to someone else. Yes, you can lick me here, touch me there; you're angry, it is okay to use me, it is fine to suck and fuck and pull and scratch and bite. It's the only place in life we do it. Someone else touches us when we're little, to have a bath or get dressed or be hugged, then our bodies walk around surrounded by air until you want someone like this, and he feels like it is only a matter of time before they are naked, but then that intoxicating thrill that says what if they don't? What if this want keeps getting bigger and nothing comes of it at all? It's that unknown quantity: add this to this, her to him, what will come out of it, they don't know. When he sees Constance looking back up the mountain toward Alistair's house or the postcard she has on her fridge from Caleb, he gets it. If Marina turned up now, he can't say he wouldn't sleep with her again. They were together seven years on and off. Perhaps some bits of love never go. He picks at his cuffs and watches the way she turns on her heels to paint the other side of the wardrobe, her eyebrows so pale and that frown she always seems to wear. Constance has to come to him. That's how it works. She must feel him waiting. He's not being obvious about it. But it's there. An unspoken question they both skirt around when having a bottle, or two, of wine, wrapped in blankets, last night on her porch. He tries not to feel like he knew her before, to imagine her face in the dark, her lips. They'd have to use his place. This is the other reason why people have jobs. So they don't stalk their neighbours. She is beautiful. He just likes her. It's not creepy. Even if Alistair is his cousin, if it is right – the family tree Vivienne has left – and he wants to tell her that he found out exactly why Vivienne bought him a caravan right next door to them, but it might mean she'd never give him a chance and right now he is too selfish to take a risk on that. The guilt sits uneasily on him so he makes himself a deal: he'll tell her in one week, and he'll look at the tree Vivienne wrote down again and he'll double-check the details. Constance finishes touching up the metal 1950s larder. The inside has already been fitted out with patterned vinyl and the door knobs are plain white; she is precise and focused as she finishes up the final touches of paint. As the hailstorm stops, the snow begins.

– Stella should be back by now, Constance says.

– Hello!

Dylan knows who it is before he even turns around. He feels angry before he even looks at him. Irrationally hostile. There is a tension in the air. Alistair grins at him and goes over to kiss Constance on the cheek, an electricity between the two of them as well, and Dylan is caught in the middle of it, some of it is diverting around him from both of them. Alistair is looking him up and down. Dylan looks down at the guy, glad to be taller. He's looking to see his mother in this stranger's face. Or his gran. It would be Gunn, if she is Alistair's aunt and if Alistair's father is possibly Vivienne's dad. If the family tree Vivienne left is right, it means the guy standing in front of him is his mum's cousin and all he can think about is that he wants to bash the bloke's face in and go to bed as soon as he can manage it, with the love of his life.

— Pleased to meet you, I'm Alistair.

He holds a hand out, Dylan does not shake it.

— What are you doing here, Alistair?

— Do I need a reason to visit you now, Constance?

She glances toward Dylan.

— I'm busy.

— Aren't you going to introduce me?

Dylan holds his breath.

— No, I'm not, Alistair. Don't come down here again until you apologise to Stella.

Alistair laughs. He is a sinewy guy with bright eyes; they are black and penetrating and he is handsome enough, Dylan will give him that. His hair is dark and he's wiry, narrow, a bit mean-looking, but Dylan's no doubt he could take him, if it came to it, arm-wrestle, Scrabble, pub quiz, fist to the face. Just if he had to. Not that he'd try. Unless this offensive-looking faux-artist was game.

— Doesn't she know we are seeing each other again, darling, he says, looking at Dylan the whole time.

— I don't know, Alistair. Does your wife know we had a one-off, darling? I can always let her know how truly mundane the whole thing was, she hisses.

— I'm making a present for Cael, he says.

Dylan steps forward and flicks him on the nose as hard as he can.

— What the fuck are you doing?

Alistair grabs his nose while looking up at Dylan towering over him, blocking out the light, squaring his shoulders even more.

— Her name is fucking Stella, he says.

— Who the fuck are you?

Alistair looks right up at him and for a minute Dylan thinks the bloke recognises him. Constance is staring between the two, a little in shock, but there's a definite hint of amusement.

— That was fucking unnecessary, Alistair says.

— No this would be fucking unnecessary. Dylan curls up a ham-sized fist.

— I cut up bodies for a living, pal, you're not intimidating me.

— Animal bodies.

— Obviously!

— I've cut up animal bodies before, for meat, not to try and be interesting.

— I'm not trying to be interesting!

— Good, cos if you were, it wouldn't be working. I never met a taxidermist that wasn't a total bore, d'ye know that?

— I bet you've never met a taxidermist in your life.

— I have and he was boring, and an arsehole!

— Okay, guys, you can stop waving your dicks at each other and I am going to go and find my daughter. I'm serious, Alistair: you want near this house, then you apologise to her, and you mean it.

— Aren't you going to make him apologise? I might call the police!

— For what? Nose-flicking? Dylan says.

Alistair crunches away down Ash Lane wearing his big Russian hat with thick furry flaps. Dylan realises his heart is pounding and his right hand is still curled up. It's just the idea of it — that this guy's dad could be his great-uncle and, worse than that, his granddad as well. He feels dizzy. He wants to sit down. He is losing it. He just flicked her lover's nose and she is quietly packing her brushes away, not look-ing at him. He shouldn't have tried to work out the rest of the family tree in Vivienne's sketchbook when he was drunk. Maybe he got it wrong. Why would Vivienne leave this kind of information to him? What is he meant to do with it? He is furious with her. He has fallen out with his mother and she isn't even here for him to tell her about it, and so that anger is just fermenting in his head. A tiny child-ish part of him thinks if he gets angry enough at her, she'll have to come back. Just to put him in his place. And she could do that. Vivienne did it plenty enough times. With that, he feels that weight of missing her and Gunn, wanting to tell them things, make a drink, annoy them by his pres-ence; get a hug on the way to his projector booth and look up mid-film to find a coffee or a beer has been slipped inside the door for him; go to Borough market and buy them olives and bread. Nothing much, yet everything. They are never coming back and he is clearly flipping out. Constance checks her phone again.

— What was with the nose-flick? she asks.

— I'm really . . . I don't know.

— You'll be Stella's hero for ever now. Her smile flashes for a second and is gone.

— We'll find her. Stella knows Clachan Fells better than anyone.

He gets a shot of fear that Stella's seen the sketchbook.

— The boys at the village hall drew a picture of Stella last month and she looked all girly, except for a pair of scissors in her hand and a dick cut off. It was at her feet, like she has to get a sex change to be a girl or she has to get it cut off, or even that they are thinking about that!

— Do you want me to go round to their houses?

— And what: flick their noses?

— Seriously, I will.

— No, I just thought they were nicer kids than that.

— It was only one who drew it?

— It was only one who drew the bit where she was . . . cut. If one of them hurt her like that, I swear to God I would track them down and kill them with my bare hands, each and every fucking one, no hesitation at all!

He looks at her.

— You might be better trying a good nose-flick, he suggests.

Constance stands with her hand on the axe, unsmiling.

— We'll drop off this wardrobe, so I can get some cash, and come back round the other side of the mountain. She was on the farm road, but I wouldn't be surprised if she's headed for the lower forest, or she'll be on the middle sister, sheltering there.

— The what?

— We call Clachan Fells mountains the 'seven sisters' — did nobody tell you that yet?

Constance pulls the edge of the tarpaulin and a pile of snow slides off onto the ground and she glances over at the caravan, wrinkles her nose.

— She'll be fine.

— It doesn't always work out like that, though, does it? I've been on the trans websites. I've seen the stats. Anyway, if more of this kind of weather comes down, we'll end up snowed in for months. It sounds bad but at least I'd know she's safe for a while, have time to work things out. Or if it gets worse than that, if it doesn't even stop snowing — you know, if the temperature just keeps dropping.

She's brittle. Moving quickly in front of him. Not meeting his eyes.

— This wardrobe is going to a farmhouse near Fort Harbour. They've bought loads of stuff from me and she wants this to put in her new garage extension. They've built a wee flat above their garage, which is easily bigger than both of our places put together.

For some reason this highly unfunny truth has them snorting and giggling and avoiding each other's eyes even more and there is a lightness now as they move around one other. Constance lifts her side of the wardrobe and he takes the other end. It's heavy, but they walk down the path with it and slide it into the back of the ambulance. She lies the wardrobe on top of an old duvet and throws some covers over the top, then uses climbing hooks to secure the rope holding it in place. Dylan climbs into her ambulance and there's a hole in the floor right through to the ground. It smells of paint in here, and oil, and her — which is a clean thing like unscented soap and hair that has the faintest tinge of wood-smoke. The passenger seat is inches lower than it should be because it's obviously been pulled out of some other car.

— She's still not answered my texts. I fucking told her not to go out!

She turns the key and pushes the clutch. The engine catches and she drives slowly. She ceaselessly scans the landscape. He touches her hand for a fraction of a second and the silence between them deepens. They are complicit. Pretending, like neither of them notices. They drive past the industrial site and a Japanese car showroom where there is some event on, people drinking wine in the brightly lit display room, and metallic red and blue balloons filled with helium are beginning to droop under the falling snow outside. They drive past the industrial estate and round a big roundabout and up a hill toward the other side of the village. She switches on the radio.

— *I mean, I don't have a problem with people eating meat, but what I do have a problem with is them telling us it's pig when it is potentially another animal or something genetically modified or even worse — what else are they putting into the food chain now? There were even rumours of —— [Bleep. Cough.]*

— *Listeners, we lost Jane from Milton Keynes, but let me ask: are you feeling the pinch, are you able to afford groceries? How are you going to get by this winter? We're expecting whole communities, whole cities in fact, to be snowed in. In Yorkshire there have been ploughs out, trying to get cars out of traffic jams, and in Aberdeen one man drove around in a snowstorm for nearly two days. Angus, a residential careworker from Scotland who said he got so lost, he had no satnav, no phone. People: you have to be safe out there; take satnav, take phones, make sure they are charged, have supplies in your car, prepare your homes for the greatest snow we are ever going to see in Britain. Keep sending in your photos of snowmen. We love them. We've put them up on the website, and will announce a competition winner for the best snowman of the 2020 deep freeze at the end of this week. Please do phone into VfR.556 and let us know how you're getting along out there. We're turning up the heating and getting our thickest socks on: now there's an image for you listeners! This is Nico's classic radio bringing you the news from around Britain.*

— Sounds like we'll have to resort to Stella's plan soon, Constance says.

— What's that?

– Drinking light.

You'd be the last monk on the island, Constance! You'd be shooting down gannets with a home-made bow and arrow, taking solar shots with the foxes. You'd be a survivalist pilgrim.

She's laughing then, that low timbre.

– There's no telling Stella. She made me vow to become a sunlight pilgrim before I got out of bed this morning, and I was so hungover. My lips are still almost black!

– Where were you last night?

– I ended up at the miners' club, drinking with Ida, then Alistair turned up. That's why he is sniffing around here this morning.

– Are you back with him?

– Does it matter?

– It matters to Stella.

– I wasn't asking that.

– Your lips are reddish-black.

– They're normally about as pale as the rest of me, she says.

Constance leans over him to take a piece of cloth from the dashboard to wipe the window, and he has that drop kick in the aortal region as blood rushes to a hard-on. She rubs at the window and blasts the air conditioner and the engine dies. She pats the dashboard.

– Come on, you old relic – just one more trip.

Cars pull out around them and everyone is driving slowly today. The engine catches and Constance is elated and humming under her breath and they fly down the motorway with the ambulance roaring and clunking.

– I know how to butcher animals if we need to go hunting, he says.

— Or people?

— I don't know why I said that.

— It might come to it: cannibalism for the last few survivors in the winter wilderness that is Clachan Fells. Who would you eat first? She grins.

— It wouldn't be you, or Stella, he says.

— So sweet, and considerate.

— You're both too skinny, he says.

— I'm not skinny — it's sheer muscle on these legs, she says, slapping one.

Dylan resists asking her to do that again; he has to rein in his impulse control somewhere this afternoon, so he looks away from her upper thighs, slim under her jeans, and fixes his gaze out of the window.

— I learnt to butcher because Gunn had a sideline going for a while. Babylon is under the arches, where the railways used to run, and they all had these big storage cellars underneath. Anyway, I came home one day when I was twelve and found a few dead calves being rolled down the beer-hatch. It completely freaked me out. They were long-lashed things with unpliant lips and hooves clattering off stone, and she was hoisting them behind barrels of ale like it was the most ordinary thing to be doing. *See here, Dylan, you insert the knife to the side of the windpipe with the back of the blade against the breastbone. Press toward the spine, three inches or so; now cut through the carotid arteries and watch out for the jugular veins. Now cut the hide around each foot, that's it, then a long slit down the middle of each leg like this and a longer cut from tail to throat and then work through the membrane. Then you can peel the skin off in one go and let gravity help you. Come closer, Dylan, hold that shoulder. Now look, here's the liver; this is the heart; follow the rump; cut with one motion!*

— She sounds like my kind of woman.

— Gunn was fucking amazing. In our kitchen there was always the smell of olive oil, thyme, garlic, onion, red wine, and sometimes she'd cook up a batch of fresh black pudding and my mum would sit at the kitchen table smoking. Gran would knock back a shot of blood (as a tonic), with a second tossed down the drain for the sick and weary.

— That's what she said?

— Aye, exactly like that. She'd play her old gramophone and I can remember, as a wee boy, hearing Bessie Smith sing 'Nobody Knows You When You're Down and Out' and watching the lights flash in the peep-shows and strip-bars outside.

— You never went in those, right?

— Not until I was twelve, and then only once a week or so.

Constance laughs.

— Later Gunn would tell me all these stories, while through the floorboards we could hear the audiences laughing or clapping below. By then my mum would be seated in her projectionist booth chain-smoking and drinking gin until the credits rolled.

— Were you close to Vivienne?

— No. I was protective of her but she wasn't maternal, she was more like an older sister really. It's like there was something missing in her, truth be told. She was distant from life in general. But she was cool. On her tombstone it should say *Here lies Vivienne, a woman who thought the purest form of water was gin* — roll credits!

This is the most he has probably said about home since Vivienne died. Constance's eyes are all grey and steely and honest, with flecks of orange as snow falls outside the window.

They turn off through farm gates and up a long pebbled driveway covered in snow. Outside an old farmhouse there are two statues. A woman looks out of a kitchen window and waves them around the back. Constance parks and jumps down, opens the back doors; she takes the heavier end of the wardrobe. Dylan doesn't even attempt to argue with her. They go up the metal staircase at the back of the garage into a flat with views out over the hills and forests. Everything smells of the stabilising influence of money. There's a stack of old home magazines and he could just sit there with a coffee. A place to lay your head. Constance smirks at him, catching his thoughts. They are giggling again when the woman from the house crunches back over the drive to pay them. She is wearing a scarf with a floral pattern and has red curly hair, and Dylan imagines she has just been doing something intricate with giblets or shallots. As they walk towards her, an outdoor light flicks on.

— Half-and-half payment okay again, Constance?

— Aye, thanks.

— Have you been watching the weather in Europe?

— Not this morning.

— There was an avalanche in Italy. My son is over there — he's fine but he can't fly out, it's pretty treacherous. Are there any warnings in place for the seven sisters?

— Not yet, Constance says.

— There will be.

— Did you hear about the iceberg — it's already past Tanby Island? Constance says.

— I did indeed. My husband's colleague's wife works down at the harbour, and the iceberg is bigger than the whole of Fort Harbour. They gave it a code, C34, but the fishermen are still calling it Boo. If all the ice keeps melting, in a few years London will be gone, Venice, the Netherlands, most of Denmark, San Diego . . . I could go on. My husband is a scientist – this is the cheery stuff he brings home to discuss with me over dinner.

– I'm glad I left London and came here then. You've got all the good stuff. Triple suns, ice-flowers, icebergs. I don't even miss the strippers! Dylan grins.

The woman ignores that.

– You won't be saying that when we all get snowed in. They certainly will be on the mountain and down at your trailer park, dear, perhaps for months!

– They're not trailers, they're caravans, Dylan smiles.

The woman counts out notes and then goes into a utility room. She comes back out with a wooden crate.

– There's fresh eggs in there, bacon and some herbs from the freezer; potatoes and a pound of good-quality butter; also some shallots and a tiny bit of honey from the farm.

– Lovely, thank you!

– How tall are you anyway? You're very tall. He's very handsome, Constance!

– Isn't he – quite dreamy! Constance says.

– If you need any work . . . Dylan, is it? I sometimes need a handyman around here.

The woman says this and flashes a flirtatious smile. He nods and smiles back. Constance mouths the words – *trailer park* – then loops her arm through his as they walk back to the ambulance. They drive out along farm lanes he hasn't seen before. Constance sends texts, one after the other, steering with one hand, and her big boots don't seem to hamper her driving style at all.

She checks her phone again, one eye on the road, then chucks it onto the dashboard, clearly annoyed. Scattered in the front are little glittery stickers that Stella usually has on her nails. Dylan peers out the window as snow begins to fall again. It's getting darker out there, and colder. Stella probably doesn't even have a torch with her.

21

CONSTANCE ROLLS a cigarette with the ambulance door open. She jumps down and hauls out waterproof trousers and walks along and passes a pair to Dylan. They are a few feet too short when he puts them on, but he tucks them into his boots. The snow is falling steadily and heavily now. She takes out a torch and a blanket. They walk side-by-side down the farm roads, snow crunching under their boots.

— Snow's not going to stop falling any time soon.

— Have you a signal on your phone?

— No, she says.

— Which way from here?

There's a big barn at the bottom of the field. They head that way without saying anything. Dylan isn't even sure he'd find his way back in this snow, Constance's nose is red and she squints at him.

— What are you thinking about?

— I was thinking about a dream I had on the night that Vivienne died. I was in this bright room and there were people, all from the Other Side, rushing around and I said to one of them: *Is she going now? Is it over?* They said yes, they said I could go now, that I wasn't needed any more. I walked out of that bright room because they were there to look after her, to take her over to the Other Side. See, you think it's bullshit?

— I never said that, she says.

Snow pirouettes around them as they put their heads down and move toward the barn, their feet disappearing up to their ankles. Constance scans further up on the mountain. The trees are clad in snow. Her eyes are clear grey in this light. Long icicles adorn branches on all the boughs. There are tiny beads of crystals on her eyelashes as she turns to look at him. Dylan bends down and cups her face in his hands. He can feel the heat from her before he kisses her, and just gently their lips meet, then the shock of her tongue, hot and wet. All around them snow falls and their skin is cold as ice, but she is pulling his head further down, leaning her body into him. When they pull apart he is dizzy, blinking, looking around, her hand curling into his, smaller, gloved. He tries to settle his breathing down to something vaguely normal as they tramp across the field.

— There's a bar in Charing Cross — it's called Yuki Ookami, it means Snow Wolf. Their gimmick was ice-chairs and an ice-bar and they only stayed open for three months, but I got mortally pissed on vodka shots after I realised Babylon was in so much debt. I ended up at some house-party in Dulwich where they were having an orgy and there was a girl in a gorilla mask, with crosses of gaffer tape across each nipple. Is that the sound of the sea?

— Yup. Just on the other side of that mountain. You were saying?

— It was lame, a shit party. I have no idea what I am talking about, I'm gibbering, he says.

They reach the barn and she grips his hand a bit harder, leading him through the barn doors. It smells musty and damp and there are a few old hay-bales in the corner and small hoof-prints across the floor. Long icicles have lengthened from the rooftop down into the dim.

— There's nothing in here, she says.

— Except that.

He points at tyre tracks from a bike, in a figure-of-eight going back out another door.

— She's gone home then, she says.

Constance is trying not to look at him. She stands in between the wide barn doors with panels of stained corrugated iron on either side of her. Behind her there are the peaks of white mountains. Her hood is up and she turns again and they lean against the wall, their tongues the only heat in a world dropping degrees by the hour. Wrapping one leg around his hip, him wanting to pull her up and into him, undoing her jacket. She pulls her hood back.

— This isn't what we're meant to be doing, she says.

— Isn't it?

She pulls away. The snow has stopped and it is much thicker in the fields below them toward the bottom of the mountain, and further up there are peaks of white, but there are still some fields too exposed to the wind to have had much snow settle.

— Alistair lives there.

She points up the mountain to a cottage with a spire of smoke and claps her hands together in her gloves to keep them warm and glances back at him. It is a traditional white-house, large sloping roof and a wide wooden platform porch all around it. The windows are dark.

– Why didn't you and Stella ever live with him?

Constance doesn't answer. She gazes up the mountain and he looks toward the field. They walk out, still holding hands. A cacophony of jagged bray and honk rises into the air and down below them there is a blue loch. Geese swagger around each other in the field next to it, hundreds and hundreds of them.

– Barnacle geese – they're late coming back from the Arctic and Iceland. It doesn't look like they're stopping, but they usually would. I've not seen any Bewick or whooper swans; we usually get them in autumn but they skipped it entirely this year.

– Is that why Barnacle is called that? Dylan asks.

– You mean Bill? No, he has been called Barnacle since he was a Casanova, back in the day, gambling away all his money and squandering the family estate on women and parties and classic cars. He hasn't even one thing to show for it now. Look up Barnacle online – you'll get the gist of why they called him that.

– It's a big-dick thing?

– Huge, she says.

– You've seen it?

– Don't be gross.

– Just checking, Dylan says.

– That was Barnacle's place over there!

She points over to the big estate chimneys poking out of the forests.

– I want to see Clachan Fells in autumn when it's all red and gold and yellow; and in spring. Even in the snow it is the most beautiful place, he says.

– It's something else, she says softly.

Birds yak away in the fields, striding in circles. The flock calls out to each other, their gaggle getting louder and harsher, before the first few take a run forward and glide up into the air and then the whole flock lifts!

He holds his breath.

They begin to form a straggly V behind the leading geese; their wings beat harder and faster as they gain height and speed and swoop down the other side of the mountain across a frozen waterfall in the distance and then up over a cluster of stone whitewashed cottages. Chimneys stick out of the forest from the country house Barnacle used to own. The geese fly toward the coast – birds falling effortlessly back so that a longer V-formation emerges across the sky. Dylan links his pinky finger through hers and she curls her finger back around his.

– They can be a bit small-minded around here, Dylan. Most of the villagers don't speak to me, just because I had two lovers all these years – or I have or . . . I don't even fucking know what I have anymore, or what I want even.

– You don't need to explain anything to me.

– I can't stop worrying about Stella, it's driving me nuts. You hear about some little kid who gets chased down in a community because they're trans, or you read the suicide rates, or even the way the local boys look at her sometimes, you know. I don't know how to protect her. When it comes right down to it, I can act as tough as I want, but I can't always be there to make sure she is okay and it really fucking kills me!

She drags her cuff across her face, blinks hard and studies the trails Stella has left with her bike, leading straight toward the farm road. She's probably back in the caravan already.

There are other trails in the snow, small ones: does or stags. Tiny three-pronged prints of a bird.

— Think: one day she's going to have to bring a guy home — to meet me!

She giggles.

— Don't fucking envy him that one, Dylan says.

Snow whirls down from the mountaintop and the tips of trees sway. All this snow is going to get so heavy they won't even be able to open their caravan door. How long can they stay in the caravans without going out? How long will the fuel last? He's beginning to think like Constance. Watching snow rise up the side of their caravans in inches. Checking the death-rates online. This winter has tripled the usual amount already, and they are barely into the thing. Wind howls up around the back of the barn, rattling the tin walls. She takes his hand, the two of them silhouetted at the big dark square entrance to the barn as she leans up to kiss him.

22

STELLA MARCHES down past the farm. She is wet and shivering. Her teeth clatter. She must keep moving so that hypothermia doesn't kick in. The farmer's dogs bark and it sounds so loud in the silence. They are all out in the grounds today. Nobody is going to be out hunting or herding sheep in this. The farm estate has a twelve-foot-high metal fence around it to keep the dogs back. She always clenches her fists as she walks by them. They can smell fear, so they jump up at the fence, jaws snapping, running up and down alongside her.

If they got out they'd just go for her.

She hates having to walk past them.

The thing is to act like she's not scared and push her bike, but the snow is deep up here and her boots plunge in up to her knees and she has to kick forward, using the bike to clear her way onto more solid ground. The dogs leap at the fence. Don't look scared. Never let them know you're frightened. Except they can smell it on her. To them she must look like walking dog-food. She keeps her face a still mask and tries to appear angry, like she would kick their heads in if they went for her. There must be thirty dogs in there. They are all different breeds and most of them are so vicious they need to be penned in. It's all teeth and slaver and flashes of pink gums with black marks on them. Last year Barnacle bought her mum an antler keyring made by the farmer's son.

A black dog runs up to the fence and rubs against the metal wire. It snarls, its fangs are yellow, it has tiny rabid eyes and its penis is out and that makes her want to vomit. She walks faster. Further up ahead on a little hill there is a separate enclosure where two dogs are kept on their own. Both of the dogs in there stand up on top of their kennels, watching her. They sniff the air. Those two are not allowed to integrate or they'd just kill the other dogs. The farmer's four-wheel drive pulls out from the front of the farmhouse and he has a big green metal barrel fixed on the back of it, with a little hatch made of four black bars.

A dog snarls from inside the barrel, crazy, a flash of eyes and teeth. If it was able to, it would shoot out like a bullet to maul whatever it found. The farm gives her the creeps. The farmer's wife lives up there surrounded by that and they hardly get any visitors. How does she do it? Night after night in the dark. All those dogs snapping around outside her house. The farmer slows down when he sees her and winds down his window.

— What are you doing up here on your own?
— I just came out on my bike.
— I can see that.
— I'm going home now.
— You shouldn't be up the mountain on your own in this weather — you're asking for trouble.
— I'm fine.

— Get in.

— No, thanks.

The dogs are barking like crazy behind them both and he drives slowly, just looking at her for a minute, and she looks back at him the way she has seen her mother look at men to let them know she is not intimidated by them for even one tiny second. He nods briefly and begins to wind up his window.

— I was only going to give you a lift back down toward the motorway, he says.

— I'm fine.

— You're not fine, you're soaking; you'd better get home pronto. Are you Constance's girl?

— Aye.

— Tell her I was asking for her. Bye.

His truck trundles down the road. His wife is the only woman in that farm all year round. There are men hired in summer time or for the hunting season to help out. Stella was up there a few springs back with her mum, sitting at their rough old wooden kitchen table, and there was clutter everywhere. Pieces of antler and bills with tea spilled on them; old oil lanterns and stacks of dog-food. The farmer sat smoking one of those clear pipe things and filled it up with oil three times while they were there. He drinks in the old boat club with the other locals from this part of the mountain. Constance says they drink so much in there it's a miracle they keep the land going at all. She has driven past at seven in the morning a few times and seen the bar lights still on from the night before.

When the winter really kicks in, the farmhouse will be snowed in for months.

It gives her the creeps.

Nobody is laughing any more. The Thames has frozen over and they are holding fairs on it and she saw a picture of Trafalgar Square with all the water frozen around the sculptures and snow on all the grand buildings. It looked like fucking Moscow! The cold is down in her bones but there is something clean about it. Honest. Nobody is dead yet on their street, but two people froze on the way home in Edinburgh yesterday. This is the coldest day so far. Stella turns out into the field behind the caravan park and she can see her mum's ambulance away in the distance. It looks like it is parked. It looks like she might have walked up to see Alistair. She remembers seeing them fight one time and her mum was so angry, Alistair goading and poking and pricking and sneaky and mean, really, really mean. Dylan, he would be the one to be there for her mum.

A truck races along the farm road.

It screeches to a stop in front of her. There are two men in the front and she steps onto the verge to let them by, but they pull up closer. There is a skinny one and an older one who has ragged hair and a lumberjack shirt. She can smell them both right away, like they don't wash, like they sleep in a room with their dogs, like they drink beer for breakfast. Stella looks along the farm road to see if her mum is walking along there, but nobody else is out. The older one winds down his window.

– You seen a dog?

Stella shakes her head.

– S'been up the back fields worrying sheep, must be a big one – you've not see anything?

– No, I've not seen a dog loose. There's just the ones penned up back at the farm.

— You the farmer's girl?

Stella nods, hoping the idea of having a father with a gun will make them move on and stop looking at her like they can see through her clothes.

— You stay away if you see the dog. It's a vicious one — it's killed three sheep, it has. We've lost four along on the other side of Clachan Fells this morning. Going to sort it out when we find it!

He shifts the way he is sitting so she can see his shotgun.

Stella takes a step back.

If her mum would just appear right now. The men sit there a minute longer; they look her up and down, then the older one nods his head and starts the engine as the younger one leers. They drive away slowly. It's good they thought she was the farmer's girl. She wasn't going to put them right on that. Her legs are shaky. They could put her in the back of that van. Who would know? She scans the fields for any sign of her mum but can't see her. Constance will be out looking for her, though, and she'll be pissed off. Stella is really beginning to freeze and her teeth chatter; she has to get inside and have a hot shower and get dry clothes on. She speeds down the hill. Snow has settled on her handlebars and it gathers in the spokes of her bike. She forces the bike over the lane, but the snow is deeper here and she has to push it harder again. Her muscles burn and her breath is tight and ragged as a knot in her chest. She throws her bike over the frozen burn where the sinking sand is, and she shouldn't go this way because a boy died here doing exactly this ten years ago, but if she leaps after it and grabs a branch — just to be sure. She jumps and grabs onto the branches of a tree to pull herself over. The rough bark is slippy with snow and frost. She grips it harder, so it marks her skin. She shoves her bike through brambles and comes out behind the garages where the gorse bushes have long shed their yellow flowers and everything is frozen. And she looks back to where the sinking sand is and stands there, just for a minute, wondering if it would suck her in.

23

STELLA FORGOT he had her private e-mail. Vito and Stella. Stella and Vito. He is going to college in a few years' time to study architecture. There is a light on in the corner to show that he is typing. *You should come to Italy, when you are older!* He types again and a thumbs-up emoticon appears, then a dancing heart, then hands clapping. She unwinds the towel from around her head and combs her hair out. She had to stand in the shower for twenty minutes before she felt warm. Snow lies six feet up the caravan outside. If it keeps going, they will have to dig to keep the windows clear. On the telly there are abandoned cars covered in snow on motorways across the country. A girl had to be rescued when she fell asleep outside and she is still in a coma now. People are being found frozen up and down the country. There is footage where troops of people are going into community halls to live because their homes have no heat or electricity, or the pipes are frozen. They wave little home-made flags on the telly and raise cups of hot soup.

That has already happened at Clachan Fells. Stella went past the community hall a few days ago and there were about thirty people using camp-beds already. Stella comes out of her private e-mail and logs back onto the website. Thankfully it lets her. It must not delete an account for a month or so. There is half an hour before she has to be at the doctor's. She goes straight to the chat forum and posts a new topic: *How to get hormone-blockers from your doctor?* The boy from Italy is there. He types in *LOL.* Then a thumbs up. He is so cute. He is sixteen. She looks at his picture. He doesn't look like he ever transitioned at all. He has a beard and a moustache and he's posing on someone's boat in front of a beautiful little bay. If they had babies he, as her husband, would have to carry them, if he can even still do that. The cursor flashes at the bottom of the screen. Over at Barnacle's front door he is making his way slowly up his steps, stooped over further into his C than ever, and he closes his door and then his light goes on inside even though it isn't dark yet. *What's the weather like there? Are you scared it's an Ice Age?* Stella finishes combing her hair while she thinks about it. She types a reply. *More scared about how to go through transition, don't know how to do it. I don't want any operations, either, not even when I'm older.* She gets up to pour herself a cup of hot tea and think about how odd these conversations seem to her at times, but how much easier it is to explain it to a stranger like Vito than anyone else. *You don't have to have any operations.* He types this and she tries to imagine him sitting in his house; people, noise, stuff. *I guess I don't know how to do this. LOL, thanks for chatting Vito.* He sends a smiley emoticon, then a surprised one, then one dancing around. *There is not any one right way.* She is glad now that she came on here. *I just don't want hair on my face.* Vito and Stella. *You are so young.* Kissing up a tree. *You can get help.* The bride was barefoot and happy. *The hormone-blockers will stop all of that happening. Get them. Don't take no for an answer, be tough!* They would live in Italy. Her mum could send post-cards of Clachan Fells all covered in snow and she would send her presents of little coloured bowls. *Our Prime Minister said recently it was better to be a fascist than a homosexual or trans. It is very macho here, they accept men dressed as women but only if they are magical, like in the stories. They tell lottery numbers or predict things, but if they do it just to be a man, or boy, as I do, or just to be a woman working in an office and having a boyfriend, they don't like that, they think it is awful. It is changing, but so slowly.* Stella buttons up her warmest cardigan and pulls on thick socks. The news is now showing entire areas of Europe lit up in red. Extreme Alert. Lots of parts of the US, Africa; the snowstorm is spreading and they have given her a name: Cecilia. *I like you, Vito.* He flashes up a bowing heart. *I like you too, little Stella, but you are young and like my little sister. I am happy to chat to you if you like to, any day.* She grins. He is a nice boy. Far more handsome than Lewis Brown. *Is it snowing where you are right now, Stella?* She looks out of the window, where snow is falling heavily again already. Clachan Fells might become a huge blanket of white snow and ice and they will all go to sleep one night like Pompeii, but frozen instead, with teddies curled up in her arms or her mum with a book by her side. She sends him a nodding emoticon. *Stay warm,* he says and logs off, she turns the tele-vision up and pulls a blanket around herself. Stella does not want to add an extra log to the fire, now they are on rations, so she is wearing more and more layers. Her fingers are still pink and her skin blotchy from being outside in the cold for so long. She should not have tried to go up the mountain.

— *Snowstorm Cecilia is the most deadly winter weather on record for over two hundred years. In a short time we expect to hit the*

The Sunlight Pilgrims

Maunder Minimum, which hasn't been seen at this particular level for three hundred and sixty years. This is the very first tip of a winter that nobody has really expected! There are meetings today at the United Nations; many of the delegates are having to attend via video conference because they cannot fly in! As you can see, leading environmentalists have been invited to attend these meetings for the first time since this winter began. The delegates are saying this must be the first honest, serious conversation about climate change! Over to you, in the studio!

24

THE DOCTOR'S surgery is so quiet. He is only opening once a week in this weather. The rest of the time people are seeing him at the community centre, but Stella couldn't do this there where other people might overhear her or even see her there and ask questions. He is looking down at her file like he will make decisions according to that, rather than what she says — his choices will be based upon what other doctors have to say and what he himself has said to them in the past. She will be asked to speak but he won't listen.

— If you don't give her the hormone-blockers, then we will need to see someone else.

— I am the only doctor in Clachan Fells region, Constance.

— I know that, but we'll go elsewhere if we have to.

— Don't you think Stella is very young to be making decisions about hormone-blockers? She only has a very small bit of body hair and her voice has not changed fully yet. What I would really like to do, Stella, is refer you to the clinic in town that specialises in hormone replacement. They will be far better able to help, in an informed manner.

— How long might that referral take?

— It could be a year, or more.

— She will begin to go through puberty long before that.

— And?

— And how would you feel if you grew breasts and got your period tomorrow, Doctor?

— That's not very helpful, Constance, let's be serious here.

— I am being deadly serious, Doctor, how would you feel about that?

— I don't think we should be thinking about emotions. Let's focus on the medical referral — realistically it might be a year, or more, before Stella can see a specialist, he says, putting her file back down.

Click-clack click-clack.

It's that tiny door in her heart.

This feeling lately that a boy is following her, ready to take over her body. She will wake up and have to walk around inside someone else's body. She'll feel like a skinny girl who is being forced to wear a sumo suit and a guy's hairy chest, but worse. When this boy who is coming turns up with his face hair and his deep voice, she won't know where she is or who she is any more, but she'll be stuck there like a witch has cursed her to stay inside someone else's form, no matter how uncomfortable the fit of skin, hair, muscles, the protrusion of an Adam's apple, a deepening in vocal tone.

— That's really depressing, she whispers.

— Do you feel sad? he asks gently.

She looks at him.

— Are you suicidal?

— No!

— I think perhaps we should prescribe you some

anti-depressants, just while you're waiting for your hospital referral to come through.

— That's not what we came here for, Constance says.

— Perhaps a light dose of Prozac, something easy to tolerate.

— She's only twelve years old and you won't give her hormone-blockers but you'll whack her on tablets that can be detrimental to brain development!

— That isn't proven.

— It makes depression a whole lot worse before it makes it better, *if* it makes it better at all! Or it can send a person properly loopy. She wants to feel comfortable in her own skin, and growing a beard is as distressing for her as it would be for any other young teenage girl! Can you imagine if your daughter grew a moustache and developed a baritone one morning? How do you think she would feel about it? Would you be telling her that somebody might get back to her in a year's time, Doctor?

He has switched off already.

Time is running away and she knew this would happen and she ordered them a year ago online and didn't think she'd have to take them, but now Stella knows she will. She feels the packet in her pocket. Looks at the doctor with his white beard and his utter conviction of his own rightness.

— Do you know about your raphe line, Doctor?

— Excuse me?

— That would have been your vagina! she says.

He opens his mouth but doesn't say a thing as she scrapes her chair as loudly as she can along the plastic floor — and walks out.

25

DYLAN IS on the left-hand side of the ambulance. Stella is in the middle. Constance has put her glasses on to drive. She looks like some kind of secretary porn star. He has a hard-on like Donkey Kong. It's seriously uncomfortable. The path down to Fort Harbour has been cleared by the snow-ploughs and stacks of snow are piled up on either side of the road. It is still snowing so much that the piles of snow haven't even turned dirty or slushy around the bottom. Fort Harbour is small with stone walls curving around it. There are little wooden boats and a few bigger ones for fishing. The masts click in the wind and make a strange keening noise. Seagulls spiral at the trawlers' baskets where there are usually lobsters or crabs. Nobody is going out in this. The sea is completely mapped over with ice.

– I have never seen anything like this in Fort Harbour in my whole fucking life, Constance says.

– Mum, this is so exciting!

– Better than going to school, huh?

– A hundred-million-gazillion times better.

– Why are you in such a good mood today, Stella?

She shrugs and looks ahead of them as the ambulance

eases carefully down the icy slope to the car park. There are tourists taking photographs of the sea from the harbour wall. Constance pulls the ambulance in beside some public loos and there is a big brass sculpture of a seal and a map of a nearby island with puffins and another where gannets nest on the rocks. They jump down and each of them buttons up straight away, wrapping scarfs around, pulling gloves on.

— Aren't you going to lock the ambulance? he calls after her.

— Nobody would steal it! she says.

The road has been heavily salted all round the harbour so that they don't skid off it and land in the iced-over water. Stella skips ahead and Dylan falls into step with Constance, slips his arm round her waist for a second and she takes his hand and they both stop as they reach the shore. Stella smiles to herself, noticing them holding hands.

— What are they? Dylan asks.

— Ice-feathers, Constance says.

Sticks have been placed all along the shore to gather crystals of water. Fronds of ice have all blown in one direction, creating feathers — some of them are taller than Stella. She stands right in front of them with her phone out and her mohawk hat on, jumping up and down, leaning in to touch one.

— This is the prettiest thing I have ever seen in my life, he says.

— Look at the ice-floes all over the bay, Stella!

— Listen to them cracking, Dylan says.

— It is so utterly strange and perfect, Mum, I love it!

Dylan and Constance stand at the edge of the shore as sea-ice drifts across a flat grey ocean. Behind them the mountains rise up and a steam train chugs out of the lower forests all the way down past Fort Harbour, billowing smoke and steam – it is black and shiny against the snowy mountains. When it is gone, they can only hear the quiet lap of water and the crack of ice out there. It creaks and groans.

– Is that what I think it is?

Dylan points to the right.

A great hulk of ice is way out there on the water.

Locals begin to point and raise cameras. They gravitate toward the shore as the iceberg turns, so they can see it more clearly even though it is still miles away.

– Fuck-a-shitting-duck! Stella says.

She cups her hands to call up the shore to them. She is walking further away and two girls stand on the pebble beach with cameras, and a cluster of seagulls sit on a crooked arc of grey-cerulean ice.

– Look at those seagulls, surveying the humans, they look like they're about to bestow a riddle on us!

– The riddle of how to stay warm in an Ice Age, he says.

– The riddle of Constance and Dylan.

Stella snaps a photograph of her mother standing in front of all these ice-feathers. Constance is wearing welly boots and tight jeans and a headscarf and a hat on top of that, and she sips a coffee from the metal travel mug she uses whenever she is out working. She shelters her eyes so she can take in the view.

– Sometimes you get a minute where it all seems worth it: all the stress, the struggling, life, death, all the shit in between. You see something like this and it all becomes sharper – oh yeah, you remember, this is it, this is it!

– It's what? he says.

— It! she laughs.

— It is minus twenty, that's what it is, he says.

— Don't try and tell me this isn't better than shining a light in the dark, Mr MacRae?

Stella has almost every inch of herself swaddled in layers and she casts a critical eye across the landscape.

— Are you missing London a little bit then?

— Nope, weirdly. I thought I would be, but I'm not.

Stella skids up toward them, she gives her mum a hug and steps back to look out at the sea again.

— You know what it feels like, Mum? It feels like snow is going to cover the whole world, even the pyramids, even the beaches and like all those deserted airports and even those big skeletons of roller coasters in those empty amusement parks that nobody has been in for ages? They will all get covered in snow too, and so will the cities and the skyscrapers and even big cargo containers out on the ocean, and San Francisco bay and all the streets in Rome and the taverns of Athens. White wolves will roam everywhere. Goths will be kings, Stella says darkly.

— I love wolves, Constance says.

— I figured that out at the bonfire party, he says.

Sea-ice bumps together and separates and the noise of cracking under the ice gets louder. Their breath is a clear mist and there is the tiniest hint of frost on Constance's eyelashes. They need to get back soon. They can't stay out too long in this weather. Dylan looks from one to the other and all three of them are staring out across the ocean now.

— Do you think the ambulance will make it back? he asks.

— I've skis in the back, just in case it doesn't, Constance says.

— You are kidding?

– Nope.

– Mum has something to survive every situation. You'll get used to it!

Stella walks along the beach to where a spiral of ice has curled out in the thinnest layers from a flower stem to create a petiole. She lifts her camera and photographs it.

– Look, it's an ice-flower!

She has to shout from down the beach while floes collide and snap at each other. Somewhere underneath the water they grind up against each other and growl. Something innately pleasing about hearing the sound of ice breaking and colliding, while your own feet are placed firmly on the ground. Dylan's wearing green welly boots – the man in the shop said he was lucky that even though he is the biggest man he's ever met, a pair were ordered for a farmer at Saint Bernadette's but he got stuck in a plough and he's dead; so lucky for Dylan. He could have them. They are good boots. Fur-lined. Just there on the ground. Not like he's hovering. Not like he's a trespasser. Like something in him comes from this rock, these mountains, this landscape, something older than time and generational – all those links to people who survived this place and thrived and lived, all those sui-cidal monks and one lone sunlight pilgrim, butt-naked and tough as hell. Each day they are chased by darkness here; it comes down at night and everyone is already going cabin-crazy. Out on the seashore ice mimics the high sounds of a whale, then is followed by the smack of a hard block against rock.

– It sounds like malcontented mermaids are about to sink every whaling ship around, Constance says.

– That's a bit poetic for you, he says.

— I must be trying to impress you!

The wind calls out, high-pitched as a baby. They stand with feet wide to brace against the elements, and moving crags of ice settle and creak.

— Mum, why is the ice making those noises?

— It's all freezing up, Stella. All those platelets will be frozen into one sheet in a few weeks. I came down a few hours ago and it was just frazil ice, so the temperature is really dropping crazy fast, to get it to solid big bits of ice like this in only a few hours. The Gaelic for it is *cuan eighre,* she says.

— Mum is basically becoming Siri, she says.

— No, I'm not!

They crunch back over to the ambulance, too cold to stay out any longer.

— Can we come back and see the iceberg again in a few days?

— We'll see what the temperature's like.

Dylan pulls on a door handle held on with string. His mind is snow. They are two bridges. Separated by a river. She likes him and she wants him, but she can't let go. Of what? Alistair or Caleb, or both? They pull out of the beach car park and the ambulance rolls slowly down along the coastline.

— Why are we going at five miles an hour? Stella asks.

— Because the ice is packed under the snow. Salt is good for grip but it's still really dangerous!

As if to back her up, the ambulance groans and slides a little along the ice and she changes gear and it screeches its way up the hill. It misfires a few times at the top and then they are onto the motorway, where stacks of snow are piled in hillocks and clods of grass jab out at odd angles and a gritter is in front of them, which slows everyone down even more. It's not that anyone is driving anywhere near the speed limit anyway. Even 20 m.p.h. feels like high speed when the roads are like this.

— It gets dark too early, he says.

— What's the temperature now, Mum?

Constance checks the temperature gauge on the bonnet and flicks it a couple of times with her nail, but the dial still hangs down.

— Cold-as-fuck, she declares.

Stella sighs.

They drive through the village and the church bell calls out in a heavy gong. Snowy council houses and narrow streets are lit by bright Christmas lights. Ornament snowmen have been attached high up on lamp posts and someone has set up a nativity scene in the square. The village shop has a display outside it of real pine Christmas trees. Round bits of cut log sit in a pile to be used as bases for the trees. The chip-shop window glows hot and greasy, with a queue of people trailing out the door. It is Friday night and everyone is getting ready to drink and eat and watch telly and not worry about the rising snow as it settles even thicker outside on gates, fences, rooftops.

— I heard Lewis Brown's mum found their dog frozen by their bin yesterday, Constance says.

— That's horrible!

— I know.

Stella taps her fingers against the dashboard. She saw Lewis on the way home from the doctor's and he waved hello. It is the first time he has acknowledged her since they kissed this summer, the two of them lying on a hay-bale holding hands and watching clouds, and then him not answering her texts and her getting battered at Ellie's Hole and Lewis pretending they never even knew each other at all, then just like that – a wave, a hello. She didn't wave back. Not at all.

There is a deadening of volume as the ambulance rolls over slush and everything goes dark, just like that.

– It's like someone switches the lights off, Dylan says.

He peers out at the streets, lamp posts lighting up the snowy pavements.

– That's winter arrived properly. I reckon we are now officially getting completely dark at two-thirty p.m., Constance says.

– I thought we were already in winter, he says.

– Not quite before, but that's it now.

– It'll be like a three-month night, Stella says.

– I think maybe we should leave the country after all. Vietnam is nice, he says.

– Some of these winter days you still get really amazing blue skies, but it is going to be bloody dark this year!

Constance switches on the windscreen-wipers as snow begins to fall.

Perhaps tonight is the right time to ask her on a date.

It's not like either of them are going anywhere.

– I found the canister to make a stove, Dylan. It's basic, but if we make sure the flue is right, then it'll keep the place warm and you won't get any risk of carbon monoxide. We could fit it tomorrow?

– Sounds good.

They drive along in silence for a good three or four minutes.

— I'm going to string the Christmas lights around the caravan tonight. It's too dark outside already. Stella, can you stop picking at your face in the mirror, Constance says.

Stella sits a fraction closer to Dylan.

— Beatniks and star children don't do well with scientists, she says.

They pull into the caravan park behind the car of a young woman with a red woollen hat pulled down over her ears and she stops at Ash Lane and gets out with a bag, and she has her nose pierced and she gives Stella a wee wave as she goes up to Barnacle's door. The girl has a mongrel sheepdog with her and it wags its tail, waiting for her to come back.

— Chip-shop delivery girl, Stella says.

Stella unclips her seatbelt and waits for Dylan to get out, then she ricochets along the path and straight in the door and into the bedroom and kicks off her boots and climbs up onto her bunk. He steps in behind Constance and she puts a log on the fire as he pulls out a bottle of wine she stashed in the cupboard below the sink. She kicks her boots off and puts her bare feet underneath her on the sofa and tucks her short hair behind her ear and flicks the television on. He pours the wine.

— I like you, but it won't change anything else, she says.

— What, like if Caleb comes back, or if you want to see Alistair? he asks.

— It is how it is. I'm not looking to settle down.

— I know, he says.

26

THEY WALK down the path together in silence. Stella can smell chips and pie from Barnacle's caravan and hear the sound of televisions playing different channels in caravans right next to each other and someone having an argument, and right on the other side of the park someone fires up a power tool. They walk down his path easily, now all the thistles are cut back and it is just snow and ice on his path, with grit lying on top of it that Constance threw down earlier. The doorway to Dylan's caravan looks even shabbier now it is not hidden by lots of thistles. Dylan opens the door and holds it to let them both walk through.

— What's in the parcel? Stella asks.

— The missing part for my gin-still.

— Excellent! Stella says.

— I'm thinking about setting up the projector next year.

— Where? Constance asks.

— I might ask the site manager if she wants to do a screening at the back of the store. Could do it outside when the weather gets better. It's a big old wall — it would work.

— I cannot imagine a cinema in Clachan Fells! Stella says.

— There didn't even used to be a coffee shop here, Constance says.

— Mum, you're such a dinosaur.

— That's nothing; if you'd told me about the industrial units, car showrooms, giant warehouses selling stuff in bulk — when I was a kid — we would have thought you were talking about some kind of voodoo! When I was a kid in Clachan Fells it was exotic to eat French bread; seriously, we thought it was from France. I remember when people started eating pasta! They'd say *Have you tried this pasta? — it's from Italy!* Or tortillas: we thought that was eating Mexican just a few decades ago, Stella. Things change fast.

— Your caravan is freezing, Stella shivers.

— That's why we're here, Constance says.

— It's an empty Calor gas canister, Mum, what exactly is it going to do?

— Give me that marker: okay, this is where I am going to weld out a door. It will need to be fixed back on and the flue will fit here.

Constance sketches onto the red canister with a black marker pen.

— I'll need to paint it black and put in tensioning latches. You need a viewing window here at the bottom and insulating fire-brick to line the inside. Then we need some vermiculite insulation, and luckily for you I have some left over from doing Ida's last winter. And you'll need a decent heat exchanger, then you can fix it up to provide hot water, if you get a back-boiler and a thermal store. I couldn't find enough pieces for that yet, but we can add them on — at least this is free and it will work for now, though. We can fix your water heating up next year and put in a more detailed system.

— I love that you're the kind of woman who keeps spare vermiculite insulation, he drolls.

— Does that turn you on, does it?

— A little.

— I have a grinder disc and welding electrodes as well, Constance mocks.

— Remind me again why nobody married you?

— Remind me again why I would want to marry anybody?

— Will fitting this stove mean that Dylan won't freeze to death in his bed?

— Stella, don't say things like that.

— How many layers are you wearing to sleep? she asks him.

— About four, plus your hot-water bottles and all the extra blankets and two duvets, he says.

— I'm not sure that's enough, she says.

— What would you add?

— A hat.

Stella goes into the kitchenette. Dylan is watching Constance mark where the hole will go for his stove flue. He looks happy when he is near her mother. He has learnt how to walk around the caravan so he is not stooping totally. He sits down a lot. This place is too small for him really. He needs to get an old barn up on the mountain and convert it, and maybe they'll all move in together and she'll take the blockers that she bought online and everything will work out okay. How does her mother do all of this stuff? She watches as Constance measures the distance to the wall for the flue and up to the roof. Dylan and her mother place pieces of pipe out and get together a saw and a mask for the welding gun, and this will probably take the rest of the day, but her mum will have the whole thing fitted out for him by tonight. Stella looks in Dylan's cupboards for biscuits.

— What's this?

Stella picks up a sketchbook.

— No!

Dylan lunges over and grabs it, puts it in the cupboard.

— It belonged to my mum — I'm still working through it, he says.

— What's there to work through?

— Nothing! Just leave it alone, alright?

— Okay then!

Adults are weird. They can't help it. They're defective. Outside it has fallen dark again and it is only 3 p.m. but it is like this every day now from 2.30 p.m. They are living in a world of night. There's something heavy and easy about the darkness, like a weighted blanket. There are some tins of food and beer and a loaf of bread in his cupboard above the sink, but not much else. She opens the cupboard to the left and finds an old-looking ice-cream tub and a Tupperware box; there's no biscuits inside, either, just a load of old ash. She goes to the front door to see if the stars are out yet and peels off the Tupperware lid and launches the entire contents of ash right across his garden because at least she can help by tidying while they do all of that.

— I don't know why you're keeping ash from some old fire, Dylan. You need to throw it out — it feeds the soil — or get an ash bin!

— What?

— Ash: why are you keeping it in the cupboard? It's okay, I just threw it over your lawn. God knows, your ratty grass will need it when the snow melts.

Dylan straightens all the way to his full height.

His face is wrong.

— What?

When he stands up like that everything seems to shrink around him and she has a bad, bad feeling; even her mum is reaching up with her hand over her mouth, a mixture of shock on her face and trying not to laugh.

— I'm only helping to tidy. What is your major malfunction? Stella asks.

Stella goes to get the second tub of ashes and he strides over with one step, looks out of the door to where ash is scattered across the snow.

— You could say *Thank you for being helpful, Stella, you're welcome!*

— Stella!

— What?

She peers in between the two of them at the front door and there are smudges of grey all across the snow on his lawn. It dusts the outline of a few remaining thistle stumps and the wind has carried it across the path. Ida walks through it with her two children and gives them a wave, and Stella is the only one who waves back because the adults are acting strange, again.

— Which one was it? Constance asks.

— It's Vivienne, he says.

— What's Vivienne?

— You just scattered my mother across the garden, he says.

They stand quietly for a full minute.

— What a way to go, she says.

— It's not funny, Stella!

– I'm sorry – I'm nervous. I didn't know! I get funny when I'm nervous, and what was she doing in a Tupperware tub? I guess if that's your mum, then I take it this Carte D'Or tub is your gran?

He takes the tub out of her hands.

– Aye.

– Why didn't you keep them in an urn?

– The urns wouldn't fit in my suitcase, he snaps.

– One down, one to go? she tries.

– Get back home right now, Stella, I will deal with you when I get there. It's not funny!

– You just scattered Vivienne across the lawn, he says again.

Stella is scared now.

Dylan doesn't look right.

He looks limp.

There are tears in his eyes and this isn't how he wanted to let his mum go, and she is crying now too and she didn't mean it, and her mother is resealing the ice-cream tub and placing it carefully on a high shelf.

– I was wondering why you had taken ashes from the bonfire? I thought you must have taken them from the bonfire. I don't know what I was thinking. Why did you put your mum in a Tupperware box?

– It's not her – it's the fucking ashes! he shouts.

– Don't shout at her! Constance snaps.

– I didn't mean it, Dylan says.

– I was trying to help! Fuck both of you! Stella hollers and runs out, slamming the door behind her.

27

DYLAN SITS on his flowery armchair with a nip glass and a bottle of whisky. It is not good whisky. It isn't smoky or peaty, but it is very, very strong. It is strong enough to burn his throat all the way down, so he doesn't care that the wood-stove is just bits of metal laid out on his living-room floor and in front of him on the table there is one empty Tupperware box and right now, while nobody can see him, he is hugging an ice-cream tub.

Dylan rolls a cigarette very, very carefully because he is quite drunk and feeling more okay, the drunker he gets. He raises another glass to Vivienne, downs a neat whisky and stoats out onto his back porch to have a smoke. They are up there or they're nowhere, or all the way up there! He sways. Look at those stars! No answers. Just silence. Vivienne saying nothing even now, just a completely unconcerned canopy of stars above him and all those moon-craters stand out starkly silver, like moon-mountains or white seas, but they are actually seas of lava. He raises his hand and sways. He KNOWS this! They had a moon-season at Babylon a few years ago. He watched every film made about the moon and he only picked the best ones, no matter what their customer-satisfaction feedback forms said, and what's more he watched them all over the space of one week. ONE WEEK! From here only three of those seas are clear – Mare Humorum, Nubium and Imbrium, where *Apollo* landed.

His garden is only lit from the moon and the synthetic yellow spilling out of his windows. Most of the caravans are dark or dimly lit windows behind curtains, and Constance has not come back. He scoops up some snow. Don't eat yellow snow, but even more so – don't eat GREY snow! There is no point in trying to save those ashes. They are scattered too far and at some point winter will pass and Vivienne will be slush. Dirty snow is the most depressing thing in the world as well, especially when it has stones in it, gravel and maybe a wee stain from a dog. Dylan takes another drink of whisky.

– Well, Mum, I can't say I did you proud on the send-off!

He slurs.

The stars are totally uninterested.

For the rest of his life dirty slush will make him feel guilty.

He could go back inside or he can just stand here and sway instead. Swaaaayyy. It is such a great word. It seems important to go through all the things he knows about the moon. 1. It is white except for when it's yellow. 2. It is far away. He snorts at this concise inventory and imagines putting it on a survey for dimlos and desperadoes, but that is not all he knows at all – oh no – he knows loads of moon shit. He is the moon man, but he's never going to get to marry a woman who polished the moon because his cousin has some toxic hold on her. He reels. The sketchbook is flat out on the deck and that horrible family tree. What it means. What Gunn had to go through. His grandmother! He feels himself crushing the glass in his hand. If he was in a pub quiz on the moon he would fucking nail it, even if he was the only one on his team. Team Moonshine. Constance should be sitting in on it with him. Mr and Mrs Moonshine. If they ever get together and rent a hotel, that's what he'll sign them in with. His knowledge of the moon is going to impress her – he can't believe he's not shared it before now; so her older guy stuffed some rabbits and put some costume jewellery on them – whoopdee-doo! Her younger guy travels all round the world. So-fucking-what! Dylan MacRae, the greatest projectionist that ever lived, is right here all the way from Babylon. A boy who was made to butcher a calf in a cellar at the age of twelve (and spent three hours puking up afterwards and who has never been able to eat a burger since then). Yup – he is the man! Dylan staggers forward and glares up at the stars. Constance Fairbairn is the most infuriating woman he has met and what she doesn't know yet is that he can tell her *anything* she wants to know about old moon-face up there.

He should probably go and tell her right now?

An owl calls out nearby and another calls back and he takes another hit.

The world spins obligingly.

There are several seas of lava on the moon and the others are called Tranquillitatis, Fecunditatis, Crisium, Nectaris and Serenitatis, each preceded by Mare. The moon is also a satellite that was – he sways on the steps – it WAS originally a part of the earth but it broke away – the earth was so enamoured with her own beauty that she created a mirror to light up her crevices in the night – to send moon-glades as adornments to her earthly mother – she was something cooler and clearer, and more than willing to play rival to the earth's much larger sun.

He's going to marry a moon-polisher.

He'll write her a song.

Make her a tiny little paper bird.

They'll have three goats in a yard outside a barn they built themselves.

Constance won't ever marry him really, but he'll propose each morning over coffee all the same, twice on Sundays, once at Easter. He'll have to tell them about the sketchbook and the news, but not today. He might wrestle Alistair to impress her. He could wrestle that grey-haired fox right into fucking oblivion!

He stares at the mountains.

This place is nothing like even his most beloved or favourite open space in London – it's not a park with brightly coloured parakeets screeching in the treetops all summer, flying in twos and threes and sometimes in packs of ten or twenty – or Soho, where he would go to see a single heron – something about seeing that single heron standing in a park in the middle of the city, it always did astound him. He goes back inside and puts his coat on. He needs a Twix. It is imperative. He marches through the snow to the site office, stoating a little to the left the whole time. And a Pot Noodle. How many years is it since he ate a Pot Noooodle? Nobody is out. Since it hit minus twenty, nobody comes outside much at all. Dylan goes into the big barn store that's also the site manager's office. The storeroom is made of corrugated sheets of iron. It has a tractor casually parked in the corner. He loves that. Excuse me, you at the crisps, while I drive behind you and casually park my great-big-fuck-off-tractor! Steel shelves are fixed all the way up to the roof. How has it come to be that his mother – a woman who loathed grass and flowers and all things natural and earthly – has become just a dirty grey smudge in a ratty garden, while he is in a cowshed in the middle of fuck knows where, looking at copies of *Hustler* on the top, top shelf? He wonders for a minute if his mother was always so sad because she knew? Something in her knew what her mother had gone through to bring her into the world?

Fucking *Hustler*!

How many years has it been since anyone got their porn from magazines? It must be a niche market. He is tall enough that he can reach them without moving along the ladder that sits at the front of the rails. Height has its advantages – peeeeple. It has its GAINS! He can't imagine this set-up passing for health-and-safety anywhere: customers climbing a ladder for a tin of macaroni cheese or a copy of *Asian Babes*?

Who still buys porn on the page?

The site manager sits at the till, smoking a cigarette. She taps things into an old computer keyboard in front of a bulky PC screen. She clicks on a kettle beside her and tips a sachet of Cup-a-Soup into it. She has a bulbous nose and she has absolutely no interest in him whatsoever. Dylan stops in front of a plastic container with curry-flavoured noodles and beside them there is a packet of fortune cookies, with a dragon on a shiny wrapper. Chinatown this is not! As a boy he used to walk past all those glistening ducks roasting in windows and smart young men sitting outside bars, and other men who wore lipstick and shops that sold dirty books and women that looked like plastic dolls, but he still thought they were pretty. One of the guys on their street took him into his first dirty movie when he was seventeen. All these guys sat around in this cinema wanking. He let the guy he was with stick his hand down his trousers. It wasn't bad. It wasn't amazing. He was almost legal. It was something to try.

Dylan walks along an aisle stacked with microwave meals.

There are spare plugs for sinks.

Tins, tins, tins.

Ida waddles by the big open door and she must have a client in today because she has her schoolgirl shirt open, her gargantuan tits spilling out, a school skirt on and long white socks, gym shoes; her hair is tied up in bunches. Over all of that she has a fur coat draped around her shoulders. He watches her for a good long minute. She must have got out of a client's car and is just about to go into her house and jump in a hot shower. Dylan grabs the first *Hustler* at the top and two packets of bacon and (it looks like a large old pickle jar) what claims to be cloudy cider. The bottles of cloudy cider come in three strengths: mellow, biting, blows-your-brains-out. He reaches out and grabs two Twixes as well. The woman rings up his purchases and has the decorum not to look at him while he waits for his change. He strides back up the park. The snow is so high that all the gnomes he saw on his first night here are now faint hillocky bumps in people's gardens. Constance appears behind him, trudging through the snow in her big welly boots trying to keep up. She is wearing her wolf-cape and her ears and nose glow in the moonlight.

— Don't comment. It keeps me warmer than any of the hats!

Dylan turns round and looks at her, with snow all around so cold he can smell it, and street lights glow orange on the path and those mountains behind them climb up into the black sky, so there is no knowing where rock ends and sky begins until the stars come out. This is the wrong time to have a hard-on and want to take Constance to bed. He doesn't want to speak. He is done with talking. There is an older one and a younger one, but right now there is just her and him and that is how it is. He is glad the *Hustler* is tucked at the back of his bag. They're not at that stage yet. If they get to the porn stage they'll use a laptop. All he needs right now is her. He takes her hand and they walk up onto Ash Lane. She grips his hand back as he walks up to his door, getting more sober by the minute — a perk of being a giant: can get pissed and unpissed if you don't go too far down the bottle. He avoids looking toward the grey patches of snow — he turns the key and they fall into the hallway.

The door flies shut behind them, caught by the wind. It howls over the caravan roof while she shrugs off the wolf-cape and slips it over the back of a chair in his lounge. She pulls off her boots, taking two steps down the hall as he pulls his jumper off — his hands are freezing on her skin, sliding under her top, finding her nipples, her breath ragged; she undoes his belt buckle — shoves him hard onto the bed and a bite as she wriggles out of her jeans, pulling him onto her, and she's wet so he pushes straight in. She grips her knees into a lock around him, taking him in deeper, until they are just tongues and sweat, and pushing and pulling and biting and tasting and touching and holding and getting tired and slowing down and starting again and forgetting that there is anything outside this bed.

Afterwards they lie in the dark not talking.

She traces his arm lightly.

A bed as an altar. A bed as respite. A bed that smells of sex. Sex is better than prayer, better than talking. They've said everything they need to now. He kisses her neck and it is cold and she smells like snow.

28

THEY LIE in the dark for hours. At one point he goes and pours them each a glass of wine. She smokes a cigarette. The duvet only reaches round under her arms and so he puts on the little portable three-bar fire and it glows in the corner and smells like chemicals.

– Would Vivienne have found this funny?

– Not in the fucking slightest.

– I suppose not.

– I'm just glad it's not Gunn; she had a weird enough death and life, it turns out, and he shakes his head.

– You didn't mention that before?

Her skin is alabaster in the dim light. Her fingers are long and with rough calluses where she has been chopping wood and smoothing down furniture and building things. Just to hold hands. Such a simple easy thing. To lie like this. Let the snow fall out there. There is an ordinariness to their strange. Like they could outlast a lot more than this first bit.

– Devil's snare – it's a fatal hallucinogen. They call it other things as well: the angel's trumpet, jimson weed. Devil's snare creates an agonising trip that never ends if you take too much, which is exceptionally easy to do, apparently.

— I don't fancy it, she says.

This is harder than he thought.

— After tripping about as far out as a person can, it creates a really, really long, slow, hideous painful death.

He's pretty sure his skin is white and he flexes his knuckles, and this bedroom is too small for a giant, this whole caravan is. It's kind of ridiculous, he's going to start scouting around for disused barns or old wrecked bothies. Constance looks up at him and rests her hand on his chest.

— Vivienne?

— Gunn.

— Why did she take it?

— The story goes, I have since found, detailed in my mother's sketchbook, she drew pictures and she has left these little notes and— He stops.

— You don't need to say anything, she says.

— I know.

— I sat and had a few gins with Vivienne, one night, she says.

— Did she mention her sketchbook?

Constance appears to be studying the roof in his bedroom.

— I found out a few things, he says. The first was that Gunn arrived in Babylon seven months pregnant, after prising the keys to the place from a corpse's fist — it was some aristocrat that owned it and he had a heart attack during a game of poker and, other than him being dead, she swore she won it fair and square. She didn't really have to prise the keys because rigor mortis hadn't set in, but it felt, you know – wrong. She went to a phone box and called someone for back-up in the islands who was working in the meat trade and he said it was best, under those circumstances, to get rid of the corpse. He picked it up in his van and took it to Dead Man's Wharf, weighted it down, slid it in. Babylon had been used for orgies, politicians, underage kids – that's what we heard much later, but she was earning a living from it by then. She brought her daughter up knowing how to run it by the time she was a teenager. Vivienne had me when she was seventeen and they taught me the business when I was a kid, but Gunn apparently said it was borrowed time. She said one day the devil would come to collect his dues and she'd take the consequences on herself. She'd take it so it didn't get passed down to us, so she reckoned the worse it was, the more she'd know we were in the clear so to speak. The day she got ill, Vivienne swore blind the devil came to the back door and asked for Gunn.

— That's fucked-up.

— I know; thing is, I think Gunn was expecting him.

— Why?

— She was religious really, she thought the devil was coming to collect his fee for her sins.

— Maybe they weren't her sins?

Dylan looks at Constance and wonders for a minute if she knows about the family tree, about him and Alistair, that a whole community and family forced Gunn out and never spoke to her again and she hadn't done anything wrong, so there had to be a reason for it.

— This was just six months ago? Constance asks.

— Aye. Gunn had convulsions for days, she was seeing things everywhere, under her skin, on the walls; all her organs shut down one by one – it was hideous and it was even worse, you know, because she was so lovely and hard-as-nails, and she *always* put me and Vivienne first.

— Did they do an autopsy?

— They said there was enough in her body to kill a very tall man, or ten. Then the night before my mother died, quite peacefully, in her sleep, she told me quite clearly at the kitchen table that she would never, ever forgive me!

— For what?

— Well, they were both pretty psychic, so I reckon . . .

Dylan points outside, where patchy areas of grey snow lie all around the porch and down the garden path. She gets up with the duvet wrapped around her and he pulls on a T-shirt, thinks about making coffee. The door lets in an icy air, which feels nice for a minute. The two of them huddle there in the doorway, his arm around her.

— This would have been right up there on Vivienne's list of fucking no-nos! he says.

— Not the way she wanted to go.

— Not really.

Barnacle's door clicks open and he comes out onto his little porch steps and looks across to see them both sniggering helplessly at Dylan's front door.

— Been on the weed again? You bloody reprobates! Get a life! Grow up!! You've got a child in there, he shouts.

He slams the door and eventually they stop giggling.

Dylan offers her a roll-up and she takes it. He goes inside and comes back out with another glass of wine and a throw, which he wraps around her shoulders. He is wearing her wolf-cape and the ears stick up, making him look even taller. She giggles again. He catches her glancing at him. His wrists, the tattoos, his Chelsea boots, she isn't impressed by any of it; what she is drawn to is something else.

— My mother never had it in her to work out who she was, she says.

– Where does she live?

– She's down south. She did every job as a wife exactly right – she went above and beyond, but he just picked at her and picked at her and picked at her until she didn't even look the same, or act the same, and he did it with us too. It's like she wasn't there in the end. It was like she never had been there. She was going through the motions. Making beds perfectly.

– The first time I saw you, you were polishing the moon.

– What?

Dylan tips her chin up and kisses her on the doorstep, where anyone could walk past and see them, and the shock of their tongues, the heat against this freezing cold, and they are apart just as quickly and he flicks one of the long wolf-legs back over his shoulder.

29

STELLA HAS five empty clear plastic bottles in the bedroom. She has cut the top off each of them and filled them with water. She drops in dried flowers and acorns and berries and mistletoe. They will freeze outside in no time and she can take the plastic off and they will be great ice-sculptures. When you scatter people's mothers into slushy mush, then the only answer is to make some art. It appears to be becoming her answer to everything. She has cleaned the house. She made some soup. She sent Vito a whole load of songs from YouTube as a mix-tape. She has cleaned her ice-grips. She cleaned the grate for the fire. She visited Barnacle and slid all the way down his path.

— It's an ice-wonderland today, she tells her mother.

— I'm going to go to the shops, Stella.

— Can you bring me back bananas?

— Yes.

— And chocolate?

— Yes.

— Is Dylan still angry at me?

— He wasn't angry.

— He *was*, for fuck's sake! Stella huffs.

— When did we give up on the swear jar? Constance demands.

— When the world threatened to end each day, and when it got so dark that it made everyone in Clachan Fells crazy. Did you see the satanist putting up pictures of pentagrams and all that weird shit all over his windows? He reckons Satan is going to rise for the second coming of evil, or some shit.

— I didn't see that, no.

— He freaks me out. I bet he'll behead his girlfriend or something.

— Don't say that!

— Oh, come on, Mum, you know Incomers can't handle the bloody darkness here, and this winter is going to be the longest, darkest, freakiest, possibly most never-ending one we'll ever have!

— It will end!

— I know: in human extinction.

— No, Stella, it will end in spring. Stop watching the bloody news!

Stella switches her laptop on and off again. Constance leaves to go to the shop. There is no Internet signal. None at all. She switches the router on and off but there isn't anything, then she picks up the phone and the line is dead too. No Internet on her phone. The telly is working but the picture is fuzzy. She waits until her mother reaches the end of the path and then she takes out the packet in her pocket. Today is the day. She didn't want to do it like this. She waited and waited for a letter about her appointment to see the gender specialist, but it didn't come. The fluff around her lip is getting dark. She will start with two. She swallows down the tablets without a drink and one lodges in her throat and, after she has managed to swallow it down, she wonders what is really in it? It came in an unmarked envelope. There is no little list of potential side-effects; just a stupid bottle on the table and it doesn't even say *hormone-blockers* on it. She found the tablets on a site where you can buy all kinds of drugs and hormones on the Dark Web. She should tell somebody this is what she is doing, but not Constance or Dylan. Maybe Vito. Lewis was in the park yesterday. He looked cute.

Vito is her only real friend, though.

And Dylan.

Except she scattered his mother across the lawn.

In their kitchen there is a pine fir tree and tonight they will decorate it with baubles from a box Mum keeps under the caravan. They will thread tinsel around it and there are even decorations she made when she was a little kid that her mum has kept all these years. She won't even open the box that arrived addressed to her from Alistair. It can go to the charity shop. She curls up on her side in bed. She feels a bit ill, now she has taken the pills. Her heart is beating in a fast, light way and fear shoots up her spine. Her skin is slick in a cold sweat. She reaches for the bottle and knocks it over. She just didn't want to have hair on her face. Outside snow won't stop falling and she is feeling really scared now, because her heart is beginning to hammer and her skin is hot. A hard shot of fear. Panic that her mother is going to find her on the floor, dead. Reaching for her phone, blurry and wanting to stand up, texting Dylan first because he can explain it to Constance later and she probably can't even get out to the hospital in this. Feeling desperate now, her heart pounding even more and the world feeling far away, like somewhere she might not be again.

Part III

31st January 2021, −38 degrees

30

DYLAN MEASURES 70cl of base-spirit out and tips it into the pot. He has found exactly the right blend of lemon and sugar to make a solid base-spirit this time; just a touch of tomato purée seemed to help and he let it cool to 23°C before he stirred the baker's yeast in. This batch has sat on a shelf above his wood-stove for seven days and even though the fermenter is airlocked, he is sure it picks up a hint of wood-smoke in the flavour. Dylan pours the mixture through the still for a stripping run. He turns the boiler on full power. It will take fifteen minutes before the next stage and he has already weighed out juniper berries, wild water mint, a few slices of cucumber, grains of paradise, bitter almond, lemon peel, orris-root powder. He pounds the botanicals down using a stone pestle in a mortar.

He has been avoiding Vivienne's sketchbook all Christmas and New Year.

It sits on the table.

Last time he looked at it he was so drunk he wasn't sure he understood what he'd found there. He picks it up and on the first page there is him as a little boy in their attic kitchen, rain behind him on the Velux window, a single flower in a vase.

There is a heron at their local park.

Her old boyfriend, Jed the Herring.

Him asleep.

Him kicking a football down the hall in Babylon.

Babylon's foyer chandelier.

Sketches of posters, of movie stars: there is Audrey Hepburn, there is Joan Crawford.

Seven pages of shoes.

Gunn MacRae dressed up like she did when she was going to greet guests for Saturday night at the movies. She'd still wear her bovver boots but she'd match them up with a twin-set and pearls. His grandma was the original grunge-woman. There is a sketch of her down in the cellar drinking a cup of tea, next to the head of a calf. There is her gin-still. Her brewing, just like he is now. Their kitchen. The old cream oven, all tatty; and then lots and lots of sketches of his mum's winkle-pickers, his old Chelsea boots, him laughing at something in the foyer, a massive poster of Godzilla behind him and he can remember her watching him – never saying anything much – sitting at night, sipping wine, and the sound of her pencil as she made sketches of their life.

He flicks through pages curled and bent from where she left the sketchbook out when she was cooking, or drinking, or smoking. On one page there are red smudges and they could be pasta sauce or it could have been red wine. Between two pages she has pressed a flower and it has been there for so long it is as thin as paper; he leaves it like that, too scared to pick it up in case it disintegrates. On the very back page, on the hard-cover insert – she has drawn a family tree.

He takes the book over to the window.

At the top of the page are Håvid and Bitta, his great-grandparents. They are drawn beside an outline of a fairly remote island in Orkney, a man and a woman holding hands outside a croft with a child – an arrow points down to: Gunn MacRae, and beside her there is a brother. He realises, peering at it this time, that the last name Gunn had for her whole life since she moved to London was actually taken from Bitta's maiden name. His grandmother did not keep the same surname as the rest of her family. She changed it when she left.

He peers at the page as the sound of the still bubbles in his kitchen. It reminds him of Gunn; she never talked about a brother, but there he is – Olaf Balkie – and his arrow runs along to a wife called Astrid.

Below they have an arrow that runs to their child.

A son.

Alistair Balkie.

Another line runs from Olaf back along to Gunn, and below them it points down to a child, his mother, Vivienne MacRae. There is a loop from Vivienne to Alistair to show they are half-siblings. Alistair's line then runs along to his first wife Christine, then his second wife Morag; it then turns away from his wife and goes left to the mother of Alistair's only child – Constance Fairbairn.

Below an arrow points to their son, Cael Fairbairn.

The name Cael has been scored out and his mother's tiny spidery handwriting has replaced it with the name Estelle.

He puts the book down.

All the sadness in her makes sense to him now: his mother and Gunn, bickering their way around Babylon at three in the morning; the brittle way they had with each other, and how Gunn always seemed to love him so much more easily than her own child.

Why wouldn't she just tell him?

He feels bad for the dead and their secret squirrel routine.

It's not like it was her fault.

Was it that Vivienne was born of love, or something worse? Either way, they would have thought incest was the devil's work on a tiny religious Scottish island all those years ago. He strides through to the kitchen, trying to get rid of tears. He doesn't know what they are good for. A stream is coming from the output pipe on the still now. He collects the first 100ml in an old milk container; this first bit has all the methanol and acetone in it, so he uses it as a cleaning product like Gunn used to do.

Dylan pours out the rest of the brewed mixture into 2.5-litre bottles until the mixture begins to look cloudy. His hands are a little shaky. He leaves the rest of the mixture in the boiler and turns it off. Outside his window there are no birds. The body has its habits. He listens for birds each day, but he hasn't seen or heard any for weeks now. They are frozen in trees or they have flown as far south as they can for winter. Only the bigger birds will remain and they are probably nesting in caves up on the mountains.

He looks at the family tree again. He feels dumb as a kakapo. He once had sex with a woman who tracked kakapos in the wild and she said that they walk on the ground, instead of flying, and if a predator comes they scurry up a tree, then fall out into a pathetic lump on the deck and then if you're female – even if you're human – they will try and have sex with you. The woman told him about this at her sister's party in Brighton on a day when he had consumed so much MDMA he wasn't sure if anything was real any more and he remembers a similar grind to his brain – an inability to grasp things – like how to walk up and down steps or drink a pint, and now he knows for sure that Vivienne did not buy this ratty-tin-bullet for any random reason. Why couldn't the woman ever just use words?

What the fuck was wrong with her?

How about: *Hello, Dylan, you have a second cousin, a child; a first cousin once removed who is also a half-uncle. They live in Scotland if you wish to meet them; no, your gran didn't ever want to talk about it again, she would tell me about it when she was drunk, then the next day she'd be ashamed as if I was evidence of her life as a sinner, as if my personality was proof that a brother should never lie with a sister, no matter what the circumstance. She thought I was off like curdled milk from the day I was born, a bitterness in my mouth from her milk, a poison in me that only deepened over the years. All my love, Mum xx.*

His mouth is dry. Ida walks down the path with a client, both of them looking highly unsexual, all wrapped up in layers with balaclavas on. She has sent her kids to live with friends. The iceberg took some fucking insane detour, but it is almost back here now and everyone is worrying it will collide and create an avalanche. That won't happen but there's no telling the locals, once a rumour spreads. He peers in his still. There are two good-quality bottles of gin there, by the look of it, clearer and better measured than the last batch. He puts the stoppers into the tops of the bottles and picks up his mother's sketchbook again.

All those little lies, left unsaid, in families; all the things that then become unsayable.

The selfish dead fuck off and leave us with half-truths and questions and random relations and bankruptcy and debt and bad hearts and questionable genetics and stupid habits and DNA codes for diseases and they never mention all the things that are coming – like a fight at a wedding, it just breaks out one day.

He can't tell Stella because she's still getting better after her hospital trip and he doesn't want to go through this with Constance, not yet. Not when they keep saying the world is going to end in some frozen version of Pompeii. Does any of this even matter? He tries to imagine Gunn leaving the islands and deciding to never go back and being ex-communicated by her family. Not one word of contact ever since. What horrible secret makes a family do that? What makes a pregnant teenager run away to another country where she doesn't know a soul, and never return? He looks at the tree again. Olaf Balkie. Her brother. Dylan curses the dead their privilege of silence.

Alistair and Vivienne share the same grandparents, Dylan and Stella share the same great-grandparents. Gunn would have been Stella's great-aunt. His brain-cogs process it bit by bit. Stella is his cousin and Vivienne's half-niece. Why would Vivienne come up here and not say anything to Stella or Constance? Unless it was too much for her, so she bailed out and left it to him.

Which sounds right.

For his mother.

Absolutely.

Dylan puts some coal over the logs in his wood-stove.

He clicks the door shut.

He sits on an old chesterfield armchair donated by Barnacle. He feels weak and cold. He pulls a blanket around him, from Constance. Ida dropped off a slow cooker that she says she never uses. There is a gnome stolen by Stella although she will not say from where. The fire makes the room glow and his Hawaiian-lady lamp-base creates a mellow light in the caravan. Dylan takes out his original movie posters, 1968: *2001: A Space Odyssey* and 1957: *I Was a Teenage Werewolf*. They were the last two he could have sold. He must have sold at least a thousand film reels and countless posters before he left Babylon. Perhaps the dead are entitled to their silence. It is not up to him to break it at all.

It is claustrophobic, all that whiteness outside his window, the incessant news. A month ago the army cleared the streets in Edinburgh so lorries could get in with supplies, but nobody can even manage that now. He is living on food from Constance's apocalypse larder and he is angry because he cannot be the one to provide right now.

He opens his mother's suitcase and finds the copy of *Hustler* he bought when he first got here. He walks through the caravan, checks himself out in the hall mirror. His beard is wide and round. It better suits his big squint-nose, he looks older and paler, thinner. He needs to buy some red meat. Dylan picks up a pair of scissors and holds his hair in a fist; he cuts it bluntly, then lets it fall back down so it is just below his ears. He keeps cutting until the hair on his head is a short, shaggy mess and his beard looks even better this way. It is years since he had short hair and now he doesn't look like someone who might be half-covered in ink underneath his clothes. He looks like someone's dad. Dylan opens the fridge. There is nothing in there but the growing realisation that Constance has been sleeping with two cousins.

This isn't going to go down well.

Not at all.

All the times Gunn said she'd never go back home until she was on the Other Side – that is what she always said. It makes sense now. His mother not saying who her father was, just 'someone' from the islands, and Gunn not even naming him on the birth certificate. Dylan sits down on the flowery armchair. Constance and Stella have had enough reason to ignore the villagers and their judgement; he doesn't see this should really matter to them either way, although he will tell them when this winter is over. A feeling skirting around him. A darkness like afternoon falling. That it wasn't anything to do with love, that nineteen-year-old girl with a child in her belly leaving the island on a ferry, nobody to see her off at the shore and no one to meet her when she arrived where she was going. It was not a mistake she made, it was not her decision at all. Although he does not want to admit it, something in him knows it is true and that is why the chromosomes in his body keen whenever he sees Alistair, because he has half the blood of Gunn's brother, and for something that wasn't even her fault Gunn felt guilty and disconnected all her days. It is funny how he always thought she was a hero when he was a little boy, but he had no idea exactly how much that was true. He cries for Gunn, and his mum, who hadn't done anything wrong in coming into the world; he cries and cries, he wants to let them know he loves them, to somehow make okay a fact of their life that they all lived within the shadow of and barely understood at all.

31

STELLA CLICKS off her phone and surveys the top of the farmer's field. She is wearing a plastic flower ring under her gloves. Vito sent it at Christmas after she got out of hospital. Every year all the kids used to go out and show off their new toys when they were younger. This year she didn't even want to see anybody, but enough is enough. Stella Fairbairn is the fastest stand-up sledger in Clachan Fells. She doesn't care what Lewis Brown says. Or anyone else. She can see them all up there, a row of children silhouetted against the snowy sky behind them. Most of them are teenagers. There's a few from Fort Hope, maybe even the boys she got in a fight with. She pulls her hat down over her ears and trudges up the hill, pulling her sledge.

– Stella?

A nod. That's all she has to give them. She's not here to make friends. There are nods from other kids – ones from her class, ones whose birthday parties she has been to, whom she sang carols with as a kid and went guising with – and a tiny bit of energy sparks along the line as people realise she is there. She is the fastest and most daring of all of them on a sledge. Every one of them knows it. They are all here for a serious reason. This is not a fuck-about.

She remembers when you used to go to somebody's door and ask if they were coming out for a kick-about and then, when you were older, it was a fuck-about; and even when she was really little and Lewis came in for her, knocked on the door and she went out in jeans, when what she wanted was to wear a goth-skirt black tutu and braid her hair after growing it long. Everybody is here today and nobody mentions anything about how she looks now. A few raise a hand to say hello. Nobody says her old name. Nobody seems to remember passing a picture back in the village hall last year and, if someone mentions it, she will punch them on the nose.

Stella walks up to the top of the hill and takes her place right in the middle of a long line of kids. The sledges are all in a row. There are big plastic red ones and someone has a smooth big old tyre and there are two tin trays and a thick plastic sack. It's going to be war. She claps her gloves together to get snow off them and cricks her fingers. Stella arranges her wooden bobsleigh. It was her mum's first birthday present to her as a girl, and she restored the sledge and treated the wood and put new metal runners on the bottom and waxed them, and on the back of the wooden seat she painted one tiny star and painted *Stella* underneath it. It is amazing to think that was over a year ago now. Stella found her new sledge in the kitchen that birthday, with a note tied on the back from a bit cut off her Frosties box: *For my darling Stella, ALL MY LOVE Mum x.* Of all the sledges, this bobsleigh is the one most people are looking at. It is to be both admired and feared. It is the ultimate racer.

Stella's feet are cold and her fingers are numb and her heart is heavy.

There is hair on her lip and her voice is getting lower.

Her hair is in braids.

She doesn't care any more what anyone thinks.

She is going to win this race.

All the caravans look like igloos lately. The Inuit in her and the wolf in her mother will keep them wily enough to survive. If it is possible. If they can. Stella stops right in the middle of the line of kids and positions her sledge.

— You racing then, Stella?

— Looks like it.

Lewis with his frizzy hair and his wide smile.

— Think you're going to win?

— I will, if you keep holding your sledge like it's a skateboard, Lewis.

He has it down on the snow, one foot on it.

— I'm going down standing up, are you? he asks.

— Always.

— Do you want to come over to mine later, I've got a new computer game?

— No, thanks, she says.

— You should come over. It's a really amazing game, he says.

— Yeah? Why don't you draw me a picture?

— I did say sorry for that, he says.

— Did you?

— Hey, Stella, are you going down standing up? another boy shouts over.

— Same as last year!

The kids are tense. It only takes one bump, one rock, one wrong fall and your neck's broke, or probably just your arm or even a wee finger, and that has happened before, they've all seen it – but you don't know which one it will be if something breaks, that's the thing. It could be irreparable. She still feels a bit fuzzy from them testing her blood and saying she'll be okay and flushing the tablets away, and she has had enough of worrying what someone else might notice about her body and bring her up short on.

This is her.

So what if they don't get it?

The little kids are all sitting down on their sledges, throwing snow at each other because they are amateurs and they don't care yet, but the older ones are clapping their hands together and checking out each other's sledges and getting ready to go. Lewis glances over at her and smiles again. He is so irritating. Stella looks down the farmer's field, which is such a steep slope that most people stumble even when they are walking down it in the summer. The snow is powdery on top but packed dense underneath, so they'll be able to go about as fast as they can handle. Once the sledges speed up, you can't slow them down unless you go sideways and then you are risking a spin, or you can use your arms or your legs or just throw yourself off the side.

It often comes to that.

Speed doesn't scare her.

All around her kids are saying things and making jokes and throwing snowballs, and Lewis is talking to another girl, so she steps onto her sledge and settles so she is perfectly balanced standing up. She pulls the reins in, getting ready to go. The rest of the kids begin to line up and put on gloves and scarves and take selfies with their friends, and one of the girls from the estate has a selfie-stick and Stella has to resist the urge to take the thing off her and beat her over the head with it. Someone has been appointed the gun-man at the end.

All this winter she has been changing.

Things she used to be afraid of don't seem scary any more.

Most of the other kids look nervous and about half of the row are not standing up, but the rest of them do and the older ones like her are kind of feared by the younger kids, and they are all watched by the ones on the side who won't even ride the slope sitting down, cos it's too dangerous. There are only five of them standing up. Stella flexes her knees and waits for the rest to organise themselves. The girl with the tin tray and her friend with the thick plastic sack are getting ready to push off with the backs of their hands. Stella adjusts her hat so it is right down around her ears and tightens her scarf. The farmer's truck is parked down at the back field and it gives her a bad omen. Last year Tabitha the Fanny's cousin broke his leg going down standing up, and they couldn't get an ambulance anywhere near here because the snow was bad last year as well; they ended up carrying him out on a grain sack pulled tight over a pallet. Right up the top of the mountain she gets a glimpse of two familiar-looking shapes making their way down and then someone calls out.

– READY!

The ground is hard underneath her sledge.

– STEADY! STEEEAAADY!!

Stella bends loosely at the knees, holding her reins just firmly enough to keep her upright.

– ONE, TWO, THREE, GO!

Just one dip at the knees and tilting the toboggan over the edge, and the world whizzes around her – two kids are rolling down the slope already, with empty sledges flying in front of them. Stella half-kneels down over a jump and the plastic-sack girl is on her side; the tin trays are right out in front and she holds her elbows in and her head down and gains speed.

Fields sparkle.

A roar.

The wind.

Her heartbeat.

Kids shouting and screaming.

Someone on a bigger sledge catches up with her for a second and then she is out in front of everyone – the world a blur on either side of her, she is going so fast – faster – faster – if she falls now, she'll break her neck for sure, but no time – flying. The doors of the barn at the bottom of the hill are being hauled back and the farmer is letting the cows out so that they charge up the hill toward her and she can't stop now!

She holds on tighter.

Kids fall left and right from their sledges and run, as cows thunder up the slope.

It is way too late for Stella to slow – she grips the high sides of her toboggan, while the roar of cows' hooves thunders right toward her and a brown and white blur. If this is the day she dies, then they'll all know she was braver or crazier than any of them – remembering when she was little and the big kids in the caravan park put her in an old-fashioned pram and pushed her off the steps for fun; they bumped her all the way down. And last year she sat on the back of the gala-day lorry with crêpe paper made into a flower-skirt and a flower-band for her hair, and that was the first year she went out dressed as a girl; and she'd put a bed sheet in their garden, place rocks on it to hold it onto the top of their porch steps, then pull it out as far as it would go and she'd climb into her tent and eat cheese sandwiches and read books, and the sun would warm it up and she'd make daisy chains and go to the park and climb the monkey bars and in the summer they all stoated around on stilts. Caleb made her the stilts and sat on their porch teaching her guitar. He always has wrinkled clothes and crooked teeth and a great smile, and he used to make home-made pizza for her and Constance. She hopes he comes to visit soon. Oddly she thinks he and Dylan would get along. He picked her up once, after she'd been running so fast she fell on the tarmac slope outside on the car park and skinned both her knees skidding along the floor, and that summer the sun was so hot she got water-blisters on her shoulders and would jump in and out of her friends' paddling pools, and they'd often skid where it was hard on the ground underneath and fall and get big black-purple bruises on their legs and she would press them when she was watching television, or pick at her scabs, and at night she'd crawl under the covers and read by the light of her torch and they'd pick rhubarb out of gardens and dip it in sugar to eat. She hasn't seen that woman in the donkey-jacket again who told her about those pilgrims, but whenever there is light in any way in life she's stashing it away like a magpie – drinking it orange to grey – and this must be how it is when your life flashes in front of you, and she grips onto the front of her sledge totally out of control again, and it is only a few weeks since she started to feel better from the last brush with death and she can see herself when she was little jumping off the cliffs of mulched paper, an imprint of light in the air and the thunder of hooves pounding all around her, and closing her eyes and only opening them when the blur of cow legs is gone and her sledge is skidding in circles across the frozen burn.

When it stops she lifts her head up.

Kids are scattered up on the slope; some have run back up to the top and others jumped the fence to get away from the cows, which are now clustered in the middle of the field. Lewis Brown is halfway down, picking himself up. He rolls over, sees her all the way down here, raises his arm straight up in the air.

– Fair play, Stella, he shouts.

Other kids look around and see she was the only one who made it down to the bottom. Stella Fairbairn is the only kid in the whole of Clachan Fells who has just sledged at 40 m.p.h. through a pack of huge Jersey cows. The farmer is out, getting the cows back into the barn again already; he let them out on purpose, though, to stop them sledging in his field – she knows it. He's heading up to the top to shoo the cows back down the field.

– Well done, Stella, someone else shouts.

– Fair play!

– You're fucking nuts!

– Her heart pit-a-pat in her ears and she has to hope that her mother up there on the slope did not see her do that.

32

Dear Mrs Constance Fairbairn,

It is with deep regret that the Sisters of Beathnoch have to inform all parents that snowfall is now measuring thirty-four inches from the school windows. They are still unable to fix the boiler system, all the pipes are frozen solid. As such, we must continue to put the health and safety of our students first. We are aware the school has been closed since November, but we are unable to reopen now most likely until spring, when we hope these winter conditions should begin to thaw. We would like to ask that you maintain your child's educational process throughout these long winter months. Focus on scripture may be especially appropriate at times such as these. We also suggest that each household places a candle in their window at night to guide and honour those who are displaced due to these harsh conditions. We are sending prayers and good thoughts to you all. If anyone is not safe in their home due to falling temperatures, then please do send them to the village hall at Clachan Fells. We will keep this resource open with basic camp-beds and we will provide cooked meals to anyone who needs them. Nobody will be turned away from our doors.

Wishing you all a safe and blessed winter.

Yours sincerely,
Sister Mary Shaun

Constance passes the letter to her.

Stella's nails are each a different colour with little stars painted on them and she is wearing a red polo-neck with an owl on the front and a bright-green cardigan that her mum found in the charity shop before it closed. She has her hair back in clasps with cherries on them.

— We should take the Christmas tree down, Constance says.

— Not until the snow thaws!

The tree looks dilapidated, so Stella sprayed it white and stuck wires in the branches to perk them up. It has a Japanese feel to it now and the fairy lights glow outside when they are walking home. It looks nice.

— What time will they be here?

— Any minute now.

— Do you think we'll see it?

— I don't know. How is Vito?

— He is fine.

Outside each snowflake is wide and slow. They fall steadily without hesitation. The sky is relentlessly heavy every day and it is beginning to have an actual weight to it. Days stretch out, each longer than yesterday.

— The snowfall feels different.

— Yup.

— I love you.

— I love you too.

The two of them glance out of the window, up at a sky that is already turning into a river of colours. There is a lemon-drizzle cake that her mum made on the counter. She spent two hours making soups and putting them in the freezer. There is a tap on the door. Stella runs to open it. Dylan swoops in. He tips snow off his parka onto the porch and gives her a grin and a hug; he seems more awkward and tired-looking than usual.

– The aurora is coming, the sky is already turning! He peers out the window.

– Dylan, you're like a kid at Christmas, she says.

– I know.

– Was your cinema totally tiny?

– Totally tiny. It had red velvet curtains, one screen, old balconies, statues, stars gliding across the ceiling. If I couldn't sleep, I'd lie in the middle of the stage just daydreaming.

– Were your girlfriends strippers? Stella asks.

– Because I lived in Soho?

– Aye.

– A few.

– Did you date any boys?

– Only good-looking ones.

– Really?

– Once or twice, he says.

– Dylan, why are you looking at me like that? Stella asks.

– I'm . . . glad to see you – you look great, he says.

– I don't look any different than I did last time you saw me! she says.

Dylan places a clear bottle on the table. His first batch of gin. He has made a label for it and it has three suns on the front and underneath he has neatly stencilled *The Sunlight Pilgrims*.

— Is that for me? I'd say you shouldn't have, but clearly you should! How many bottles did you make? Constance picks it up and turns it round, her face lit up.

— I made exactly the right amount to get us through an Ice Age.

Barnacle appears in the doorway.

— Is this some kind of party? Do you need an invitation?

— Come in, Barnacle, we're just getting ready for our little aurora party. How are you?

— Crippled as ever, darling, but good. I couldn't half use a drink, though!

— Of course Stella decorated outside for us and we've got the chimenea up on the roof, so it isn't totally freezing — gin? It's Dylan's, he made it all by himself!

— Bloody well done, Dylan. A gin would be to die for! I brought my telescope, not that we'll need it!

He has pleated his beard to keep it out of the way and he has silver rings on; a mouth organ pokes out of his pocket and he looks more like a sailor with his blue eyes and his lined face, glancing up at her, a little smile. Stella can't remember any more why he used to creep her out.

— So, you're still here then, young Dylan.

— No choice, mate, can't get anywhere else.

— Charming, Constance says.

— It's just as bad down south. The Thames has been frozen for months now.

— You must miss something from home, no?

— Sushi.

— That's it?

— You could always catch some fish at Fort Harbour and chop them up raw, Stella giggles.

— Hilarious!

— What are those big holes in your ears? Barnacle asks him.

— Flesh tunnels, Constance says.

— It sounds so sexy when you say it like that, Dylan says.

— Dylan and Mum are a bit of an item now, Stella says.

— Not really, Constance says.

— Oh, stop resisting. You'll be a normal woman one day, with just one old man and nothing exciting going on at all, Constance, Barnacle says.

— Really? Shoot me if that happens.

— What: the one-old-man bit? Dylan demands.

— The nothing-exciting bit, she says.

Outside the sky has turned green. Stella stands at the window and takes a photo for Vito with her phone.

33

A VAST road of stars trails across the sky. It looks like he could just walk along it to some other place. It feels like it won't be much longer in these temperatures before they all might do that, but he has to shake away thoughts like that. He gets a brief image of that cloud on the mountain when he first got here, beyond the veil where there were barmen with long, narrow teeth ready to siphon the souls of humans and send the energy up into the universe to that . . . that river of green light.

He has chills down his back.

It is all rivers of green light in the sky, which turn purple, then red.

Constance has strung glass lanterns all round the back garden. They sway from branches, candle flames flickering. Stella is laughing at something Barnacle says, as he opens Constance's door wearing a cap on his head and a glance to the right to make eye contact. Constance comes out behind him with her cheeks unusually radiant. She slips on her wolf. Barnacle hands Dylan a large glass of gin with ice and cucumber and Constance is smoking a tiny spliff.

— To winter and all who sail in her! Barnacle says.

They raise their glasses (apple juice for Stella). Dylan is sure he can hear something creaking, like the sea as if it was frozen and going to crack, as if the snow around them is shifting.

— Have you seen Dylan's tattoos, Barnacle?

— Not really, Stella, no.

— A smile around the edges of Constance's eyes.

— The wind has just dropped, we are not going to be out here for long, Stella, okay?

— Do you have a lot of friends down south then? Barnacle asks.

— Nope.

— Lone wolf?

— Little bit.

— So's our Constance, he says.

— What would you do if you didn't have any friends, Mum?

— You only need one or two good ones.

— But if you didn't have any.

— If I needed to, I'd go out and make some. Plenty of people out there, she says.

— I had friends from the theatres around Soho. I've not seen most of them for years — they all ended up scattered across the globe. I was the last one left at home, Dylan says.

— I love the theatre. I always fall asleep, though, in the box, and sometimes at the Lyceum in Edinburgh there's this same homeless guy who turns up, and he has a big rucksack with all his stuff in it and he queues up because they give out four free tickets for each preview. He gets in the circle and sleeps, all warm, for the whole thing. I love that: a theatre where a homeless man can sleep whilst listening to Faust. A good fisting from the devil, ay—

— Barnacle! Constance warns him.

— Most of the homeless are dying in doorways, Stella says.

— True. If the site rates go up next year, I'll be joining them. I can't see me fitting a rucksack on this back, though.

— Dylan is trying not to watch Constance as she smokes. A thin stream of smoke curls out of her mouth and it gives him a hard-on. He looks away from her, back to the sky. Stella wears her brightly coloured mohawk hat and gloves and she is holding her mum's hand.

— I have mulled wine up on the roof, heating up on the little chimenea stove. We'd best get up there before the alcohol burns off? Constance says.

— I'm a bit scared about getting up there, Barnacle says.

— Don't worry, Mum will bring the Bentley round.

— Constance runs down the path, then rumbles back along the salted gap in the snow, in a little forklift with a big wooden board over the front two prongs.

— I've never seen a wolf drive a forklift before! Dylan says.

— You do see strange things around these parts, Barnacle says.

— Where did she get that?

— Borrowed it from the storeroom. She used it to get up on top of the roof and tarmac it a few months ago as well – the woman's a tomboy.

She reverses the forklift down the side of her caravan and the satanist kid up at the end is standing at his door drinking a beer. She raises her wolf-paw and the kid raises his back.

Stella helps Barnacle climb onto the platform at the bottom of the lift and he grips on, chortling loudly as the machine buzz-whirrs up. There's an almighty clunking noise, then Constance is neatly turning the forklift at the top to slide Barnacle right onto her roof.

– Come on then, Incomer, he calls down.

Dylan climbs up the ladder at the back of the caravan with Stella in front of him. The roof is a perfect viewing platform. The chimenea burns. There are four deckchairs around it and a blanket in each and cushions and a telescope set up on its own.

Barnacle places another log on and a spray of sparks come out as he puts the lid back down. There is a small pot next to the chimenea and it looks like a black cauldron with a single gas flame underneath it and the smell of cloves and cinnamon and red wine and orange spices. Two wolf-ears appear at the edge of the roof and then two paws and Constance climbs up, and he pours some wine out with a ladle and everyone gets a glass to warm them, even Estelle. The moon is a perfect half and each crater is dark and grey. An owl twit-twoos. Dylan tilts his head back to see cream-and-brown feathers in a flurry going past in the dark, and the light of the chimenea catches the owl's eyes. It sits in the holly tree, which has inches of white on each sprig. Stella is wearing brand-new moccasin boots, which she admires.

– Where did you get those?

– She glances at her mum.

– Alistair.

– You finally opened his Christmas box?

– I was bored.

– No tartan shirts. Shame, you can never have too many of those! Barnacle says.

Stella looks at her mum and giggles.

The light is changing each of their faces from one moment to the next, and the colours, energy flowing over them, stars sending light from years and years ago and only reaching them now and a feeling that it is all just how it was meant to be. Dylan takes another glass of wine, wanting to drink, to drink for the sake of warmth, and the owl turns its neck all the way round and blinks. There are tufts of feathers on top of pointed ears and then it spies something in the field and swoops.

– Did you see that?

– What?

Stella turns round.

Barnacle is sitting in his deckchair, looking the other way to the mountains, and the forests are white but the thick dark fir trees still stand out in layers all the way to the top. To the right of the biggest mountain is a smaller one and there are willow trees bent under the weight of snow. Constance stands on the front of the roof with her feet placed wide and lights a cigarette. Spirals of light unravel across the sky until they are sweeping arcs of green and purple.

– It's the aurora! Stella squeaks.

Circles of green light are shot through with white dashes – horizontal iridescence shoots down in zigs and zags from somewhere above the sky. Stars sparkle through a moving river of light and colour and it turns the tips of Constance's wolf-ears green, and she turns her face to the side so he can see her silhouetted – with the universe spreading out behind her.

Those great hulks of stone and tree and bark and soil and clods of earth and the deer up there, and the wildcat he likes to imagine is up there, and the farmers' dogs barking in the night – all of it is so cleanly real.

– The sky is my wife, Barnacle says.

– And how spectacular she is, Constance says.

At Barnacle's feet there are three old rear-view mirrors, so when it hurts his neck too much to look up and out he can still see everything by looking down. Stella dances up and down the rooftop and Constance taps her on the shoulder to stop, lest she fall off. And the girl stands with her hands stretched up into the sky above her and she is radiant.

– I always wanted a wife that was the sky, so I could admire her every day of her life, so she'd never stay the same and I'd always be watching for the changes, Barnacle says.

Dylan sits down next to Barnacle in a big stripy deckchair and lets the old astronomer refill his wine glass with a ladle. If he had to grade life on the best days and the worst, he'd say seeing his grandmother on devil's snare was the worst, and this – the best seat in the house to watch the universe unfold, with a woman he loves, and a kid he loves too and a neighbour who is affable and a tin box for home – is as good as it gets.

The aurora unfolds, it moves, it's never still. The light alters each second and it appears as a being, an entity older than they themselves will ever be. Down below them cara-vans are lit up, lights in windows; nobody is out, why would they come out? – they wouldn't and even Ida has gone back inside. The caravan rooftops and the mountain are eerily lit by green light and the faint river of purple moving through it now, and a silhouette appears on the mountaintop – of a sole stag.

– I bet you that's the giant red. Barnacle sits up a bit.

– Three hundred pounds and nine feet tall, the giant red doesn't exist, Constance says.

– Are the farmers out tonight? Stella asks.

– Better hope not, cos they'd shoot that one, Constance says.

The sky above them is opening – that's what it is – the sky is opening and they are looking out and the lights of little cottages up on the mountains glow orange.

– Can you see it? Barnacle whispers.

They follow his arm, which is pointing over to the nearest peak of the mountain, and his head glancing up, glancing, glancing, and they are all following his directions and it is there – silhouetted – a green sky behind it and around it and somehow below it: on the closest peak of the mountain a second stag with his antlers wide and curved round and just a silhouette.

– Is it the white one?

– I don't know – get the telescope.

Stella takes the little lid off and places it down at eye height for Barnacle and he is looking, looking. Constance claps her hands together because the temperature is dropping further. They can't stay up here much longer.

– I can't tell if it is the white one because it looks purple from the reflection of the sky, Barnacle says.

Dylan can see the shape and it looks like it is white – then another appears and the two stags face each other, right up on the peak, with the aurora around them as if it's radiating out from behind them and even from here: the size of them!

— This qualifies as the best aurora party ever, Constance murmurs.

It is like the caravan is in motion — like they are sailing into skies of purple and green — like this is their spaceship boat — and there are a few figures out now, in other gardens across the caravan park, all different people looking up.

— It reminds me of Iceland, Barnacle says.

— Do you get polar bears in Iceland? Stella asks.

— One swam two hundred miles to get there not long ago; they shot it when it arrived.

— Why? Stella asks.

— They've got a policy. They won't let them be reintroduced again.

Barnacle has somehow reclined in his lounger in a way that makes it easier for him to look round, his back still bent, but he seems more comfortable and the colours of the sky intensify like it has an energy of its own. Treetops across the forests jut up into the purple aurora and behind it a cluster of shooting stars.

— Did you tell them about Coatlicue, Dylan? Stella asks.

Barnacle tilts his head as the Milky Way snakes right above them, so many stars. Dylan couldn't even imagine seeing quite so many stars so clearly ever in his life.

— Nope.

— Who's Coatlicue? Barnacle asks.

— Soul-collector, Dylan says.

— Sounds like my first wife, but she went after bank accounts too, Barnacle says.

— She gave birth to the stars and the comets. From the moment they appear, the death-wish comets are on a trajectory to complete self-destruction; they burn so fast through the universe so that they can return to the nothing they came from — they want to go back there and see what nothing is made of, so they burn, and burn, and burn, using up all the energy they can as fast as they can. Coatlicue has snakes in her hair and her skirt is a ballgown made out of skulls; they are tiny little skulls at the top and they get bigger all the way down, and when she walks across the universe they move out around her and talk to each other in whispers, and she collects souls that have been lost out there and puts them back in the river of Lethe so they can return. They say out there somewhere there is a bar beyond the veil where they siphon off the souls of humans. Funny thing is, when I first got here and I was up on the mountain a cloud drifted up over where I was standing and I had this feeling of being right on the edge of the other side of life, you know, and it was littered with these hideous, long-toothed skinny creatures who wanted to suck up the last bit of humans' soul energy — you know, siphon off any goodness they had left and send it up into the universe to give it more energy for stuff like that! Dylan points up.

— And I thought I was the goth, Stella says.

— She sounds hot — she can collect my soul any time, Barnacle says.

— You won't die for years, Stella says.

— Why not?

— You eat too much frozen food. The additives are preserving you.

— I don't believe in holding on. I want to be like an old

Eskimo, just go out in the snow one night and fall asleep. Wouldn't that be peaceful?

— Peaceful like drowning? Stella asks.

— How does anybody really know if drowning is peaceful? Constance asks.

— Because they record the brainwaves afterwards or something, Barnacle says.

— Bollocks! she says.

— That is the brightest half-moon I have ever seen, it is so pretty!

Constance gazes up to where her child is looking. Stella stands up on her tiptoes at the front of the caravan and holds her hands above her head in a curved steeple until it looks like an earth-child has captured the moon.

Barnacle has gone back through to his caravan to bed. Dylan carries Stella over to the bedroom and lays her on the bunk, tucks her in. He looks at her for a minute in the dark. They share ancestors. They both love her mother. Somewhere in the park he can hear someone blaring dance music and there were two fights earlier. People are going cabin-crazy. It would take police hours to get out here and they are unlikely to turn up for anything small; Clachan Fells is more lawless by the day. Stella's mouth is squint and plump and childlike, as if her dreams take her right back to a place ruled by the innocent and the free.

— The plates and cups and ashtray and everything are still up on the roof. I should go up and get them, Constance whispers at the door.

— Get them in the morning, he says.

They step outside and she leans in as he lights a cigarette

for her, and she looks at him with her white hair and her grey eyes with their orange rim, which is now always going to remind him of the parhelia. She takes his hand and they just stand there, neither of them feeling even the remotest need to begin speaking.

34

STELLA GOES over to their sun mirror and combs her black hair so it shines. She braids each side neatly and puts on a tiny slick of lip gloss. Her tiny wax strips are in a pouch in the bathroom and she's been using one each week, even when she can't see any hair on her upper lip. She pulls up her polo-neck under her chin and buttons her cardigan over the top.

— *Winter is proving to be the worst that has been seen in the UK in living memory, generating unseen conditions across the whole of Europe and indeed many countries worldwide. We will take you across the map now. Russia, as we can see here, is at an utter stand-still, fatalities in rural areas and cities have reached a crisis point. Nobody is able to get in or out on the roads and a main cause of death is cold and hunger. Chicago is on city-lockdown; we saw a forty-car pile-up in Chicago due to black ice on the road only few weeks ago; there have been riots across parts of the city, with wide-spread looting and violent crime; there are reports of home owners shooting anyone who enters their home without cause, and police are no longer intervening in these cases because there are just so many. Morocco is under twenty feet of snow this morning; we saw a demonstration against local government for the number of street children and families who are literally being left to freeze unless someone takes them in, and many ordinary people are opening their homes to others if they can do so. The northern British Isles are mainly frozen over, with icebergs at the furthest tip of the Orkney Islands; another iceberg — the biggest ever recorded outside the Arctic — has entered an area of Scotland called Clachan Fells; whale-pods are migrating through the Atlantic at vast rates, birds are changing route and in fact in the UK there have barely been any bird sightings for weeks now. Those that are in nests have just frozen. Rivers are frozen. Blackouts across the grid can be seen lit up here, here and here. We are not sure how many fatalities this harsh weather will create, but thousands and thousands of people are dying due to dangerous conditions, and this is only the beginning. We can confirm the weather in the UK will be minus fifty before the next few weeks are through. The whole of Europe has come to a standstill. The entire planet is being impacted upon by the collapse of intricate weather systems that are vital to survival, just a few degrees lower than is manageable for human habitation, and we could be plunging into an Ice Age.*

As of today, the Prime Minister has released a statement saying people must stop panicking, but it seems the public do not agree. A man walked into Tate Modern on Tuesday and shot dead thirty people. There are widespread reports of violent crime having reached epidemic proportions. In the US you can see in this footage that families are traipsing from their main residencies to garden-bunkers that are sometimes equipped with up to twelve months of food and water. For the next few days the temperature is anticipated to keep dropping rapidly and, as of now, there is no definite conclusion as to how this will end. We will keep you updated, with ITV proving a main point of contact while Internet connections are down. We will be back with you at eleven p.m. tonight, at ITV with leading

scientists, politicians and religious leaders meeting to try and offer
some guidance at this time. Until then, from us here in the studio,
stay warm and stay safe!

The news reporter is wearing a scarf and the window
behind him is completely black, with snow in mounds halfway up it.

Stella glances at her mum and they both look back at the
television again. Constance squeezes her shoulder. The sun
has been up for hours and the sky outside is a whitened grey
and it feels ominous. From their windows there are icicles
hanging all the way down to the ground and she is thirsty.
Stella finds her army boots and puts them on and keeps her
pyjamas underneath, but slides her waterproofs on top of
them, then she drags on a big jumper and her Eskimo coat
with the furry hood and her mohawk hat and she opens the
metal door.

It is so still outside.

Dylan's caravan is quiet and his windows all bare because
he still hasn't got curtains, but at least now he has a tiny
crooked metal chimney sticking out of the roof and smoke
wisps up and curls into the cold air. There is a skitter-patter
sound as a dog walks down the pathway; he cocks his ears at
her; he has a clever face and a black-and-white coat and his
tongue hangs out, and then there is a dog-whistle sharp and
short from somewhere in the park and he turns and runs
over the field, so his back legs almost seem to move forward
as one motion and his front paws plunge down into snow
too deep, until he is a furrow moving forward through a
white field.

She traipses around the back of their caravan – the tarpaulin over the wood-stack is heavy with snow. She lets one

corner down so the snow all slides off onto the ground, then she puts it back into its peg to keep the logs dry. The only bit of furniture they have left to sell is the 1950s metal larder, and the snow-chains on the ambulance are holding out but the engine doesn't start any more.

Inside her mother's garden food store there are half the amount of tins that were there before and only one crate of wine. The bags of rice are triple-wrapped in cling-film but they have still frozen. She closes the door again. Stella takes the axe out of the tree. Icicles hang from the windows and they are clear and almost as thick as her wrist at the top, then they taper right down to the ground. She doesn't want to get any of the bits that are frozen onto the caravan or they will taste like metal. Stella taps at the icicle a few inches below the windowsill, and small chips fly away into the air. She keeps tapping gently, with her left hand ready to catch it as it falls, and it does, in one piece.

Stella holds the clear tusk out in front of her – puts it up to her head as if she is the unicorn – she spins around, holding the icicle out in front of her as a spear – jabbing it into air to show the spirit-plane that she is her mother's daughter – that the child of a wolf may not feel like she has fangs until she finds herself facing the moon, but they are still there the whole time regardless. Stella crunches down on the tip of the icicle and clean, pure water chills her tongue. The sky is so dense this morning that it is hard to imagine any stars were even there last night. She looks in the window and her mum has lain down on the sofa and closed her eyes. Stella goes back into the kitchen and the wood-stove has almost gone out and she cannot be bothered to clean the grate right now, so she just adds some paper and kindling and two logs;

it catches and it will keep the fire going for a while at least. She grabs a pair of old binoculars and a plastic bag she prepared a few days ago. There are no carrots in the fridge, so she takes an empty can of deodorant with a bright-blue round lid.

Stella heads out along the paths, down past a caravan with cartoons blaring out of the window, and a woman shouts at her children with the kind of harsh tone that is as bad as a punch.

Stella turns to look toward the open window. A little girl is staring out at her and she looks so miserable and lonely and hungry. She pushes down in between the scratchy gorse bush on the lane and then right across the car park, where the snow is up to her knees and then nearly to her thighs, then she is in the field and she can stand with the snow just touching the top of her boots. These are perfect conditions. The motorway still has movement. Over at the industrial park the lights on the big stores are all yellow and fake and somehow welcoming all the same. The car showrooms are closed, but they have bright lights shining down on four-wheel drives with shiny interiors of leather and just one of those cars would cost four times more than their caravan. There used to always be young flash-looking couples from the city coming out to buy a car or go to Ikea or to pick up paint, but there is nobody visiting the industrial parks now.

She feels angry. This stupid snow. Her voice is lower all the time and her mum is not sleeping again. Stella makes a snowball, pressing it down as hard as she can in one hand, and pats it with the other hand until it is really solid. It all comes from this one snowball – that's how it all starts – and it has to be a good one and super-hard so the rest will stick to it and keep the shape. She rolls the snowball across the white expanse and the snow is so high she doesn't even have to bend down properly until it gets bigger and heavier. This is good for her fury: the exertion and moving forward and shoving this big ball of snow forward with a vengeance in her. She rolls the big ball and it leaves an indented path behind it. She rolls and rolls; her legs hurt. She has to pat it down and make it solid again before she turns it and rolls back the way she just came.

By the time she is no longer able to push the torso, she is near the entrance to the city dump. This is the best thing – creating something out of nothing. A landscape creates a snowman and later he uses these big long feet to walk across to Ikea, and he leaves a watery trail behind him as he takes over the tannoy to tell stories of all the creatures who came out of nothing – all the beings like him who came out of the snow, who have no idea where it is they return to. By the time she has rolled it all the way back to the torso, the head is ready to go on. Stella carefully places the head down on the body. She opens her bag. The nose goes on first: it is the miniature can of deodorant with waves on it and she sets it firmly there, so she can rest the binoculars on top of it. He is a snowman scanning a landscape. She can hear cars in the distance. His deodorant-can nose is perfect, with its round blue cap sticking out, and the binoculars sit well. She wraps the black scarf around his neck. Her snowman scans the landscape. There are vast layers of snow in every direction. Behind him are the mountains and the caravan parks. She pulls out an old suit jacket from the bag and she has to work to get it to fit around his wide neck; she has to recurve the shoulders so that he wears the thing like it was tailor-made.

She steps back and looks at him.

Three stones.

That's what he needs.

She finds them right at the bottom of the bag, which is wet with ice and snow, and she places the buttons down the middle of his open suit jacket and now he is sharp. He is super-smart. She can see herself in the reflection of the binoculars and she looks like a radiant elf. Stella checks out her snowman one last time and he is solid. She'll bring Mum down to see him later. She wades back across the fields toward the gap in the fence where she can squeeze back onto the caravan-site road and Lewis Brown has been standing at the back of his caravan watching her. She gets the feeling he has been there the whole time. He raises his hand. She pretends not to notice, so he climbs across his fence and wades toward her.

— Stella!

— Lewis.

— You didn't answer my e-mails, he says.

— You didn't turn up at Fort Hope when I got a kicking-in from all those guys you like over there. What was the matter: couldn't face it? she says.

— I couldn't stop them, he says.

She pulls up her hat and parts her hair and points out the scar going up into her head.

— You are a coward, Lewis Brown!

He watches her wading through the snow away from him.

She turns around and he is frowning, all that snow around him, but just as handsome as he ever was.

– I'll call you! he says.

– Oh, fuck off, she calls back.

It was a good day until she saw his face. She hopes he freezes out there in the field, with nobody to watch him die but her snowman.

35

THE MAN on the tannoy says something while big televisions play news footage on repeat and everyone in here is
glued to them – cannot stop watching, cannot look away,
only getting up to get food or go to the toilet. The snowfall
is heavy outside and people text anxiously. Even in here it's
Baltic. There's a tired guy on the tannoy talking about
the medi-aid in Bargain Corner and free soup up at the
cafeteria. They've opened Ikea as a place for the community
to get medical aid and shelter, buy food, get heat. He is curiously exhilarated to be sitting here looking at meatballs and
fries and gravy and extra cranberry sauce. The tannoy
person starts speaking in depressed tones again.

– You are welcome to stay in-store until further notice.
We will bring you weather updates throughout the day and
you *can* see news footage on televisions throughout the store.
The food in our restaurant and the shop downstairs has been
reduced, to help those who are unable to attend jobs at
this time. There will be songs, sung by the staff each day
at 1 p.m.

The tannoy boy clicks up and goes off somewhere to com-
mit suicide.

Dylan feels better walking around here with all this space. The caravan is giving him cabin-fever — that and the snow and Vivienne's sketchbook and feeling guilty whenever Constance lies in his arms and he doesn't say anything. He goes over to the condiments and stuffs packets of sauce, vinegar and sugar into his big pockets. He gets a tray and goes over to the hot plates. What to have now? The ciabatta with bacon? He has sold four bottles of gin this week, so he can afford this. There are always ways to make cash and the more this temperature drops and the higher the snow stacks up along the roads, the more people want to drink. It's an ideal beginning for his brewing empire. On the way out of here he will buy as much food as he can for Constance's larder. The guy further up Ash Lane, with his alien badges, gave Dylan a lift all this way and is off to get himself a new office desk-type thing to put his new alien transceiver box on; he zapped Dylan this morning on Ash Lane and Dylan staggered back a few steps. That's what nailed him the lift.

He pushes a little metal trolley ahead of himself with two trays on it, and the hot counter is bright and the boy with his yellow uniform stands there with his badge, which says *Happy to Help!*

— I'll take a cooked breakfast, please.

The boy has a white hat on and he scoops up beans; he uses tongs to add two sausages, mushrooms, potato scone, hash brown, bacon, a little folded-up yellow thing that appears to be masquerading as a miniature omelette. Two brown rolls. Dylan slides his bank card in with the faintest hesitation — what if there's nothing in there? He is relieved when the guy hands him a receipt.

Dylan pushes his trolley over to a table at the quiet area around the corner, where big windows look down on the store so that customers can admire fake flowers and brightly coloured plastic chairs. They have pinned up banners of material around the walls in all different colours. There is a green sheet covered in third eyes: two smaller eyes on either side, then a big one in the middle looking right at him. The pattern repeats throughout the open-plan area below. He soaks up bean sauce with a buttered roll. The sausage tastes dreadful and there is a completely fake feeling to the egg omelette, but the tattie scones are delicious. Gunn loathed this place. Wholly detested it. It was Vivienne who used to make him drive her all the way out to Croydon and, when they had lunch, she'd always get one of those little bottles of white wine and a Dime-bar cake. Then another bottle of wine. He smiles to himself. Dylan dunks a chunk of sausage in brown sauce. It's edible. Needs sauce, though, and that egg thing. Like a yellow brain. Airport food on an Ikea plate. That's what it is. Dylan pushes the food away and it is uncomfortable to sit for too long. He goes over to the big window where the mountains and caravans are all covered in snow. If snow keeps falling, it will soften noise across the whole world and everyone will have to pipe down a while, put down their weapons, stay home, make soup, talk quietly.

Over in the farmer's field there is the most amazing snowman. It's tall and wide and dressed with a suit coat and a tie and suit trousers and scuffed trainers and a big tummy and buttons, and a coloured-in deodorant can for his nose and binoculars that look familiar. Cheap Japanese binoculars for watching black-and-white films. Stella must have pinched them from his caravan! He needs to watch that girl. He taps his boots on the ground and behind him a woman is crying to her friend and the people going downstairs to the market hall all looked pinched and haunted. Constance is sleeping a lot this week too. He'll get back, soon, but first he will find a living-room area to read a paper, one with a working lamp and a blanket and a footstool. It is so good to walk around somewhere that seems even vaguely normal for a while. Dylan makes his way out of the cafeteria and begins to follow the arrows and he is tempted to steal a teapot for Constance. How clever of this store to stay open in these conditions. Great for community relations: it says *We are here to support your family through the fucking apocalypse, people — come back here for the rest of your life to buy corner sofas and clever Scandi kitchenware; we are all the extended human race: you, me, everybody!*

Outside the window a digger rolls through the snow.

For a minute he gets an image of Stella on her bicycle, an imprint of light behind his eyes. She is standing on his pathway, holding a gobstopper aloft like a poisoned apple.

36

THERE ARE still no e-mails from Vito. He has been eaten by the snow. Northern Italy is a white mass and when she looks at their news everyone is scared, and they look like that in the village at Clachan Fells this week too. Perhaps Vito has had enough and he is living with a piccolo player in Azerbaijan. She dreamt of Gunn MacRae last night. The woman came right into the caravan and took a bottle of Dylan's home-made gin.

— He got it wrong on the mint, Gunn said.

She screwed up her face and drank three shots in a row.

— The branding's good, though, she said.

— Why are you here?

— Aren't you getting up, Stella?

— Why should I get up?

Gunn sat down at the table and put her boots up on the chair so that mud got on the cushions and she burped and lit a cigar. She pulled the bottle of gin over to herself.

— Coatlicue is on her way, she said.

— On her way where?

— Poplar Path.

— Where's Vito?

— They took his hormones away, he's standing on a bridge in Pordenone.

— I don't want him to do that.

— You'll meet him one day, don't worry. He's going to be fine.

She had a chess board with her and she set it up on the table and they passed Pawns and Queens and Bishops and Rooks and Knights, and Gunn told her all about rocks and men and how everything could be settled with sex, and how her value was only going to be as solid as she decided it would be and how little anyone knows about anything and how they all play dress-up and let's-pretend, and that she has to work out how to make some money and how to keep it coming in and that is the key, and don't stay with a man who plays games with your emotions and always have a lover on the side or you might as well be dead.

— You look a little like me, she said.

Stella pushed forward her Knight to claim checkmate.

— What about the real sunlight pilgrims, who were they?

— Those fucking crazy monks?

— Yeah.

— You're descended from the one that was left on the island, Gunn said.

— The one that didn't eat gannets.

— The one that drank light until his eyes glowed like lasers in his head. I had a toy like that once, a little wind-up metal monkey, and it had two red lights for eyes and it played the drums and stamped its feet a lot. It was my first true love, she said.

— Why aren't you visiting Dylan?

— That boy's brain couldn't take it — he's figuring out a few things right now.

— He's heartbroken since you both died.

— He'll get over it, Gunn says.

— You miss him.

— I do.

— He was your favourite, over Vivienne?

— By a long, long way but I'm not proud of that. It wasn't Vivienne's fault, you know.

— What wasn't her fault?

— Any of it.

— Why come to me?

— I'm just doing the rounds.

— What are you, a milkman?

— Just seeing the family, she said.

When Stella woke up she felt like she hadn't slept at all, and rolling over and looking at their kitchen table and no mud-prints on the cushion and no cigar in the ashtray, only the dog-ends from her mum's joint and cigarettes and glasses on the drying rack. Stella opens the curtains. Outside the sky is a clear, clear blue and the snow has stopped. Crystals sparkle across everything, over the lumps and hillocks of things hidden by the snow. She can hear Constance turn over in her bed. There is no sign of last week's skies, which were so white and dense and heavy it seemed it was pressing down onto Clachan Fells. Lewis Brown walked past their caravan three times last night. Everyone knows you only walk past someone's caravan if you want to stick your hands up their jumper. She will get Vito over here and he will drive through the caravan park in a big fancy car and park right outside Ash Lane and all the kids will watch her as she climbs inside. She'll wear a headscarf and big glasses and blood-red lipstick, and she and Vito will neck for ten minutes in front of everyone before he starts the engine and his car flies right up into the sky. He will drive her to Gretna Green and marry her. Just the two of them. Maybe her mum will come, and Dylan, and Barnacle, and she'll stay with him for ever. He'll be the only man she'll ever kiss and even when she is old he will sing her songs.

Stella goes online.

The usual news is there.

Strange people doing even weirder things.

Ugly things.

Weather reports coming in from everywhere. A new coalition treaty to deal with environmental issues. A lorry gone off the road in Plymouth and straight through a house. A gunman in Florence. Migrants stuck off the coast of Sicily, Greece, Turkey. A man trying to sell a child outside a bingo hall. No e-mail from Vito. He was last in the chat-room three days ago. Now he is gone. She wants him back. She makes some tea, drinks it so hot that it scalds her throat and she checks for hair on her face – just soft down and it is not growing in so fast any more with this waxing, but they have still not got the hormones from the clinic, although it is only a matter of time now. She pulls on the moccasins that Alistair gave her. He must have taken ages to make them and it means something, although just because her feet look pretty in them doesn't mean he can retrace his steps, but these moccasins are clearly not designed for a boy. Her bio- logical donor has never called her by her real name, but he has stopped using the boy one and he did not give her shirts this year; he spent months sewing together the prettiest little moccasins she has ever seen. The laces are strong lea- ther and she ties them up, tightly. On the radio a DJ is commending the emergency services and hospitals for stepping up, despite the cuts that keep going, due to a general economic decline that they are saying can only end in a complete collapse. He talks about the bankers and the government and big business but in a sad way, like the only thing he really has to look forward to is the cheese sandwich he'll eat later on. They break for the weather. It is always on the radio now. There should be a spring one day, but not for at least a month or three.

In essence:

– It's going to get a whole lot colder.

They don't know if temperatures will rise.

37

DYLAN GETS his parka, pulls his boots on, clicks the caravan door shut. He crunches along Ash Lane. He heads down along past the park and for no reason at all he decides to take a left and go down through Poplar Path instead of the other route behind the garages, just for variety. He had an urge to have a gin this morning. He had to quell it with tea and loud music and burning a few logs on the fire. For today, in that, he wins. He saw Alistair going into Constance's last night — that's what did it, he was in there for an hour. Dylan paced for another hour after he left; the man still makes him want to turn to violence but he needs to rein it in. He turns onto Poplar Path and stops.

Down at the end of the path there are two black boots.

They stick up from the snow and it is clear some dog has gone past and scrabbled around and exposed the boots, otherwise they would be completely covered in snow.

He looks behind him.

Nobody is about.

As he walks down the path it appears to elongate.

He brushes the snow off the boots.

It is clear already from the body shape. He dusts snow off

and his fingers can tell that what he is touching is solid as granite and twice as cold. Barnacle's eyes stare up at the mountains. Clear. Frozen solid. They reflect the tall shadow of Dylan as he flicks snow off the guy's collar, shows off those two badges on his lapels, one with a pure pristine world from space, the other celebrating a revolution. He steps back and the garages are reflected in those eyes as well. Barnacle must have walked here last night and sat down like an old Eskimo, like he said he would, that night on the roof. Snow falls off his arms, and his hands are out in front of him like two claws, like he is sitting in an armchair and is just about to get up.

The world turns.

People are somewhere talking, doing, being, driving; there are work places, there are strip-lights.

He dials 999 on his phone.

Barnacle's eyelashes are frosted white and solid – he still has the pleat in his beard where he wanted it out of the way so he could drink and eat and laugh, and words are coming back to Dylan as he listens to the ring on his phone: Constance asking if Barnacle was going to stay with Ida, or at the community centre and Barnacle saying he'd rather just sit down in the snow – Dylan takes a few steps back.

– Which service do you require?

– I have found a body frozen in the snow, it's my neighbour.

Dylan gets a feeling of motion, all the mountains blurring slightly around him until he kneels down, tears again, brushing them off his face, furious with everything.

– I am sorry to hear that, sir. We do have a designated service for these calls now sadly, please hold!

He keeps checking behind him, hoping Stella won't appear and see Barnacle sitting here like this, his hands held out before him like two dinosaur claws.

— Hello, can we help you, sir?

— Yeah, I found a body.

Barnacle is leaning right back, so he is still in a C-shape but he is able to look up, he has gone like that — lying there watching the stars, watching night turn to morning and waiting for the sky — his wife.

Part IV

or

The End Has Almost Come
19th March 2021, −56 degrees

38

THE LANDSCAPE is brilliantly lit, flawless — the mountains look like somebody has cut them out of the sky. The skies are clear and blue, but the wind still bites and nips at any exposed inch of skin. Each of them wears snow-goggles so their eyelashes don't get frosty, and balaclavas pulled up right up over their face and nose. The cold is clangorous. It vibrates. Shrill and deadly. They argued about it for two weeks before coming out to do this. Constance has enough food to get by for two days, a shelter in her backpack. They have three charged phones. They were going stir-crazy in the caravan. Stella is just behind him now and there is the crunch of their feet on soft powdered snow over the hard-packed ice layer below it. They wear ice-grips over their boots, and gloves and scarves like they are moon travellers setting out into this landscape alone.

— How old are the polar ice-caps?

— Up to fifteen million years old, Dylan says.

Stella stops and looks at him, he puts out his hand to help her up the slope and they walk on.

— So this winter has happened really because of water melting from the ice-caps, which means this winter started out, in

Jenni Fagan

a way, about fifteen million years ago? This is all sort of time-travel! We've kind of gone back in time – this was fifteen million years in the making. Stella gestures around them.

– Shouldn't you be playing with My Little Ponies or something? Dylan snaps.

– Is my existential goth-angst bothering you, Dylan?

– No.

– Is.

– Is not.

– Mum, can you see the iceberg now?

– You couldn't miss it!

Constance calls out from the top of the mountain, where she is looking down on the other side. She has begun to wear lots of thermodynamic layers, so she can still move pretty quickly. She is adjusting to conditions. Fluid. Sinewy. Wolflike. The elbows of her old ski-jacket are patched over with gaffer tape. She lifts up his old binoculars and sweeps across the entire landscape.

– Why don't you want to scatter Gunn in the islands any more? Stella asks.

– I just don't.

– Do you think someone ever collected Barnacle's ashes?

– There probably weren't any ashes; he would simply have been chucked in with some other people. I am sorry, Stella, I know it isn't nice! He would have been, though. I mean, I don't even know if this really is Gunn in here. It's probably the ashes from forty different Londoners who died on the same day. I'm probably scattering the ashes of a whole crew of Russian gangsters who got shot at point-blank range, he says.

– That's pretty cool, Stella says.

— I have no interest in your opinion on ashes, child!

— Child! You're the one who was watching cartoons when I got up this morning! Anyway. What did they do with Barnacle's body when they got to the morgue?

— It takes weeks to defrost a fully grown man, Stella. It's best not to think about it, Constance says.

— How do you know that? Dylan asks.

— She slept with a mortician, Stella mutters.

— Is nothing sacred or secret in my life any more?

Constance stands at the top of the slope ahead of them, with the sky as her backdrop.

— It is so hard to walk in all these layers, Mum, can I take my coat off, or just the balaclava?

— No, you can't. No! You'll freeze — we're not stopping here for long, Stella, we need to keep moving!

— Okay, Mum, don't get hysterical.

Dylan tests the ground ahead of Stella with a ski-pole to make sure they won't fall into deeper snow. Words are like crystal when it is like this; they hang on the air, it carries them up to the trees on the mountaintop, all those frozen willows he can't help but see in the shape of a C, their long arms frozen. And somewhere in the cherry blossoms away down on the farm lane there are the tiny buds just waiting for a thaw that might never come round.

— Come on, keep going. Wait until you see this! Constance calls.

— Is the iceberg as big as they said it was? Dylan asks.

— Absolutely! That's not all, though, you are going to love this!

— What?

— Hurry up and you'll see.

She turns away, looking back out over the mountains and down over the coastline. Stella reminds him of Gunn more and more lately. He doesn't know how he didn't even notice that she looks like Gunn. He has to stop his tall frame taking bigger steps up the mountain, slowing down so Stella doesn't have to hurry to catch up, and as they reach the top the whole landscape emits an ungodly silence. The silence hollers! Stella steps onto the ridge and her voice trails away to nothing. He has never seen anything like this in his life. The breath is gone from him for a second. He reaches out for Constance's hand and the three of them are on the top of the smallest seventh sister, looking out across thousands of penitentes; the tall, peaked snow-figures all march down the mountain toward Fort Harbour where the sea is iced over as far as the eye can see, and almost touching the harbour wall there is a great hulk of iceberg wider and taller than he could ever have imagined seeing in real life – he accepts the binoculars from Constance and stares at it; his eyes can't take it in yet.

Dylan's throat burns from the icy air.

His eyes water behind his sunglasses.

Constance turns to him and he can see himself, bearded and bespectacled in polarised lenses, and up behind her the trees have spears of ice jagging down from each bough.

Blood pulses in his veins.

All those years in Babylon watching life instead of living it.

Light trails across his cornea.

There is the dull thud of his heart, in his ears.

A want for her that won't dissipate.

All those peaked figures of ice, like all of their ancestors have been caught by the elements on the long walk home, their souls captured by ice and snow, and below them the North Sea cracks and groans as ice-floes creak and collide.

— They call them penitentes, don't they, Dylan? There must be thousands of them! Constance says.

For that second she looks just like she must have done as a girl.

Stella puts her arm around her mother's waist.

A bird of prey soars down from the sky in slow circles and alights on a tree beside them. It is shocking to see one, when they haven't seen any birds for months, but this one is massive, his wings could easily be a yard wide each. The feathers are brown, but it looks bigger than a hawk. Its claws are like human hands, four long digits with a sharp, pointed talon on each one. They curve around the bough, gripping it steadily. It must be a sign. They can't feel it, but perhaps the thaw is finally on the way somewhere in the world, a tiny shoot of green way down in the soil somewhere, ready to reach its way up toward the light. Behind them they are sheltered by forest and tall pines, and the smell of clean sap rises from pine needles and underneath that the clean pure smell of snow, always at the edges of every smell now, and under that there is the faintest hint of eucalyptus.

The bird faces away from the forest, looking out at the panorama.

Yellow eye-rings circle black eyes, which dart around at all those mountains. The bird flies straight down through the trees and snow falls through branches onto the forest floor. Dylan is buzzy in the head. Hyper-aware. There are more marching snow-figures than he can count, they must be at least five feet tall. Stella stands next to one and puts her arm around the thing to hug it and Constance takes a photo on her phone and laughs, easier than she has seemed for weeks. His eyes ache from the brightness. Constance offers him a hand and he takes it and steps onto the highest ledge of the mountain.

— They must be sixteen or even eighteen feet high, he says.

— What are they, Mum?

— Penitentes are something to do with the sun and dew and carbon and ice. They must have been forming up here for weeks — maybe all month — and that iceberg, look at it!

— Mum, look, there's news crews down there! They must be here to film the penitentes and the iceberg. Do you think Clachan Fells will be on the news tonight?

— I think it probably will, yeah.

Constance wraps her arms around her daughter and kisses her head and holds her tight. Stella nestles into her mother. Constance's grey eyes scan the horizon and she looks down behind them to the caravan park, and behind her the peaks of snow-penitentes march like snow-people, all soaking up sunlight until they sparkle and appear to be moving just as clearly as they are standing still.

— We would never have seen these properly if we hadn't come up here, Stella says.

— The weather is turning. We should get back, Constance says.

— It looks okay, Dylan says.

— It isn't. I can feel it.

Away down in the caravan park he can see Ash Lane. The farm road is quiet, with no snow-plough out — it has already been this morning. Stella digs the toe of her boot into the snow.

— We should have a quick nip for the road then, Dylan says.

He takes out his little pewter flask.

Constance takes a hit of gin.

— What are you drinking to? Stella asks.

— To a man who took the sky as his wife, Dylan says.

He raises the pewter bottle up and takes a swig and Constance has another and Stella clicks her water bottle against the flask.

— Come on then, get out the Carte D'Or, she says.

A little smile drawn on the sticker on the side of the ice-cream tub. He drew that in Babylon, surrounded by a cold building that had made up their family home for ever — it feels like a million years ago already. He checks the wind, makes sure it won't just coat them or lie thick on the snow, reaches right out as tall as he can until a gust of wind carries the ashes down out over the penitentes. He taps the empty ice-cream container off the solid ice, taking another nip — at this altitude everything begins to blur seamlessly into lines of ice and ease, and a gladness in him that she is out there sparkling across the snow on a day like this, rather than stuck in a dark cupboard in a caravan.

He feels lighter.

— So, if winter has come to us now from millions of years ago, then time-travel is really possible. If the world has fifteen million years of frozen geology there and it can enter the present and melt and bring forth another Ice Age, then it's like the planet has kept them as an insurance system.

— Insurance against what?

— Humans. I took my first hormone-blocker this morning, Dylan, she grins.

— HIGH-THE-FIVE! he says.

Dylan puts his hand up to high-five her and instead of high-fiving him, she makes her hand like a paintbrush going up and down his, in one fluid movement. It has become their own private in-joke lately.

— That iceberg could be up to ten thousand years old, Constance says.

— Let me see, Mum!

Stella holds her hand out, excited. He follows her gaze down toward the coast and the sea is mapped over with ice-floes; right by the harbour the chunk of ice juts out and up, like it is mocking the mountain by holding such a similar shape out there on the ocean.

— It must be three hundred feet long, Constance says.

— It looks like a pyramid.

Dylan takes the binoculars and looks down towards Fort Hope. There are boats moored by the harbour wall and tall stacks of frozen lobster crates. He can see the shack that sells chips and home-made banana bread and cups of tea to fishermen and tourists who would normally be getting on ferries, but now they are all simply enthralled to be here when something so astounding is going on. Clusters of people hold up camera phones. The iceberg is peaked at one side with a smaller spike at the back and streaks of blue and cavities. The sea is still enough to reflect the mountains as the sun begins to go down, and the sky turning from blue to white and Constance looking nervous and the temperature dropping, and just like that out over the sea they see the snowstorm coming in, a whorl of white and grey moving toward Clachan Fells.

— What the fuck is that? he asks.

— Mum, that looks really, really bad!

— Right, get your skis on — hurry up, Constance says.

She is reaching in her backpack, undoing the strap holding the skis on. Dylan watches the snow turn in the air, heading low over the sea; people are scattering from the harbour below.

— Mum! I'm scared, Mum!

— It's okay, stop freaking out. Come on, get your snow-grips into here, quick — keep your head down, come on, hurry up! We're heading for Alistair's, we won't make it back to the park. You're going to have to go fast, Stella, are you listening to me?

Constance is shouting; she straps on her own grips and Dylan has already snapped his into place, a feeling of dread all the way down his gut. They can't see the frozen sea behind them now, it is just a thick white blizzard, and cars and news crews skidding out of the harbour.

39

THEY FLY past the farm where wild dogs used to bark outside. It is eerily silent. Further on they reach Alistair's croft, feeling the snow storm catch up behind them. The windows are lit yellow. A first blur of snow passes overhead as Constance hammers on the cottage door. Stella has her head tucked down and she is holding onto her ski-poles. Alistair opens the door and ushers them in, and he has to shove the door shut on the storm until the wind and snow are locked out. Dylan ducks his head in the cottage hallway. They take off the skis and stamp their boots in the hall to get snow off. He can already feel the heat of a fire. Alistair places his hand on the small of Constance's back, a quick smile from her to him. Dylan wonders if he would be better off out there in the snowstorm.

— Come through, Dylan, nice to meet you under different circumstances. Perhaps it will go a bit better than last time, what do you think? Constance, it's really fucking scary out there, what the fuck were you doing up on the mountain in this?

— The weather reports were fine earlier. We were going crazy down in the caravan — we've been in there for weeks without going out!

— How's your nuclear food-bunker holding up? he grins.

— Not well, Constance says.

His smile falters.

— Hello, Alistair, Stella says.

Alistair glances over at Stella.

— Hello, he says.

Stella's face falls.

— What are you looking at me like that for, Dylan? Are you going to try and flick my fucking nose again? he says angrily.

— You flicked Alistair's nose? Stella says.

— Not hard.

— It was hard! I don't actually have to let you stay in here, Alistair says.

— Are you going to throw me out?

Dylan is so tall his head almost skims the roof of the little cottage. Outside the world darkens and the mountain feels like it is rumbling under their feet.

— Mum, is that an avalanche?

— What's your fucking problem? Alistair says.

— No, that's not the question, arsehole. The question is: what's your fucking problem?

— Hello, Stella!

Alistair snaps the words out and his face has grown red, the blush beginning in his neck and going all the way up.

— Didn't fucking kill you to get that out then, did it, mate!

Awkward. Moments. Passing. Stella scuffs her socks on the wooden floor and Constance flicks on a few lamps. She knows where they are, of course she does. Alistair goes into the kitchen and clicks on a kettle. Constance follows him and Stella sidles up to Dylan. He puts his arm round her and gives her a hug.

— Sorry if that got awkward, he says.

— Thanks for sticking up for me, she says.

— Do you want me to beat him up for you? Dylan asks.

— I don't get the feeling you'd be doing that for me, Stella whispers.

Constance is laughing in the kitchen. She comes back through with hot tea.

— At least that rumbling noise is stopping outside, she says.

— I think it was just the snowstorm going over the forest, he says.

— Has there ever been an iceberg before in Scotland? Stella changes the subject.

— There was one in Treshnish in 1902, Constance says.

— I love the way your brain stores random trivia, Stella says.

— There was another in Sumburgh Head in 1927.

— You need to start reading some non-factual books one day, Mum. Are people older than icebergs?

— Modern humans are nearly two hundred thousand years old. They think the family tree could go back six or seven million years, though — earliest fossils of the genus *Homo* were about two-point-four million years ago, Constance says.

— Why are there black patches on the ice in winter?

— Wind can get trapped in there, Alistair says.

— Or bad spirits? Stella asks.

— There are no such things, Alistair says.

— I wouldn't be so sure about that, Dylan says.

He is looking around for photographs of Olaf and imagining Gunn, just her, and thinking of Stella saying she saw an old lady in a donkey-jacket — it is too odd to be a coincidence.

— How old's the earth then, Mum?

— The earth is about four-point-five billion years old, and they think it coalesced from material in orbit around the sun and split away, then another part of what made the earth broke away to make the moon. Some of the old myths say that the earth was so enamoured with her own beauty she needed a hand-mirror to hold, so she could gaze upon herself in admiration.

— So we were orbiting the sun and then we broke away, but we stayed close?

— Well, we weren't, Stella! But the planet was, pretty much.

Dylan tries to stop jiggling his legs, let the adrenaline go down; he shouldn't be so annoyed at the guy — okay, so he's clearly a trans-phobic womanising fuck-tard but Constance still seems to like him.

— That's why we need light, anywhere we can find it. Do you think the matter that was orbiting the sun came from the sun? Stella says.

— I don't know, Constance says.

— If the moon broke away from the earth, then surely the matter that made earth could have broken away from the sun? I bet it did, or we were close enough to be made of the same stuff that the sun is made of. If the universe is mostly black matter and we can't survive without light, or the moon, then it makes sense that part of the matter that made the sun and the moon is inside us. So, if we don't get light, we will die. We're essentially made of carbon and light.

— Plants need sunlight for photosynthesis or we can't grow food. You could probably raise a human without it, but their bones wouldn't form properly, they'd be all sort of sinewy and floppy and they'd have long, thin, ratty teeth, Constance says.

Dylan looks at her.

— So we're surrounded by dark matter, but we came out of it into the light, which is a planet, or stars, we know that dark matter is all around us in the universe, if we can even feel it out there — and as we all know, goths have a direct line to any source of authentic darkness — but dark matter has no atoms, is that right?

Constance nods, grins at Dylan, who is shaking his head at the two of them. Alistair sits on his sofa looking awkward and confused.

— Where's your wife, Alistair? Dylan asks.

— She's with her sister in the city, she didn't want to risk being snowed in here with me.

— No shit! he says.

— Stop it, Constance says.

— You two are an item as well then? And you have an issue with me — is that what is going on? Alistair asks.

Dylan ignores him completely as if he hasn't heard a word.

— So if dark matter doesn't absorb light and it doesn't reflect light, but we do, then we need to store that shit up, so when our souls get catapulted out into the universe, we have our own battery to keep us going, and you know how bad it is here if it gets too grey, and it's because when matter separated from the sun, the atoms that were going to make us went with light in it, with energy to create life, and we know if we stick our toe out into Coatlicue's river, then all around it there is total darkness and if we go into that, horrible things will happen — we'll be taken as light-slaves by the universe. Our cells crave light because that is what we started as, it's what we are. All humans are sunlight pilgrims. Except me. Cos I'm a goth. I could totally live without light, Stella says.

Constance grins.

— She's so your child, Dylan says.

— Truth.

— Mine too, Alistair adds.

— Is that your father, in that picture? Dylan asks.

— Aye, Olaf and that's his wife.

— Big family?

— Not really.

— Did he have any sisters?

— One. She ran away.

— Where to?

— Australia was what they told me.

The snowstorm is howling down the mountain and he feels Constance place a hand on his leg and, just like that, he gets the feeling she knows. Constance looks at the picture of Olaf and back at Dylan.

Then the lights go out.

— Fuck's sake, not again! Alistair snaps.

— Is the generator charged?

— Of course it is, Constance, I'm not some city idiot!

— Stella, don't move!

— I'm not bloody moving, Mum!

The two of them head outside the cottage, banging around.

— If the snow never stops falling and we don't ever get out of here, I will never have sex with Lewis Brown, Stella says.

— If the snow doesn't stop, your mother will build an igloo village single-handed, he says.

— I don't think so. Archaeologists will dig us up in years to come: the frozen community of Clachan Fells, the year of the freak winter, Stella says.

Alistair stamps back into the room and the generator

kicks in, the lights flicker back on, but everything is a little dimmer than before. Dylan looks back at the photograph of Olaf.

— Constance, you did mention you got drunk with Vivienne one night?

— I didn't say drunk.

— What did you talk about, exactly?

— Nothing, Dylan.

— It's all fine — nothing to panic about, just owerblaw, blin drift, skirlie. Honestly, I have got enough roadkill in the freezer to last until summer, I reckon; well, maybe four weeks, and me and your mother and Dylan here, we'll be civil, won't we, Dylan? We'll play Monopoly and cook soup, we won't run short of fresh water.

— What about firewood? Dylan asks.

— Enough for a month.

— We won't be here more than a day, Constance says.

— I wouldn't count on that, Alistair says.

— Can you get a radio signal?

— No.

— Has anyone got a phone signal? Dylan asks.

A small pitiful chorus of *No*.

— They will find us in here, all frozen to death, next summer, Stella whispers.

— Stop that right now! Constance says.

— I'm scared! She grips her mother's hand.

— I don't know why you're scared, Alistair says.

— Why's that? Stella asks him.

— Well, when we run out of tinned food, then roadkill, which will take a while, after that I reckon it's me that will get eaten first. You know it's like that joke about the kid bear that goes into the forest and it says I'm scared, and the guy bear says: I don't know why; you're not the one that has to walk back on your own.

They all sit listening to the clock tick.

— If you do eat me, though, could you do just one thing?

— What's that? Constance asks.

— Well, I'm so glad you are not contradicting me — if you *do*, could you keep my bones, get them ground down, made into a nice bit of china?

A barometer on the wall reads minus seventy, Dylan and Constance glance at each other and as he looks back it drops one more degree. Wind batters at the door, so loud he could put a face to it. There is a booming noise up the mountain as ice expands and cracks.

They sit on the sofa in a row. Alistair, Constance, Dylan, Stella. The fire flickers and the windows glow yellow against a dark that is as complete as any of them will ever know. Constance takes Dylan's hand. He cannot see if she is holding Alistair's on the other side. Stella curls into him and he puts his arm around her too, pulls her in and holds her safe. They can do this. It's fucking snow. It's ice. No electricity, but wood. They can cook with the fire? He can't think. He is woolly and tired. As soon as they get through this he will go to a city, just for a visit; he'll go to a decent pub and he'll get some new tattoos — a sunlight pilgrim, a wolf-child, a moon-polisher, an iceberg and a vintage projector that shines a light in the dark. It will have to be a full sleeve. They can go over some of the old tattoos. Olaf looks out at him from the picture on the wall. Vivienne must have told Constance when they were drinking gin one evening, and all this time she's never said a thing, not to Stella, either. Cos she liked him. Right from the start she didn't want to do anything to stop it happening, either. She has left it up to him. If they had to eat Alistair, there's no way he'd pound those bones down for china. He'd throw them out of the door for the farmers' dogs. Odd thoughts lacing together in his mind, wondering if this is the beginning of some kind of snow-cabin fever.

The only noise in the cottage is the crack of the fire.

Outside the snowfall grows thicker and heavier.

He'll go outside when it stops falling. See how much of the village below is lit up. There's probably electricity out in homes all across the region. People sitting in cold houses without heating. Knocking on their neighbours' doors. Snow piling up higher each minute. The cottage windows look out onto sheer darkness. Stella is asleep, leaning on him now. Constance stroking her thumb along the palm of his hand. Firelight making shadows dance. If they can make it to spring they'll be okay. Unlike Barnacle. Poor guy. Dylan can still picture each eyelash encrusted with frost and his eyes frozen wide open, like a man cursed only to see the world straight on when he was laid out on the floor in the worst snowstorm in 200 years. Staring at the sky. Clouds drifting over his old, tired corneas, Constance curling into him as his eyes close too, just, so tired, all of them, their bodies gang into hibernation mode, just to rest here, like this, just for a few hours.